PERFECT LIGHT

Marcello Fois

PERFECT LIGHT

Translated from the Italian by
Silvester Mazzarella

MACLEHOSE PRESS
QUERCUS · LONDON

First published in the Italian language as *Luce perfetta*
By Giulio Einaudi editore s.p.a., Turin, in 2015
First published in Great Britain in 2020 by

MacLehose Press
An imprint of Quercus Publishing Ltd
Carmelite House
50 Victoria Embankment
London EC4Y 0DZ

An Hachette UK company

A CIP catalogue record for this book is available from the British Library.

ISBN (PB) 978 0 85705 675 7
ISBN (Ebook) 978 0 85705 676 4

10 9 8 7 6 5 4 3 2 1

Designed and typeset in Cycles by Libanus Press Ltd
Printed and bound in Great Britain by Clays Ltd, Elcograf S.p.A.

to the Survivors

CONTENTS

"You tell him
that, despite the fact that he has gone to live by
the sea, nothing is satisfactory and no-one can be saved . . ."

My mother, in a dream

I was expecting something to
happen, and my waiting for this was my expectation . . .

T. MALICK, "The Tree of Life"

PART IV

Even Later

Gozzano, January 1999

HOW SHE MANAGED TO REACH THE PRECISE PLACE WHERE she now found herself, Maddalena Pes would never have been able to say.

The morning before, carrying a small suitcase, she had caught the ferry from Porto Torres to Genoa. That had meant getting up before dawn to reach the port in a hired car, then waiting all day to board the ship in the evening. Alarmingly, during those dead hours, she had even been tempted to give up. But she was a woman who had been forced to learn tenacity. She had known far worse periods of waiting during the course of her forty years. After the ferry she had caught a train from Genoa to Torino, an unprecedented experience for a woman who had never travelled anywhere by train in her native Barbagia. Then finally, by means of a local train from Torino and a coach, she had reached Gozzano, a place whose address she had learned to write down perfectly and which turned out to be quite a small building of fairly recent construction. To be honest, it had the atmosphere of a clinic. Or a school for priests. Or a seminary, which is what it was. In fact, the whole village seemed to hint at honest sobriety. A cold compassion perfectly in tune with the freezing weather gripping it. January was showing its fangs, and Maddalena Pes realised she had not dressed warmly enough. Sighing, she pressed the doorbell a couple of times. A lock snapped back and the front door opened.

The deserted corridor inside was dominated by the smell of the kind of floor-wax dear to ecclesiastical housekeepers. Its walls featured a few naively creepy images, a few posters advertising missions, and shelves decorated with little vases and doilies in the childish style sometimes favoured by nuns and elderly women when chance throws them into contact with all-male communities.

Taking a few steps forward, Maddalena passed one closed door on her right, then another. Before she could reach the third it opened, and a tall man dressed in grey came out. He looked no older than twenty-five, and when he saw her he gave a smile of enthusiasm seemingly unrelated to her presence.

"You must be Luigi Ippolito's mother," he said. "We've been expecting you." Maddalena nodded. "Let me," he continued, reaching with nervous politeness for her suitcase. Maddalena did not resist; she was tired and cold, even though the building was warm inside. "Luigi Ippolito is busy at the moment with the boys, but he'll be here in a moment." The young man had the condescending good manners of someone impatient to get back to whatever he had been doing before he was interrupted.

Maddalena forced a smile. The man did not respond, but led her into a modest room furnished with bulging brown leather armchairs, their back rests decorated at shoulder height with coarse pieces of multicoloured cloth crocheted from woollen scraps. He put her suitcase down on a chair and straightened up almost as if expecting a tip. Glancing at his wristwatch, he repeated, "He'll be here in a moment," then stood to attention with his hands crossed over his bottom as if to make clear that he knew it was his duty to escort and guard her until her son arrived.

"We've heard what happened," he murmured as they waited. "Such things are not good, but the Lord helps us to get over them."

Maddalena studied him carefully for the first ime: he was a very tall youth, well built and well groomed. "And what have you heard?" she asked sharply.

The man stammered a reply: "Luigi Ippolito has told us about his father . . . yes indeed . . . about the accident . . ."

"Are you a priest?"

"A novice. Still some way to go . . . If Christ accepts me, I'll be a priest soon. People think we decide these things for ourselves, but the decision is entirely His."

"You mean Christ's?" Maddalena added, to be quite sure she had not misunderstood.

"I mean Christ's," the novice confirmed.

This was followed by a silence filled with noises. It was only then that Maddalena noticed that the room was just what the late-lamented Marianna Chironi might have called an "eating area" rather than a drawing room, kitchen, studio or antechamber. In fact, it was a room that only existed in terms of what it was not. Where Maddalena came from most things now thought of as modern had come into houses via the "eating area", which was the main reason why old and once precious pieces of furniture had been sold off cheaply or chopped up for firewood. Such "eating areas" would feature an ancient television set that was never turned on, and be decorated with scraps of cloth similar to those on the armchairs in this room, though this one was smaller, and also contained a little vase with a couple of artificial carnations.

After waiting for several minutes during which nothing happened, Maddalena decided to sit down. She chose a plain chair rather than one of the armchairs. The man hinted at a smile, as if approving of her decision to be comfortable.

"So Luigi Ippolito has told you about the accident," Maddalena said unexpectedly.

Shot out like this, her statement was almost an accusation. "It's impossible not to realise how much it has affected him; there are times when no words are needed," the novice mumbled.

"I can well believe it." Maddalena allowed herself a touch of sarcasm.

"Luigi Ippolito has done a lot of praying," the young man assured her.

"Of course, that's only to be expected. I mean, that's what you are here for, isn't it?"

The novice stiffened. "Yes, exactly. Here we pray," he answered as if avoiding compliments in order to respond to a challenge. "Sometimes we also pray for those who do not pray themselves," he added.

Maddalena looked at his perfectly shaved face and impeccably cut hair, his autumn-green eyes, high cheekbones and slender neck. "You're a good-looking man," she said aloud, not quite able to hide the fact that what she meant was "too handsome to restrict yourself to a life of chastity". Just as the clients of some prostitutes can't help saying "you're too beautiful to live this kind of life".

The man opened his arms as if to stress that he had implied nothing of the kind, and changed the subject. "Luigi Ippolito should not be much longer."

16

Nor was he. The boy arrived slightly out of breath and took a step or two towards his mother without indicating in any way that he expected her to embrace or hug him. She took his face in her hands, pulling him against her breast and kissing him on the forehead. The novice hurried out so as to leave them alone.

"So you've met Alessandro," her son said, using this as a pretext to disengage himself from his mother's arms.

Maddalena made a non-committal gesture. "You're looking well," she observed with ill-concealed disappointment, as if she had expected to find him injured or emaciated.

"I am well, in fact."

Maddalena reflected that apart from the fact that he was the shorter by a few centimetres, he could have passed for a clone of the novice whom she now knew was called Alessandro.

"With your hair cut and a little extra weight, you're certainly looking well," she confirmed.

Her son nodded.

The ugly room, the multicoloured doilies, the calendars with pictures of dogs and cats, the armchairs like plump Phoenician beauties, and even the little vase with its plastic carnations, seemed to be spying on them.

"They all say you look as if you're my sister," Luigi Ippolito said eventually to break the silence.

"How do you mean 'They all say'?" Maddalena was surprised to have been noticed, since she had not seen anyone, apart from the young man who had received her.

"All the others," her son explained, as if that were an adequate answer.

"I've seen no-one." A touch of irritation was creeping into

17

Maddalena's voice. She did not like situations where she was not in complete control.

"But they've seen you," Luigi Ippolito concluded as though that was the only thing that needed to be said.

"Must we stay in here?" Maddalena asked. "I'd like to see your room. Where you live, I mean."

What she meant was quite clear to Luigi Ippolito. "It's nothing much," he said evasively.

"But all the same," she insisted drily, as she always did when she felt a need to remind her son that although he may well have been sent into the world deliberately to antagonise her, she had no intention of accepting this.

"I have a single bed, a desk, and a wardrobe," he said, doing his best to make the list sound banal and tedious. "What do you want to see?"

"A single bed, a desk, and a wardrobe," she repeated pedantically, trying to echo the exact tone of his voice.

He changed the subject abruptly. "I thought I'd take you out to supper."

"Is that allowed?" Her mockery was palpable.

Luigi Ippolito refused to be drawn. "We can go out."

"But you won't show me your room. What's this room we're in now, anyway; a special place for interviewing visitors?" She swept her arm round as if to include the whole of it.

"I've never thought about that," Luigi Ippolito admitted, also looking around. "I've hardly ever been in here before, to tell you the truth."

"You mean you've not had many visitors."

"What I said is exactly what I wanted to say, Mamma." Judging by the way Luigi Ippolito pursed his lips, Maddalena's own approach of pre-empting people before backing off was beginning to bear fruit. It was something he had done ever since he had been small, pursing his lips like that when he wanted to stay in control. Every time he had to deal with being denied or criticised. Every time anything was not going the way he wanted. He had been a difficult child.

"I'm not stayjng in this room," Maddalena said. "You were going to take me out to supper, remember?"

"Yes." Luigi Ippolito's expression had the same immobility as the ferocious January weather biting the mountains to pieces almost as if they had been nothing more substantial than slivers of chocolate.

"I must stop by the guest house first . . ." she said. It had grown dark outside. An inscrutable gloom, foreign and hostile. "I feel I'm being a burden to you," she confided, after a short pause.

Luigi Ippolito came up with a smile that made things worse rather than better, but remained silent.

"Have you nothing to say?" Maddalena asked, as if longing for him to contradict her.

"What is there to say? As Babbo used to put it: 'a paragulas maccas uricras surdas'." Luigi Ippolito's Sardinian was carefully nit-picking, as if to tease.

"You've always been the best at 'deaf ears', but I win when it comes to 'silly words'."

"I didn't mean that seriously," Luigi Ippolito felt he had been too harsh. "Can't you take a joke anymore?"

"No, no, for goodness sake . . ." Maddalena buttoned up her coat ready to go out.

Luigi Ippolito preceded her into the passage, and just before reaching the front door grabbed a padded blue jacket from a coat-hanger.

The cold took no more than a few seconds to swallow them up. And it wasn't six o'clock yet. When they passed the guest house, Maddalena dropped her suitcase off and the landlady lent her a woollen scarf.

"Are you hungry?" Luigi Ippolito asked when they were finally sitting opposite one another at a table for two at the trattoria which, perhaps not entirely by chance, had been called Osteria del Prete or "the Priest's Inn". He said in an encouraging voice, "The food they do here is simple but good. What would you like?"

Maddalena tried not to show that she never liked eating out. She was a woman who had always considered eating on a par with washing, something extremely personal. Even so she could not help smiling when she remembered the many times her husband had tried to take her out to lunch or dinner. "No-one but you could ever have got me into a restaurant."

"Restaurant's a big word. But the food's excellent and the prices are reasonable."

"And the prices are?" She couldn't resist teasing him a bit.

"Reasonable." It took him a moment to realise his mother was making fun of him.

They both laughed. Like the time many years before when they had played a trick on his grandfather Giuseppe, whom everyone called Peppino. Luigi Ippolito had had to pretend he'd been abandoned at home on his own . . . How they'd laughed to see how fast the old man ran to his grandson despite the fact he never stopped complaining how much his bones ached . . . What fun to see him run so clumsily though rather dangerously, like an enormous irritated boar. Which reminded them that for a short time mother and son had been partners in crime. But it also forced them to remember how quickly that complicity had come to an end.

The Osteria del Prete served chestnut puddings and Luigi Ippolito knew how much his mother liked such things: that was why he had taken her there. And why he had made her walk so far despite the cold. It gave Maddalena the chance to try the best marrons glacés she had ever tasted. Sometimes choosing a particular eating place can mean a lot.

"You do know I wanted to come back, don't you? For the funeral, I mean." It became clear that Luigi Ippolito had been waiting to say this from the moment he had seen his mother.

"But you didn't come," she observed, wiping a smudge of marron glacé from the corner of her mouth. She could expect anything from this creature who had started life inside her body but now seemed intent on stressing every possible difference between them. Children may term this progress even if their mothers, privately, call it desertion.

"No, I know I didn't. When it came to the point, I didn't feel up to it." It was suddenly clear to both that the "love" they had once had for each other had been transformed into a battle for advantage. So while Luigi Ippolito was still trying to seem like someone who had no need for self-justification, he remembered a time when his father Domenico had said: "You are utterly without pity." Which he had said as if talking to an adult rather than to a child of nine. Luigi Ippolito was indeed pitiless, there was no doubt about that, because if he had ever felt compassion he would

21

never have been able to cope with what was currently happening to him.

"Yes, of course, that's obvious . . ." his mother interrupted, having been aware of every one of his thoughts.

". . . I had planned everything . . . But you know what they say here?"

"No, what do they say?"

"That if you want to make Our Lord laugh, tell him your plans."

Maddalena had wanted a miracle from her son. She had specifically asked him to stop being so hostile to her. And even if she thought she was aware of the origin of that hostility, she pretended that, just as children cannot choose their parents, it is no less true that parents cannot choose their children. She had clear in her mind the exact moment when she had understood, beyond any possibility of doubt, that life with Luigi Ippolito would be a constant battle. Her long labour when she gave birth to him had influenced this belief, because it had taken twelve hours from the moment her waters broke to his birth. Twelve hours of bitter struggle like a violent negotiation between mutually hostile states, full of threats and modifications and mixed with blackmail and second thoughts thrown in. And when the creature finally emerged and Maddalena was forced to look at him, everything became clear to his mother. He had turned on her a terrible gaze of profound malice, and defying every instinct, had clamped his mouth shut against her nipple. The birth of Luigi Ippolito had inflicted labour on her in the fullest sense of the word. And she had had to admit, in relation to him, that deep down inside her, from that moment every single word had carried its full meaning.

"Aren't you even going to ask me why I've come all this way to see you?" she asked as they made their way back to the guest house. Through some twist of climate, now that night had fallen it seemed less cold.

"I knew all I needed to do was wait," Luigi Ippolito answered.

"I gave it a lot of thought after the death of . . . Domenico." She could not help laughing, because instead of saying "your father" she had heard herself opt at the last moment for "Domenico".

This did not escape her son. "Babbo," he corrected. Maddalena waited for him to go on. "You had to think hard about that . . ."

Maddalena nodded. "But you, haven't you ever wondered why you were called Luigi Ippolito?" she asked point-blank.

He hesitated for a second. "After our close friends, the Chironi family," he ventured.

"Of course," Maddalena said.

"But what has that got to do with it?"

The lights of the village were flickering in the rocky darkness of the valley.

Maddalena pulled the woollen scarf more tightly round her neck. They were walking the deserted streets with their arms entwined like young lovers. The mother in her thin clothing and borrowed scarf, the son in his immaculate and ample blue-grey suit.

"Naturally, as a future priest, it's understandable you attach importance to appearances," she threw in, letting her previous remark take its course.

"The Order pays less attention to appearances than you did with me, Mamma. From that point of view, as far as I'm concerned little or nothing has changed." Luigi Ippolito's answer seemed affectionate, if distant.

This detachment was painful to Maddalena. "Surely it's not my fault?" she asked.

Luigi Ippolito, who perfectly understood this apparently obscure question, stood still and looked her in the eye. "You will be the first person from whom I have ever had to ask forgiveness."

They began walking again.

"At the funeral everyone asked me about you, you know how it is in Núoro . . . Some people even wondered if there had been any problem between us."

"Naturally, that's the way they are." Luigi Ippolito was careful not to miss the turning for the guest house. "I hope you took no notice of them, explaining too much is as bad as saying nothing at all."

"Well, dear, you know how I am . . . I did say something."

"The only thing that matters to me is that you should understand why I didn't come. I prayed for you to understand!"

Maddalena shrugged. A way of lying without necessarily telling a lie. A way of saying that she understood only in the sense that she was his mother, that she was the person who had loved him, and that she loved him even more now that he was out in the world. She knew she had become a mother too soon, but she also knew that being so young had given her more time to hope this runaway son would come back to her.

"Come in for a moment. There's something I'd like to show you," she said when they reached the guest house door.

Luigi Ippolito swallowed a mouthful of frozen air and shook his head. "Tomorrow. You need a rest. We both do," he answered as though speaking to one of the boys in his care at the seminary.

Maddalena realised she could not bridge the gulf his simple, almost subdued, refusal had provoked between them. "Tomorrow will do just as well," she conceded, taking care not to seem in any way disappointed. "Come and find me here."

"It's very beautiful round here," he said. "I'll come and get you at midday, I've promised the Father Rector to bring you to lunch with us at about one o'clock, so you can show me anything you like then."

"I don't want to waste your time."

"Of course you won't be wasting my time, what do you mean?" he protested but without force, as though just mimicking words for the sake of it.

"I understand," she said, suddenly brisk.

"So everything's alright then?"

"Everything's fine," his mother confirmed, as she always did when she was irritated and wanted to conceal it. "I'll go in now," she said, taking a step towards her son. Luigi Ippolito, surprised by what he imagined to be an attempted embrace, instinctively pulled back. Maddalena changed her aborted embrace into a clumsy farewell, as if taking her leave of someone who had boarded an already moving train.

Luigi Ippolito waited until she had vanished up the first flight of stairs. Then he turned towards the seminary.

The night had become pungent, its frosty acidity drying his palate. He had faced up to what remained unsaid and outdone himself. He realised he was sweating, and throughout the evening he had been unable to relax his shoulders. "Control", he muttered to himself, exactly like it had been when as a child he had been aware of how difficult it was to work out if you chose or were chosen.

Without being conscious of it at the time, he had told himself back then: "Control, control . . ." followed by "Here I am, if you want me take me." His mother's presence had reminded him how much strength he had needed to master that kind of tenacious flexibility. The sounds of the world, echoing round the mountains, were tense arches in his temples, chirping like a machine in action, like the clicks of well-oiled springs; there was nothing silent about the night though nothing seemed to be moving. The frost was merely a crystal bell on an old decorated clock. It was not a time for him to fall back into a whirlpool of reproaches, but to accept his own savage destiny. "You are utterly without pity," his father had said.

"I have never had any time for compassion. For as long as I can remember. I believe that everything that I am, everything that I have become, derives from one absolute truth: which is that I have absolutely always avoided compassion. In relation to my parents, but also in relation to myself. Beyond that there's not much to be said: I cultivate doubt, but not much, though I don't let it be seen, within the mud of my obsessions. For example, my obsession with kindness, and the idea that in the last resort kindness does more for the person who exercises it than for the person who receives it. Is not kindness actually a form of pride? If it had been an ordinary feeling why would the Saints have invented it? In any case, what are the Saints if not simply professionals or champions, those so proud in their exercise of altruism that they are even capable of self-destruction, and thus of raising themselves through the altars up to the highest point in the sky. And what pity did He ever have when He abandoned me to my delirium? I was, perhaps, nine or ten years old, and I remember a maddening sky, and everywhere the stunning scent of prickly broom. What pity when

I suddenly found myself at the centre of the whirlwind, a vortex like those described in the hagiographies every time the divine reveals Himself? Oh, I was innocent, so I opened my arms to offer my soft flesh to the downward slashing blade."

Luigi Ippolito repeated these words as he bent down towards the pavement under his feet, as if talking to himself with head bowed like this signified surrendering to all the evidence, attempting an ultimate exercise in humiliation to cure the huge pride that had afflicted him only eleven years before, when he had explained to his parents what had happened to him, or what he thought had happened to him.

That day, at home, seated at table, he had heard himself speak in a language unfamiliar to him, and as if inspired by the very flame of Pentecost, he had dutifully described particular things he should not have known. He had spoken about himself, the sky, the smell, the slashing blade. At that midday meal every sound had been interrupted: the rhythmic throb of the pan, the drip of the tap, the chirping of cicadas, his mother's breathing.

His father for a long time had not said a word, waiting for him to finish; then finally, "You are utterly without pity."

In the cosy intestine of corridor that led to his own room he seemed to feel better. For no particular reason, the invasive smell of boiled cabbage from the refectory made him happy. Once in his room he threw himself on his bed without undressing or even taking off his shoes. Like a dead man ready for burial.

Next morning he made his way to the guest house at ten minutes to twelve. It was a beautiful day, glazed and pure. Nothing seemed to have been left to chance: points and sharp edges, roofs

27

and aerials, gutters and chimney pots, the tops of fir-trees and whitened peaks. The scene was like a Flemish painting, its crisp edges dominating every possible roundness. And the compact turquoise of the sky seemed to contain no sunlight to fade it or the flight of any bird to stain it.

But when Luigi Ippolito reached the guest house he found Maddalena had departed by bus a few hours earlier for Torino. She had left a packet for the landlady to give to him as soon as he appeared, and this the old woman was careful to do. He accepted the bulky envelope as though it might be dangerous, and holding it tightly to his chest, hurried back to the seminary. Once in his room, he opened the package to find a collection of pages, some handwritten and others typed.

PART I
Before

THE ANCIENT OF DAYS

Núoro, February 1979

ONLY A MOMENT AFTERWARDS, IT ALL SEEMED TO HAVE been absolutely impossible. Cristian fell back on the bed as if, far from slowing him down, his orgasm had given him renewed energy. Maddalena watched him reach for the underpants he had flung on the carpet and step into them as if the only thing that now interested him was no longer to be naked. In fact, with his underclothes on, he seemed calmer.

"We can't do this to him," Cristian said suddenly.

"What a shame you only think of such things afterwards and never before," she remarked calmly.

"Domenico's my brother. It's not right."

Then they fell silent; Maddalena realised how much Cristian needed her. She knew he was trying to make up his mind whether to get up and escape or whether to stay, but he ended up doing nothing. Maddalena liked him weak and vulnerable like this, a snake that had just shed its skin. He sat down on the bed with his back to her. His skin was the colour of well-baked clay, a small mole prominent just below the broad nape of his neck. She knew every millimetre of his skin, because what she felt for him was not just attraction or love, but hunger. If after that secret afternoon, when the naked trees outside the windows were slashed with grey, they

31

had asked her what she felt for Cristian, she would have immediately said hunger. And what did she feel for the other young man? For Domenico? Affection. Affection is what she would have said.

"Then go and talk to your brother," Maddalena said, reaching out to stroke his back.

He shuddered, but carefully pulled himself away. "And what shall I say to him? What shall I say to him? Everything's been planned, you know that as well as I do."

Maddalena nodded, in no way concerned that he had his back to her and could not see her. "The fact is," she burst out, "you don't want me to speak to him, and you don't want to do it yourself either. But which would be better?"

"That's not easy." He decided to state a foregone conclusion. "Domenico loves you . . ."

"I know. Of course, Domenico and I have loved each other, but it's different now . . . isn't it?"

Cristian put his head in his hands. "Maddalé," he said after a brief pause. "If something like this had happened to me . . ." He didn't finish the sentence.

She cut in. "Well, let's leave things as they are, then."

"That's not what I was trying to say." Cristian was confused. "I just mean, it's all been arranged now, the engagement party and everything . . . what can we possibly do?"

"We have to talk to him, that's what we can do." Maddalena was firm. She got to her feet and went over to the window. Beyond the misted glass a vicious winter was honing its blade, but in the corner of her eye Cristian's bare back, strong and compact like the leather cuirass of a legionary of long ago, was heaving as rhythmically as a pair of bellows.

If only he could recapture his innocence, but that had already been lost before the first time he touched her. There had been no innocence since the first moment he even imagined he might touch her. "Right, I'll speak to him then." Cristian addressed the floor. "I'll have a word with him before he leaves for Carrara."

"Will you?" Maddalena turned back to face him.

"Yes, really," Cristian confirmed. "There's a consignment of marble we have to order for one of the yards . . . I'll speak to him before that."

"And what must I do?"

"Just wait a few days," Cristian answered, turning, "then we'll see." He wished he had the strength to push her hand away or at least restrain it; she had begun stroking his chest, but he realised he could not do it. No part of his own body had seemed so right once he had learned to see himself with her eyes. His slightly prominent breast-bone – "like a ship's keel", the paediatrician had said long ago; the little oasis of reddish down in the middle of his chest, the slight adolescent bulge of his belly, and the deep navel like a tiny crater in karst stone. If all this appealed to Maddalena, and she swore it did, then it must be absolutely right. Sometimes it seemed to him that love must be no more than being completely aware of oneself, a feeling he had never before experienced, even when he had previously imagined himself to be in love. Beautiful. But the prospect of talking to Domenico and telling him what had happened and was still happening between him and the woman who was about to become Domenico's official fiancée – this disturbed the serenity he believed he deserved, now that he was finally able to feel utterly beautiful and perfect.

*

It is not easy to say how long a previously unexpressed passion needs to brood before it takes over completely. Cristian and Maddalena felt they had known each other for ever, and most likely something would eventually have developed between them now that they were no longer teenagers. Though coming from a fairly prosperous family, Cristian had never known his father, and at the age of eighteen had also lost his mother Cecilia, cut down by a terminal illness. Just when a mutual attraction might first have become reality between him and Maddalena, he had had to cope with the slow and painful dying of his mother, while Maddalena had simultaneously been subjected to the persistent courtship of Domenico Guiso, two years his senior.

Everyone assumed that Cristian and Domenico were related, but in fact this was not the case, even though Cristian addressed Domenico's father Giovannimaria as "Uncle Mimmíu". Their families had been connected since 1943 when Cristian's father Vincenzo Chironi had first arrived in Sardinia from Friuli. In fact, Mimmíu had been Vincenzo's first and most important friend in Núoro. On Christmas Eve 1959, the day Vincenzo killed himself, it had been Mimmíu who found him hanging in his office. Vincenzo Chironi had decided of his own accord to say goodbye to the world without giving any reason for doing so. And without knowing that his wife Cecilia was pregnant.

An unhappy family, the Chironis, but for Mimmíu they had been closer than relatives. When his own son Domenico had been born, in 1958, he had wanted the Chironis to baptise him. Even if, in his heart, he had known this was making an unfair demand on them as well as doing them an honour. In fact, till then, despite repeated efforts Vincenzo and Cecilia had not succeeded in producing a surviving child of their own. But fortune, with her inevitable irony, had thought good to arrange for the birth of this latest Chironi, Cristian, exactly nine months after the burial of his father Vincenzo. This was how Mimmíu had come to be accepted as Cristian's "uncle" and Domenico as his "brother". From a genetic point of view this may have made no sense, but in practice it was enough to influence an entire life.

After Vincenzo's death, his Chironi heirs Cristian, Cecilia and the elderly Marianna, had made an agreement with Mimmíu Guiso for the administration of their inheritance. As an associate of the family firm, Mimmíu had been entrusted with the task of keeping this inheritance intact for the next generation. The arrangement suited both sides since it enabled the Guiso family to expand their range of business interests at no cost to themselves, while the Chironi family were able to entrust the care of their property to a virtual relative.

However, before signing any power of attorney, Marianna had taken the trouble to study every single line of what was in fact a very complicated document. She had been born into a world where the ownership of wealth encouraged suspicion rather than trust. So taking nothing on trust, she had insisted on having time to go through every single paragraph and footnote of the document. So much so, that Mimmíu took offence. But having buried most, if not quite all, of her own family, Marianna was unmoved by the suspicions of other people. During the course of her life she had seen hopes rise and be swept away, only to be born again, and then finally come to a definite end. It would take something stronger than suspicion and resentment to shake her. So she reminded Cristian that he was a Chironi, at the same time pointing out to Mimmíu that to be a Chironi was one thing, and to be a Guiso something quite other. So, irrespective of whether she was literate or illiterate, she had explained to the notary that while she believed that the agreement was no doubt on the whole correct, she must nevertheless, as a duty to the Chironi interest, take infinite time and trouble to study every single detail of it for herself. And Mimmíu had spread his arms wide, as if to say that what has been born fish can never turn into red meat.

Meanwhile Cristian and Domenico developed a stronger form of brotherhood than many real brothers. They were two years apart in age and differed in appearance. Cristian was tall and slim, Domenico solid and heavily built. One was fair, as occurred intermittently in the Chironi family, while the other had exceptionally dark hair and eyes: "*píchidu*", as they called it in Núoro.

When Domenico aged six started the first year at elementary school, both boys wept because it seemed to mark the end of their joint life together. But Cristian's mother Cecilia knew her son well and did her best to explain to him that all he needed was to grow a little older because, in life, the older you get, the less time you need to spend waiting for things. And she even added that one day he would miss those long periods of waiting that were currently tormenting him. Cecilia certainly did not expect her son to believe what she was telling him. In fact, some years later, in her private room at the Cagliari oncology hospital, where Cristian seemed more impressed by the novelty of the colour television than by the condition of his terminally ill mother, he – by then eighteen years old – found he had to admit that this extremely simple concept had revealed itself to be as obvious as it actually was. Because at that moment, when he was faced with a television screen showing a documentary about a Caravaggio painting in the Cappella Contarelli in Rome, the two years he had spent waiting for the results of his mother's transfusions and chemotherapy seemed to have flown by in a moment. It was only later, when he looked back, that those two years seemed to have lasted an infinity. It was as if he had reached the age of eighteen without being able to wait a single moment, with the genetic urgency of a cat so desperate with hunger that it is forced to hunt its prey at all costs while wondering why.

This was where Maddalena came into the story. Cristian had always been attracted to her, but so had Domenico. And until she appeared, the two had always shared everything. Now, by accident, they had both become interested in the same girl. Both were bright enough (one now fifteen years old and the other seventeen) to understand that the rhetoric of male friendship is always shattered by the arrival of a woman, when real life is supplanted by drama. It so happened that Domenico was the first to declare his interest and, so far as could be seen, the girl did not respond negatively. So things moved forward with what, to Maddalena, seemed not so much timidity as simply a lack of conviction. This generated the sort of vague, smoky evaporation that wine-makers call the "angels' share", that is to say the two or at most three per cent of the product that escapes as fumes during fermentation. In any case, Domenico never said anything to Cristian about his interest in Maddalena and how it was progressing.

37

In age Maddalena was exactly half way between the two boys, being a year younger than Domenico and a year older than Cristian. And the latter, despite himself, could stand on his own two feet. He was becoming a man who had little need of small talk. One of those men who particularly intuitive women feel they are talking to even when they are silent – and Maddalena was one such woman. Cristian had inherited his rough complexion from his father, and from his mother Cecilia the indefinable colour of his eyes, somewhere between grey and green. But, his aunt Marianna claimed that his amber-coloured hair and downy skin came from his great-uncle Gavino, brother of his grandfather Luigi Ippolito. Cristian was a Chironi who had turned out particularly well. And, unaware that Domenico had declared his love for her, Cristian was the first to ask Maddalena for a serious assignation.

We can never know another person really well until we are able to compare them with ourselves. And that afternoon, not long before he reached the age of sixteen, Cristian realised he would be capable of lying to Domenico. Because when he claimed he had to do some revision before the end-of-term exams, Cristian had omitted to tell Domenico that that very morning, in one of the school corridors just before the end of break and with exquisite serendipity, he had asked Maddalena to meet him after school that afternoon, and she, worrying about not being late for class when he spoke to her, had simply said yes.

So instead of going home he had hidden in a corner of the little overgrown garden behind the school, where she had joined him on the bench exactly on time without seeking to claim any advantage by being a little late.

Sitting down beside him, she had stared at a small plane tree which was clearly struggling for lack of water. She found herself saying someone ought to care for those plants. And Cristian agreed that it was disgraceful that a public garden should be so badly kept.

Then for a time they said nothing more, neither feeling any need to speak. Then it occurred to Cristian to squeeze her hand, and when he did this she did not object. She asked him how much time he had and he said there was no hurry. So they sat there, hand in hand, until Cristian leaned forward to kiss her. But Maddalena drew back, pointing upwards to show it was getting late and that this was not the right time and place for such a thing. A crow cawed above them and the air was full of the smell of cut grass. The few clouds shading the sky were like a tulle veil and a scattering of dead leaves and bits of paper were blowing about near the ground in the wistful atmosphere of late autumn.

Then, without warning or drama, just like when she had sat down, Maddalena got up, turned to look him in the eyes and promised that the next day, at the very same time and place, she would kiss him.

Cristian felt unbearably stressed by the suspense of having to wait so long, and after Maddalena had disappeared beyond the dusty box hedge he could not bring himself to stand up from the bench. As if frozen to the spot, he became aware that evening was not touching the earth delicately or lightly, as people said, but was slithering roughly down like a rush of fluid. He told himself what he was witnessing was not so much an extinction of light as a huge outpouring of darkness. And that the only purpose of this revelation was to force him to accept that evening was falling rather than rising. So he waited for the lamps in the street beyond the forlorn garden to spread the ground with yellow beams before getting up to make his way home.

Going into the house, he was aware that something had happened. Aunt Marianna caught up with him in the antechamber so she could be the first to give him the bad news that his mother had been taken ill at work. She had come home, but this had not helped her to feel any better, so she had phoned Marianna to come to her before calling the doctor. And so it had been; Marianna had run across the road like a young girl, despite the fact that she was now over seventy. It had been inscribed in her genes that she must always carry tragedy on her shoulders, and if she had outlived so many others it was precisely because this curse had been laid on her. Cristian ran straight to his mother's bedroom but did not find her there. Marianna explained that Doctor Marletta had had her taken immediately to the San Francesco Hospital. Something very bad was feared, because in all probability Cecilia had suffered an intestinal blockage, and needed an immediate operation to find out what was wrong.

That same night, her stitches still fresh, she had been transferred from Núoro to the oncology hospital in Cagliari, for the first of a series of admissions that would continue for two years until her death.

The next day, at the arranged time, Maddalena waited for Cristian on the bench in the school garden, but he did not come.

The whole of the next week he was off school. So, without realising why, Domenico was able to profit from his head start and assume that since Maddalena had never said "no" in response to his clumsy declaration of love, she must have actually meant "yes". Their relationship had barely begun, and there was nothing whatever for them to learn about each other except how quickly melancholy and disillusion can develop into something that can resemble strong feeling. To give oneself every chance by throwing oneself in at the deep end is the only true privilege of youth. Maddalena asked herself whether she could feel satisfied, and Domenico asked himself nothing at all. She never wondered what had happened to Cristian, being fully aware of the brotherly link between the two boys, and Domenico said nothing.

When Cristian reappeared in the school corridors wrapped in the mystery of his absence, he realised something had happened while he had been away. It was as if twenty years had passed rather than a mere week. But how can such a disruption compare to the beat of a heart full of new excitement?

At home that evening, learning that his "Aunt Cecilia" was ill, Domenico felt able to confide in Cristian that he had kissed Maddalena. Just that. It follows that one who trusts himself to be guided by the blind will necessarily fall into the ditch, just as remaining silent can mean the same as not intervening in a disturbing course of events.

So bewildering was this, in fact, that Maddalena, having previously sworn that there could be no comparison between Cristian and Domenico and intending to favour the first, now began to notice subtle nuances and fascinating little details in the second.

It was many months before she knew why Cristian never appeared in the garden that second evening when she had waited for him in vain. Then she called herself stupid, telling herself that there must be some way in which she could retrace her tracks. But even if she had been capable of it, Cristian would never have dreamed of inflicting such pain on his dear "brother".

So all three remained tied down by things that had not been said.

Until 1978, when Cecilia died, and Cristian and Maddalena were finally forced to account to each other for everything left unspoken during the previous two years.

The grief of a mother still young, forced to leave her son at the mercy of destiny when he had already lost his father, was terrible. It had the full force of a visceral drama, entirely a matter of the flesh, with no opportunity for rational thinking. Nothing made any sense faced with Cecilia's coffin. Even her beauty, serene in death, seemed meaningless.

When Domenico sobbed, everyone assumed he was at last able to shed tears he had suppressed when his own mother had died when he was not yet four years old, while Mimmíu now clenched his jaw so fiercely that he was afraid he would break his teeth.

Beside them, Cristian was staring straight ahead as if trying to grasp something that had escaped all the others.

A story relating to his family came back to Cristian's mind whenever he had to cope with grief: the legend of how his great-grandmother Mercede had never seen the sea until her sons decided to take her there. And how, faced with the wonder of seeing the sea for the first time, she had lost control to the extent of reverting to childhood. This brought him peace because in some way it helped him to grasp such a feeling of anticipation and wonder, and also to understand how far every ending might be from its beginning. He knew that well, because not long before the death of his great-grandfather Michele Angelo, he had himself as a child experienced the same wonder, standing on thin legs at the edge of the sea with waves tickling his feet and ankles, in a light he could not describe, but which was precise with a precision shared by very few other moments. Solemn and peaceful.

Aware of this, Cristian believed it could not be wrong to die after suffering as much as Cecilia had suffered. Even though she was his mother.

Maddalena was standing to one side behind Domenico, as if to detach herself from the open grief all around her. The funeral was nearly over before she found the courage to reach for Cristian's hand, and when she did so, without moving from her position behind him, he did nothing to discourage her touching him. But he felt a need to control a sudden devastating delirium. He imagined Maddalena close to him in his vision of himself as a child with his feet buried in wet sand up to his ankles. He had found her again and now he could turn to her, in silence, in front of the sea as it ebbed and flowed. In that perfect light.

They made love that night, without stopping to ask what night it was. Probably it was the very night when Cecilia was crossing the muddy ford to the underworld, naked because ordered to take off the clothes that Marianna had selected so carefully for her burial, and pale and bruised after two years of chemotherapy had made her skin so transparent as to emphasise the network of her veins, and trembling because she had been an unusually shy and modest person, something even death cannot change.

Cristian and Maddalena began meeting as secret lovers do, pretending in public that they had no intimate connection. So much so that Domenico was convinced there must be some sort of hostility between his girl and his brother, even if he could not explain why.

On reaching his eighteenth birthday, Cristian was able to sign the documents that confirmed his Chironi inheritance. No small matter, since he was sole heir to the Chironi estate. That is to say, to the business that had made balconies, grilles, gratings and the like, modelled in his great-grandfather Michele Angelo's forge, as well as providing large quantities of iron for the foundations of buildings – not to mention the much newer fixtures in anodised aluminium produced by Cristian's father Vincenzo that would play an important part in the construction of even newer buildings, all this created with the participation of the small but flourishing firm run by Mimmíu Guiso and his son Domenico.

The Chironi, so people said, had always fallen on their feet, because although it was their destiny to be permanently on the point of disaster, ultimate disaster never actually struck. When Vincenzo died so suddenly, for instance, everyone said that must be the end of the family. But it wasn't the end at all, because Cecilia in the very act of burying her husband had discovered she was carrying his child.

So it was, in short, that Cristian signed his first official document just six days after his eighteenth birthday; when Domenico was twenty years old, Mimmíu sixty-one and Marianna seventy-seven.

The next event was the official announcement of the engagement of Domenico and Maddalena.

A soaking wet afternoon of rain, such as happens when the weather decides to turn nasty and no longer show any friendly expression. It is not easy to understand what involuntary action could have caused this, but the fact was, that was how it happened. From the air, from the sky, in the earth, in the very light itself, a subtle hostility transformed melancholy into anxiety. Of course, you could say it was no more than a tremor or spasm marking the changing of the seasons. But you could equally well have hoped that such change might have occurred more gently, without such an expression of ill will.

It was during that fearful afternoon, shaking rain off himself, that Domenico came into the kitchen from the Chironi courtyard, and greeted Marianna who had lit the fire and was huddling close to the hearth.

They exchanged conventional platitudes about the awfulness of the weather, the hostility of the season, and so on. Then when Cristian appeared in the kitchen, Domenico, in stark contrast to the weather outside, contradicted every meteorological trend of the moment by giving his usual beautiful smile. He announced that it had now happened, that his engagement to Maddalena Pes had now been confirmed, involving all the necessary agreements between families and everything. As was still the custom in that stubborn bastion of archaism, every member of the new extended family was required to approve the couple's engagement.

Marianna looked over her shoulder to give her assent, which was her way of conveying enthusiasm, while Cristian, struggling to smile, went up to Domenico and embraced and congratulated him, though with the slightest hint of distress, which did not escape old Marianna; in fact, she now turned properly for the first time to look her nephew in the face, and crossed herself.

"What are you up to?" she asked Cristian, as soon as Domenico had gone. Her question surprised him. "What's going on with

Maddalena?" she said more specifically, so there could be no mis-understanding.

Caught unawares by these direct questions, Cristian shrugged. "Nothing's going on, why on earth should anything be going on?"

"Naturally nothing should be going on," the old woman stressed, but with a conviction Cristian had not shown. "Because God does not want the sort of things to happen that I believe have happened," she finished. Her nephew said nothing, needing time to work out whether the old witch actually knew anything or was just pretending she knew. "But you take care, because others may understand what I have understood. You young people think you are so clever . . . What, do you think Mimmíu's a fool? Even if you manage to pull the wool over Domenico's eyes." She pronounced these last words with her shoulders while pretending to adjust the fire.

"You'll see, nothing will happen," Cristian answered finally, speaking as though hypnotised, with a tonelessness that in fact revealed maximum effort.

"But you know, for many years people have been saying you were not your father's son," Marianna said point-blank. She waited for Cristian to respond in some way, but when he said nothing, she continued: "Seeing how Vincenzo decided to end things, and how Cecilia found herself expecting you shortly after that, people naturally added two and two together and said your mother must have been expecting another man's child." Marianna paused again but Cristian remained obstinately silent. "And who do you think this other man was who was said to have been your real father?"

"Uncle Mimmíu?" her nephew answered, barely giving her time to finish the question.

"Exactly. Mimmíu. Can you believe it? So when his wife died, everyone said now everything would fall into place; and the widower would marry the widow and put an end to all the gossip. But in fact no. And do you know why not?"

"No, why?" Cristian realised his old aunt was trying to steer him somewhere he had no great wish to go, but he also understood that he was on a taut leash and had no chance of escape.

"Because there was nothing whatever that would fit. No secret relationship and no illegitimate son."

Cornered, Cristian decided to attack. "How can you be so sure of that?"

"Because all anyone needs to do is to look at you to see you're a Chironi and not a Guiso. To suggest anything else would be like mistaking black for white. When your father Vincenzo first came home to that door in his patched trousers, he never had any need to say who he was: he was so clearly a Chironi. You remember your great-grandpa Michele Angelo? May he rest in peace!" Cristian nodded. "There, he never asked who the boy was, as soon as he saw him he understood instantly, because whoever Vincenzo had imagined himself previously to be, as soon as he arrived here it was immediately obvious that he was a Chironi."

"Why are you telling me this?"

"Because you are looking straight at me," Marianna said, getting closer to her nephew and pointing at his eyes, in the light of the rekindled flames of the fire. "And you are trying to tell me that nothing has happened between you and Maddalena Pes?"

Cristian looked away; this was a battle he could not win. His aunt was a survivor and her maternal love by proxy hid a harshness he could almost scratch. He remembered that at Cecilia's funeral he and Marianna had been the only two not to weep – everyone has their own particular way of dealing with things. Cristian had not wept from rage and disbelief, while Marianna had not wept because she no longer wept at funerals, she just felt angry that so many people were departing this life. "That woman will never agree to die even if they kill her," people said of Marianna, not realising how absolutely right they were. Marianna no longer went to church though she still observed everything that could be expected of a good Roman Catholic: she turned her rosary beads, prayed for souls to be freed from Purgatory, crossed herself as protection from evil, and cleaned the statue of the Madonna of Lourdes that she kept in a niche in the corridor. The popular view was that she had not set foot in a church since June 1974, that is, since the day she told the parish priest that she had declared in public that she had voted NO in the referendum on the repeal of the divorce law. And this with the aggravated circumstance that she had perfectly understood that NO meant voting in favour of divorce and YES voting against it. People believed she must have had political reasons for this. Because if the truth were told, these Chironi – starting with their forebear who had founded the whole family from nothing, and continuing with his son Gavino who had got on the wrong side of some local fascists, and then Vincenzo who had been asked to stand in an election for the Communist Party – they had always been thought of as Communists. But the real reason Marianna had stopped going to church had been quite different: she was utterly fed up with having to go to so many funerals.

"Weren't you going to help me with the plants?" she asked Cristian now, as if to change the subject.

He agreed he had promised to do that.

"All you have to do is lift the pots for me because I can't do it with my back," she went on, continuing to glare at the boy like a god capable of creating tragedies. "But in any case, give plenty of thought to what you are doing," she finished.

Cristian went ahead of her into the yard without answering, and headed for the damp corner Marianna pointed out to him, where hydrangeas and wild jasmine were flourishing in great earthenware pots. These had to be moved and taken out of their pots, so that their roots could be cut shorter like human hair before they were put back to hibernate. That would keep them healthy. As the old woman saw it, the only way of keeping these plants healthy was to cut back whatever was depriving them of nourishment. And if you did not have the courage to cut off enough of their roots, they would simply exhaust themselves without giving anything in return. Which is why she and her nephew had to do what needed to be done. Marianna concentrated fiercely without saying a word, because what needed to be said seemed to have been said, and because she had succeeded in getting Cristian to deal with her plants in the way she expected him to deal with his own life.

"I know it isn't right, I know that," he mumbled, almost to himself, as he pressed down the soil threatening to overflow from the pot. Marianna let him get on with it. "It's stronger than me," he added, meaning he had tried to keep away from Maddalena.

"Can't you see that you are a Chironi?" Marianna shook her head disconsolately. "All the men in this family have ruined themselves for something stronger than they are."

"Then what should I do, in your opinion?" Cristian begged her.

"I don't know what you should do, but I'll tell you what you absolutely must not do. You mustn't say a word to Domenico."

Cristian threw himself down on the granite bench where for

thousands of years, it seemed, Michele Angelo had spent warm afternoons waiting for his missing wife to return from the far beyond.

"Is that quite clear?" Marianna insisted, sensing Cristian was no longer concentrating fully. Instinct was telling her it might already be too late, and that the weight of the Guiso family silence might be due to the anguish of knowledge rather than the serenity of ignorance. If anything was proof of the curse that afflicted Marianna, it was that there could be no doubt that she had a remarkable understanding of the two-legged animals known on this earth as human beings. And, basically, she had not liked the look on Mimmíu Guiso's face, nor his tone of voice, when he said certain things. So even if Domenico had never suspected any intrigue between Cristian and Maddalena, his father had certainly smelled a rat.

A few days earlier, Mimmíu had appeared early one morning at Marianna's house. She had offered him coffee which he had accepted and drunk calmly, savouring the sugar at the bottom of the cup. Then, as if it were nothing, he had asked the old woman whether she knew where Cristian was. And when she said no, he started to say things like Cristian was not in a position to understand who he was mixing with, and that, with the best will in the world, it had to be said that the lad had a tendency to be unwise, failing to understand the implications of things he did. For example, when it came to choosing his friends.

"Boys will be boys," Marianna admitted.

"At their age I'd already been at work for a good two years . . . Yes, signora," he added forcefully, seeing her shrug. "But do you realise the sort of times we are living in now? You have a television and you never switch it on!" Mimmíu pointed to the set hidden on its stool in a far corner of the room.

"I've no time to waste," the old woman said obstinately.

Mimmíu, who had seemed to be on his way out, stopped as though suddenly changing his mind, and sat down again. "No time? What have you got to do all day? Look, things out here are turning bad." Marianna simply curled her lip as if to say she had already amply foreseen every possible problem. "There are bastards out there killing people every day. You should go out more."

"Why? I'm perfectly happy in my own house." To judge from Marianna's tone, Mimmíu could perfectly well have spent the rest of his life trying to convince her of the opposite without getting anywhere.

"Look, these are not easy times, not like it used to be when life was simple and it was if you kill me, I'll kill you!"

"Those were easy times to understand perhaps," the old woman interrupted, "but it was never as simple as that, Mimmí. Perhaps you have forgotten that there was a time when you always carried a gun for fear people might rob you, just because you'd earned a little money. We might have been gentlefolk, but we always made a show of living as though we were dying of hunger. It was anything but easy."

"All I'm trying to say, Aunt Marià, is that the times have been changing too quickly, and now there are certain people, long-haired hippies and drug-users and all sorts, and since Cristian is of a responsible age he should not hang around with them," Mimmíu tried to continue.

But now Marianna was seriously annoyed: "What exactly are you trying to tell me?"

Mimmíu needed a little time. He went to the sink, turned on the tap, took a glass from the sideboard, filled it with water and drank thirstily. "I'm talking about politics . . . about politics. And other things," he added.

"What other things?" Marianna asked, fully aware the conversation was about to reach its intended destination. "Bad company, and what else?"

"More personal things, though it's just gossip at the moment, and I don't want to believe it . . ." Mimmíu drank more water. Marianna waited for him to continue. He went on: "But take care, what we are talking about here must be kept between you and me. I haven't even mentioned it to Domenico, but there's a rumour going around involving Cristian and . . ." Marianna did not move a muscle. ". . . and Maddalena. But it seems too serious to suggest and I can't believe Cristian would have done such a thing to Domenico, who has always accepted him as a brother."

"No," Marianna felt a need to intervene. "No, he hasn't merely accepted him, he's always treated him as more than a brother."

"And I believe Domenico has felt the same." The battle for positions had begun.

"Exactly. Then what are we talking about?"

"About the fact that Maddalena and Domenico are about to get engaged and the fact that, all exaggerations apart, you know even better than I do that when people talk there's usually a reason for it." Mimmíu's voice was sharp.

"People used to talk about Vincenzo too, saying he did what he did because you and Cecilia . . ."

"Oh, that! Never in this life!" Mimmíu reacted.

"Well, then, you and I can agree that people sometimes talk

nonsense. Then let's do it this way, Mimmíu, so as not to waste time reading or writing about it, let's fix a date for this engagement for your son and I'll make the house in via Deffenu available for the ceremony, so that anything anyone says will end up being nothing more than hot air.

Mimmíu, staring at a fixed point in the room, very slowly nodded yes. "That'll work, that'll work . . ."

"And if it doesn't work, we'll make it work," Marianna finished by saying.

Mimmíu knew how to live in the real world, he knew that before allowing a scandal to break, absolutely everything must be done to try and prevent it because too many different interests were at stake. In particular, now that Cristian had come of age and owned more than half the business, it was essential not to throw the baby out with the bath-water. Such prudence favoured Marianna: making the most of her pretence of not knowing, she needed to ask her nephew to pull back. So this she did, with infinite diligence.

It is often not so much movement that causes things to move, as, often, lack of movement. So in order to be sure that nothing would happen, it was essential to take action. Marianna was absolutely convinced of this.

"I've set a date with Mimmíu," she told Cristian, when she and her nephew had finished repotting the plants.

Cristian looked at her, hoping not to have understood, but of course, he had.

"Two weeks from now, Domenico and Maddalena Pes –" Marianna pronounced name and surname with deliberate detachment – "will promise to marry and thus become officially engaged.

I have offered the house in via Deffenu which is large enough for the ceremony." End of part one. "If you young people want to organise something for yourselves, maybe for the following day, go ahead, since one no longer understands what you people like or don't like . . . But this engagement will be done properly and with everyone's agreement, understand?" End of part two. "And a trip to the barber won't do you any harm, I'll pay for that." Third and last part.

Cristian watched her as she went back into the house. His hands were stained with soil, his chest and collar sweaty, his breathing carefully controlled as though he were about to jump and was just waiting for the right moment. "Aren't you going to water those plants?" he said to the old woman's shoulders as she was reaching the house.

"No need," Marianna replied, without even turning.

In fact, astonishingly, it now began to rain. Regular large drops printed themselves on his shirt which had been washed too often to still have any natural colour. The rain fell from a clear cloudless sky, as if in generous homage to his work. Soft rain, which tasted good, and was specially and entirely for him. Cristian opened his mouth wide to it, like when as a child he had swallowed snow directly from the sky before it touched the ground.

Marianna, watching him from the kitchen through the French window, moaned silently and begged for some kindness from the motionless sky. "My love . . ." she murmured. "My love, my darling . . . Accursed, accursed . . ."

WHEN IT CAME TO PREPARATIONS FOR DOMENICO GUISO and Maddalena Pes' official engagement no expense was spared, even though the Guiso family lived with the modesty of the truly rich of Núoro, who found it more unbecoming to flaunt their wealth than to accumulate it without inhibition. Over the years, Mimmíu had come to understand that having friends in key positions was more important than hunting down lucrative commissions. Soon widowed and never remarried, a successful businessman who had started from nothing, always catching up rather than leading, Mimmíu had built up a considerable fortune, though this was not obvious. People who described him as the type to have a mattress stuffed with banknotes, were wrong. They laughed at him for wearing heavy boots and corduroy trousers when he met important people, but that was a misinterpretation too. They said he avoided eating so as not to have to shit, that he was stingy, and that his attitude to economics was basic, but that was another mistake. They also claimed he had grown ever more barbarous with the passing years and that from having once been a young man in step with his own times he had become a sort of closed, ignorant and savage troglodyte, but here again, as always, they were wrong.

On top of that, everyone, without exception, believed him to have been miraculously rescued by the Chironi family. They saw Mimmíu and the story of his life as that of some kind of domestic animal, a stray dog perhaps, befriended by that Vincenzo who had had everything and then for no apparent reason decided to take his own life. In fact, to hear people talking, you would imagine that Vincenzo Chironi's suicide had been the very cause of Mimmíu Guiso's fortune. People are terrible, they can never count beyond the fingers of one hand and imagine everything to be utterly obvious. Vincenzo had no children and never even knew any in his lifetime; such was the Chironi curse. His wife Cecilia's pregnancies had never resulted in living children. But when Mimmíu married, his wife had immediately given him a son. Which brings us to the Christmas dinner party of 1959. This was said to have been a very ordinary family party, with all the usual presents, best wishes, too much food and consequent exhaustion. Then Vincenzo vanished in the middle of the night, and after a search he was found dead, hanging from the rafters of the building that had served as his firm's office. But who found him? Mimmíu, of course. And a month later it was revealed that Cecilia, by some miracle, was pregnant again. So what?

Despite all this, the matter that should have made everything clear but instead caused a mass of complications, was the new fact that the engagement of the Guiso heir was to be held at a Chironi residence.

During the whole of the preceding week, sweetmeats had been made for the party: meringues, sponge fingers, amaretti and petits fours, as if the purpose were to mimic an actual wedding party.

Small ivory-coloured invitation cards were printed, announcing that Domenico Guiso and Maddalena Pes were pleased to announce their engagement; and that their happy families looked forward to welcoming relatives and friends at the Chironi house at via Deffenu 20, Núoro. This was where Marianna had once lived with that Fascist husband of hers, and later Vincenzo with Cecilia.

It was entirely pointless for Domenico and Maddalena to object to all the fuss. Despite themselves they had been bounced back a century to an age when families were mainly united by the formality with which wedding contracts were established.

Maddalena realised she had been trapped by Cristian's silence; his decision to talk to Domenico had melted away into an inconclusive muteness. Since the afternoon three days earlier when they had made love, she had not been able to find time to be alone with him – not even so much as time for a quick nod. She saw herself as an emancipated woman, but knew she was not strong enough to admit on her own in front of everybody that she loved Cristian and thus could not go through with the sham that this engagement party promised to be. When Domenico, a little embarrassed but also touched, showed her the cardboard invitation cards that Mimmíu had had printed, she said nothing.

The evening before the official ceremony, when everything was ready, Domenico insisted that Maddalena and her family walk together on foot to the house in via Deffenu. To her this seemed unnecessarily theatrical, and to all intents and purposes so it was. But it had been discussed so often that the thread of the argument had got lost and turned into something else.

It was a remarkable February, dry and extremely cold. Not just dry, but airless. Maddalena looked out at the empty street below with its motionless electric cables and far off, beyond the clusters of new houses, the countryside. To her this seemed entirely real, like a great stage set created entirely for her own benefit. She imagined her future like a precocious fruit-tree, a peach flowering in a deceptive spring-time, in a season turned to stone.

She could detect desperation in Domenico's voice as he tried to control his anxiety: the steady obstinacy with which he tried to dismiss the possibility that she might not love him, loading his words with passion in the hope of making them last for ever.

Yet what he was saying was simple enough: that he understood and he was waiting with teeth clenched. He said that this satisfying of some sort of delusion of Mimmíu's would make it possible for them to live in peace. That was not too much to expect, surely?

And Maddalena, recalled by his voice from the settled world she had glimpsed through the window, found herself agreeing with him: Alright, alright; it was as if she was telling herself, all we need is an end to this nonsense.

The ultimate purpose of the party was to prepare for the reality of the wedding. After another year Domenico and Maddalena would meet on the square in front of the cathedral. He dressed up to the nines and she in white, not like those modern brides who no longer wore veils but approached the altar in coloured clothes. Nor was there any more talk of organising a traditional reception in some decorated hall or tyre-salesman's emptied workshop. For this wedding a hotel would be needed, as was the custom on the mainland. With dinner and formalities included and guests who had nothing to do beyond making their way from the church to the restaurant; then maybe a little dancing to a small orchestra, all done tastefully and without any long-haired hippy musicians.

Domenico checked himself from head to toe while Mimmíu adjusted his tie. "But have you seen Cristian?" he asked.

Mimmíu said no; it was two days since Cristian had even been in the shop. "I thought he might be ill; I asked Aunt Marianna, and she said no, he wasn't ill, but she hadn't seen much of him either. He must be busy with other things . . . but he'll be at the party, you'll see."

"Damn right he will," Domenico remarked, before going over to the mirror to check that the hair at his neck and the quiff on his forehead were looking right.

At Maddalena's home an unnatural calm reigned; her family were anxious at this public exposure, afraid they might let the side down. The girl came from a humble but dignified family: her father was a council workman, her mother a housewife. Of her two brothers, one was already married and had been in Belgium for the last seven years. The family lived in a flat in a public housing block. They had bought the engagement dress in instalments and it was worth it, because it was "fashionable" without being eccentric, just above the knee but not excessively short. Maddalena worried that she might feel cold, as she looked at herself in the large sideboard mirror beyond the sitting-room table, dressed up like a young cinema star, raised on high heels and slimmed by the bell-like dress to a geometrical fantasy of orange and mustard, her hair coiffed to fall in firm curls along her cheeks. The beautician had defined this style as "*alla Cleopatra*" but in Maddalena's opinion it just made her look ridiculous. So she shut herself up in the bathroom where she could finish her make-up carefully with only the lightest touch of gold on her eyelids and a faint pencil mark along the edge of her lashes.

Then she joined her family: her father Peppino, her mother Nevina, and her younger brother Roberto together with a maiden aunt, Vera; her elder brother Raffaello had been unable to get leave from his work abroad. The Pes family. Each one stylish with the elegance of people about to step onto a stage, though each feeling insecure in his or her own particular way. All were now gathered near the door, waiting for a sign from the party girl, all with the anxious expressions of people who would worry all evening about getting dirt on their clothes.

Maddalena looked lovingly at them. "Let's go," she said. "But is it raining?" she added, noticing her mother and father were carrying umbrellas.

"No, but it looks as if it might," Peppino said, clearing his throat. He did not find talking to his daughter easy, not because he did not love her, but because she was, as they say, one who had "ideas of her own" about things. Someone who had to be persuaded about everything. This engagement, for example, which had been arranged as though the most important thing about it was to be seen. For Peppino Pes, a municipal gardener, this emphasis on appearance was absolutely the worst thing possible.

"Put a handkerchief over your head but don't tie it too tight," Nevina advised her daughter.

"It really is wet," Aunt Vera added, adjusting the shawl round her neck yet again. It was obvious that, though they were ready, no-one wanted to be the first to leave the house.

Then suddenly, as if in response to an agreed signal, the whole family moved together. But when Peppino opened the front door of the flat, Maddalena begged them to wait a moment and ran back into the bathroom.

Cristian opened his eyes wide. It was as if he had woken up a little too soon and come to the conclusion – without being exactly conscious of it – that he had no idea where he was; his becoming aware of himself and opening his eyes wide had been a single action. It came to him that he was in some unknown place, a bedsit with a miscellaneous jumble of furniture, and in an unknown bed with a mattress laid on pallet boxes painted red, and that he was entirely naked and sleeping beside him were a girl and a boy who were both naked too.

He sat up. The girl, opening one eye, said "Good morning", in a sleepy voice, and reached for Cristian's thigh. "Feeling better?" she asked. Cristian looked at her as if trying to fit her into some recent event in his life. She burst out laughing. "I'm Federica," she said. "Don't you remember me?" Rather than answer, Cristian turned towards the boy sleeping beside the girl. "That's Raimondo," she explained.

Now fragments of the previous evening began to return to Cristian. The bedsit had been full of people discussing in heated voices the necessity of violence for creating change. He stared round the walls: there was a poster looking forward to Sardinia leaving Nato, and a 1977 Pirelli calendar. He paused to wonder whether there might be anything creative in all that brightly repainted charity furniture, and the lamps with paper shades slightly burnt by heat. Dirty plates were stacked in a bucket and the ashtrays were overflowing with butt ends, filters and joints.

"What's the time?" he asked the girl, who had lit a cigarette.

"About four . . . Or maybe five . . . Who knows, my watch has stopped."

"Fuck," Cristian remarked, struggling to his feet.

"Aren't you going to stay?" Federica asked.

Meanwhile, beside her, the boy called Raimondo had turned on his back, revealing an unusually hairy chest and bearded face. "What time is it?" he asked in his turn, yawning. "You going? . . . What's your name?"

Cristian realised no answer was needed. In fact Raimondo, not expecting a reply, had got up and was now peeing with the bathroom door open. He was certainly the hairiest person Cristian had ever seen in his life: even his shoulders were covered with thick dark fur.

"Fuck . . ." Cristian repeated, searching for his clothes. Some of them had fallen under a small table in the dining area.

"Perhaps this is what you're looking for." The hairy caveman held out a pair of briefs. "So you wear underpants," he commented, "how bourgeois can you get?"

"Has no-one got a watch that works?" Cristian asked, beginning to panic.

The girl pulled a square alarm clock from under the bed. "It's five-thirteen," she pronounced in a singing voice.

Domenico took a step back, puffed out his chest in front of the mirror in the entrance hall and fastened the middle button of his tight-fitting jacket. Then he moved forward towards his own image almost as though about to kiss himself, checked his two sideburns were identical in length, and smiled to himself. He straightened the large knot of his tie. It was not easy to feel elegant when you had to stand straight, hold in your stomach and fight for breath with your shirt-collar completely buttoned up. He began to worry about a host of small details he had never given a thought to before, such as how much weight he had been putting on. You could not call Domenico fat, but he was certainly robust and well-covered, solid in both body and attitude. Mimmíu noticed this with hope and anxiety, because he knew how important this could be and also how dangerous it could become. He knew, for example, that many women who claimed to prefer strong, reliable men, would end up falling desperately in love with a weak man who inspired no confidence. He knew this only too well, Mimmíu did. And as he watched his son examining himself in the mirror he felt a sort of angry tenderness, because he knew that after the first moment of compassion, he would have to warn that big happy boy about the fate that lay in store for reliable men on this earth.

"Cristian?" Domenico suddenly asked. Mimmíu paused, then shook his head. "Where can he have got to?" Domenico added, more or less to himself.

"He'll be at via Deffenu already," Mimmíu cut in, smoothing the folds on his son's shoulders. The turn the conversation was taking worried him. "But I never expected him to do this to me . . ." Domenico said, unthreading the pockets of his jacket with his fingers. "I mean, vanishing like this," he added, since his father said nothing more.

"You know what he's like," Mimmíu ventured.

"Well, what is he like?" Domenico asked as if to catch his father off guard, even more worried.

"He has a mind of his own," Mimmíu said, trying to sound

63

more positive. "After all, he's a Chironi and they always . . ."

Domenico laughed. "At least there can be no doubt about that. But I wish he could be happy," he said, as though wishing for something were enough to make it true, and firmly smoothed down his pockets. Mimmíu had to control himself and closed his eyes as if they were burning him. He didn't want to talk about Cristian's unhappiness. He was too old not to understand its origin, but not old enough to be tempted to explain it to his son. "It's not important," was all he said.

Domenico seemed to need a moment or two to take this in. "It's important to me," he protested.

"I mean, it's not important at this particular moment. You know what Cristian's like. That's all I was trying to say." Mimmíu seemed to be excusing himself.

Domenico looked at his father; a sort of embarrassment surfaced in him whenever their conversations verged on intimacy. "It's because I know what he's like that I can't understand it," he insisted obstinately.

Rain was threatening, and Mimmíu looked around in search of the right words. "Your mother should have been here," he said clumsily; "she would have known what to say."

"There is nothing else to say. When something's not right, it's not right, it's as simple as that," Domenico insisted.

"I think it's going to rain," Mimmíu said. "Go and get your raincoat."

The young man nodded and headed for his room. Mimmíu was on the point of going after him and explaining that what the boy was just about to do might turn out to be the worst mistake of his life. But he resisted the temptation and stayed where he was, standing between the hall and the small dining room, waiting for Domenico to come back in his coat.

Now that her nausea seemed to have passed, Maddalena forced herself to look in the mirror. She could barely recognise her face.

Whether she should respond to the instinct that was desperately urging her to escape, she could not say: she knew that outside the bathroom her whole family were waiting, though not wondering why they were waiting for her. She was well able to understand the despotic element in the unconditional love she expected from her father, because at this point he would not even have dared to think of stopping her. She rinsed out her mouth, applied more lipstick, and added a touch of powder round her eyes, which the force of her vomiting had shaded. She tried to relax the tension she could see in her eyebrows.

She winced when she found her mother on the other side of the bathroom door, standing in her overcoat and carrying an umbrella, just as she had been when Maddalena had left them all to run off and be sick. Her mother stared at her.

"It's getting late," Nevina said.

They continued to look at each other.

"What's the matter?" Maddalena said, set on edge by her mother's impatience.

"Only you know what the matter is. Tell me." Nevina waited for her daughter to speak. But Maddalena said nothing. "If you don't want to go ahead no-one is forcing you ... but just remember, you got yourself into this on your own."

A forced laugh escaped Maddalena. "I'm a bit nervous. Weren't you nervous when you got engaged to Babbo?"

"No," her mother said abruptly. "Not at all. Are you quite sure you're alright?"

"Well, obviously we're different." Maddalena was still struggling to keep her voice calm.

"Quite sure?" her mother asked again.

"Quite sure of what? What do you want of me?" Maddalena shouted to include the rest of the family, none of whom had moved.

Nevina bit her lip and prayed to God, in the hope that what she suspected was not the case. "Tell us when you're ready," she said, joining the others in the hall.

Cristian dressed in a hurry with his back to the bed. Before leaving he turned to say goodbye to Raimondo and Federica who, both still naked, were sitting on the mattress. Raimondo was rolling a joint, austere and concentrated as an Armenian prince, with Federica in waiting like his admiring consort.

"I'm off," Cristian said.

Both acknowledged this neither dismissively nor with conviction, carrying on with what they were doing yet at the same time clearly not meaning to be rude. "See you around," Raimondo said, skilfully licking his cigarette-paper. "Great, wasn't it, last night?"

Federica smiled at Cristian. When he reached for the handle of the door to the hall, she said, "We're not all the same." Cristian stopped in his tracks. "Last night you said we're all the same, but we're not."

Raimondo lit his joint and deeply inhaled his first mouthful. "Quite sure you don't want to stay a bit longer?" he said, interpreting Cristian's hesitation as second thoughts.

Cristian left without answering.

Outside, the air, heavy with incipient rain, carried a hint of salt and bile. Like the bitterness of some beaches at night when there is a storm at sea. But perhaps it was more the horrible taste on Cristian's palate. He had been smoking and drinking non-stop for two days, and there had been sex too, though he had no exact memory of that. All he could remember was bodies, hands and mouths. Suddenly he felt a need to vomit, which he did on reaching a relatively remote lane. Then, wiping his lips on the back of his hand, he headed for home.

Luckily the house was empty. Marianna had gone early in the afternoon to the via Deffenu house with the Guiso women to get the party ready.

That gave him plenty of time to change, wash and shave.

He wept at how life had made a mockery of him, but he wept calmly, almost with resignation. Washed and shaved, he stretched out on his bed looking for a reason, any reason, why he should not get up again. But not finding one, he sat up with difficulty and put on the smart clothes Marianna had left ready for him.

He was feeling cold in a way that seemed to come from somewhere outside him, from the room and the bed. The cold, he was certain, was from another world, an accumulation of all the sufferings that accursed house had seen.

No-one would ever have wanted to change things, and this made him feel even colder. He knew only too well that neither he nor Maddalena, having reached this point, would have wanted to throw everything away. Not because they could not, but simply because they did not want to. And to romantics everywhere, this could mean that they did not love each other enough, though to them it meant that you could not be happy if you loved to the detriment of others. So, unhappy at being unhappy, they had decided, without even needing to say anything to each other, to be unhappy with other people rather than on their own. On their own they would have certainly had regrets, but not unhappiness. They loved each other beyond all measure, but could not, did not, want to possess one another. How to explain that? No explanation was possible. They could only move on.

For the last two days they had felt through the pulsing and contracting of their temples and stomachs as though they still needed to vomit but no longer had anything to throw up. Buttoning his shirt collar was harder than Cristian could have imagined possible, so he left it undone and did not tighten his tie. He put on his jacket and combed his hair in front of the large square mirror on the chest of drawers, pursing his lips so as not to weep. The man facing him in the mirror was making an infinite effort, as if stripped down in just a few hours to his most basic form. Freshly shaven, he looked so young, no-one could have imagined he had reached puberty. If Marianna had been there she would have been able to make a pedantic assessment of how many Chironi family members could be detected in the face and body of this suffering youth: Gavino, his great-uncle, who shared his hair colour, his grandfather Luigi Ippolito who had had the same grey-green eyes, and his father Vincenzo who shared his dry complexion.

No sooner had he covered the first two or three hundred metres after leaving the house, than it started to pelt with rain.

Luckily the downpour did not start until a few minutes after the Pes family reached the house in via Deffenu. Apart from Maddalena, none of them had ever been there before, nor had they ever expected to go there. But the fact was, that was where they were. Leaving their umbrellas and overcoats in the hall, which seemed to them big enough to be an apartment in itself, they were led into the main room where everything had been prepared for the reception. Nevina studied it all with precise curiosity: the way things had been arranged, the tableware, the crystal glasses. She tried not to show how much she resented as mother of the bride-to-be not having been involved in any way in these preparations. But it was quite clear that the Guiso and Chironi families had no intention of mixing with the Pes family if they could avoid it. Marianna emerged from the back of the room specially to welcome Nevina, thus making it clear that Nevina's resentment was not entirely unfounded. "So much work . . ." Nevina commented to the lady of the house, forcing herself to appear calm.

"Don't imagine we did all this ourselves . . ." Marianna replied, addressing Nevina in the formal third person. "We got others to do the work; we have long passed the days when we would have worn ourselves out doing such things ourselves . . . It's all quite different now, even we women insist on our freedom: no, we ordered everything in."

"Oh," Nevina said, "if you can afford it . . ."

This brief exchange was interrupted by a burst of applause as Maddalena came into the room.

"What a beautiful girl," Marianna remarked; "My most sincere compliments."

Nevina looked at her in astonishment. "Compliments? All we did was bring her into the world; others have transformed her into this." She cut herself short, trying to keep her tone neutral, so as not to seem arrogant.

Meanwhile, Maddalena was looking around for Domenico. She caught a glimpse of him as he appeared from the corridor drawn in by the applause, then went up and put her arms round him in front of everyone. More applause. Mimmíu, dressed unusually smartly, greeted the gathering and invited them to help themselves.

Marianna and the Guiso women really had organised everything exceptionally well. Some seventy or so carefully selected people had been invited: many of them friends and relatives of his, a few of them hers. There were also a few representatives of the local community: Maresciallo Idini and his wife for the Carabinieri, the notary Sini, who was a widower, accompanied by his unmarried eldest daughter; and even Doctor Marletta, now considerably stricken in years but still in good shape, and also, naturally, the parish priest from the Rosario Church, Father Tanchis. In the main room the young people had formed a group of their own. It was obvious that the party would have been different had they organised it, and in fact they were only there at all under pressure from the older generation.

"Cristian?" Domenico whispered in Maddalena's ear.

"No idea," she answered looking around.

"You look lovely." He tickled her neck.

"Thank you," she answered. "So do you."

Domenico gave a nervous laugh.

"Thanks to you, doing this for me . . . all this, I mean," he added, inspired.

"For us," she corrected. "It's for us."

Then they said things like how great she looked with her hair done like that, and how he ought to wear a tie more often.

Marianna sat in a corner of the main room contemplating

what had once been her own house as though she had never seen it before. From that very position, years before, she had heard Cecilia losing a child for the second time. That had been in 1956, when a snowstorm like none before it had smothered Núoro like a precious object covered in cotton-wool. It was also where Marianna had laid out the body of her husband, killed in an attempted kidnapping back in 1932, when it had been so suffocatingly hot outside the windows that the corpse had to be nailed into its coffin before it swelled up. Yet she also realised that that terrible time had suddenly come to seem the best of her life, filled with expectation if only bearable because of the prospect of some compensating reward in old age. A reward that had never come to her. Now a young Guiso girl came up with a trayful of small meringues, which Marianna refused. At the other end of the room Mimmíu and Maresciallo Idini were deep in conversation.

"You were right about Cristian, Mimmíu," the Maresciallo was saying.

Mimmíu was alarmed. "Has he done something he shouldn't?"

"No, not at all, at least not yet . . . but he keeps bad company. A certain Raimondo Bardi, for instance, who is under surveillance for possession of drugs and weapons, even if, so far, we haven't been able to pin anything on him."

"Ah." Mimmíu sighed. "But Cristian has no connection with anyone like that, Marescià . . . he may be a bit special, but he's a good lad."

"Lots of them are good lads till we find proof to the contrary, Mimmí. I know you're no expert in these matters, but you'd do well to drop a hint that he could keep better company. You know

71

what awful times we're living in now, you don't need me to tell you that."

The worse the times we're living in, the more valuable beauty must be. That was what Mimmíu was thinking, though he didn't have words to express it. But it was enough to see Domenico and Maddalena in each other's arms for physical proof of what he could not put into words. He was glad now he had not yielded to the temptation of warning his son about the common gossip doing the rounds, that the exceptionally beautiful woman now holding him in her arms in full view of everyone, had already given herself to Cristian Chironi. He looked for Marianna among the guests, who were crowding round the buffet tables just as people did in the homes of the rich on the mainland. Marianna saw him searching for her and they exchanged an almost imperceptible nod: the solution they had agreed on had been the only one possible.

The rain got really heavy just as Cristian was about to start down via Ballero. He had no umbrella, having assumed that, despite the menacing clouds, it would not actually rain. He had clearly assumed wrong. He began running, but in no time at all his socks and elegant mocassins were completely soaked. The padded shoulders of his jacket absorbed the downpour and sent a constant trickle down his back and chest. His fine hair, so recently and expensively cut, began to stick to his skull.

When he reached the house in via Deffenu he remembered he had not been there for nearly a year, not since his mother Cecilia died.

He was greeted at the door by the little girl who had offered meringues to Marianna. "I don't want to spread water everywhere,"

Cristian told her. The child agreed, but seemed not to understand what Cristian needed more than meringues. "A towel!" he exclaimed, pulling off his jacket. Suddenly understanding, the little girl vanished into the main room from where the voices of the guests could be heard.

A minute or two later, Marianna emerged with the towel. "Where have you been?" she asked him sharply.

Cristian started rubbing his dripping head, while his shirt had become one with his skin.

Totally soaked, with his hair a mess and the towel over his shoulders, he crossed the main room and slipped past the guests. But Domenico saw him and waved, while Maddalena was suspiciously slow in turning round.

In the room that had once witnessed his mother's terminal illness, he was able to change into dry clothes that Marianna had found in the corridor cupboards between the day rooms and the bedrooms.

He had just put on a pair of dry underpants when Domenico burst into the room. "Why are you doing this to me?" he demanded, as if continuing an argument interrupted earlier.

Cristian did not dare to answer back. "I don't know," he said.

"You should be happy. I would be, in your place."

Cristian said nothing. He looked round for a pair of socks, but not seeing any, gave up.

"Can't you even try to be happy for us?" Domenico insisted, as if this was something essential for his survival.

"I am . . . really I am." And the funny thing was that as he said this, Cristian was certain it was really true.

Domenico stared at him. Cristian was more naked than clothed, slim and scrawny as a monk, and immensely sad in a way only children can be. "Everyone thinks I've not understood anything," Domenico began softly. "But I know very well that all this has been imagined because of reasons that you know of . . . but I refused to believe it. That you ever could have done such a thing to me. No. And I would not believe it even if you insisted the opposite was true . . ."

Cristian went up to him, took Domenico's candid face in his hands and, pulling him closer, kissed him on the lips. A long, soft kiss. Domenico stood his ground, not moving until Cristian stepped back, merely stretching out his arms. "That's enough now," Cristian murmured with chilling gentleness. "I have to get dressed."

Apart from a polite word or two, Maddalena and Cristian did not speak to each other during the party, as if confirming that everything was just as it was supposed to be. Under Marianna's vigilant eye, this gathering that everyone in Núoro must have been commenting on passed off without incident. After strong drinks and cakes, after salad and wine, came the presentation of the ring. Followed by a cake in the form of a would-be wedding band that imitated its model so accurately that it moved everyone.

Finally, with the rain slackening, the guests began to thin out. The Guiso women and Marianna did the clearing-up without letting Nevina Pes help. Domenico and Maddalena took their leave before the last guests had gone, just as if it had been a wedding reception.

Cristian announced he would stay and sleep in his old room. Marianna did not protest, though she realised what a profoundly self-punishing decision this must be. She knew every one of the ghosts that lived in that house, but took care not to warn her young great-nephew; she had long ago given up advising anyone about anything. So, once everything else had been sorted out, she just got his room ready. Cristian tried feebly to protest, but was too tired even to understand how tired he was.

"We need to talk." Mimmíu had sprung up from nowhere behind him.

"Yes, tomorrow maybe," Cristian said, looking desperately for somewhere to sit.

Mimmíu sat down in front of him as though Cristian had not even spoken. "But do you know how much the business is worth?" he began. "Have you any idea?" Cristian indicated that he had. "Then what are you getting up to?"

"What?" Cristian was seriously confused.

Mimmíu gave him a long stare. "Nothing, you are really contributing nothing, let me tell you that. Apart from going around with the most disreputable people. We work in the public sector, remember that . . . respectability is everything. What's going on?" he asked, leaning forward and tapping Cristian on the knee.

"I don't know, I don't know . . . I feel so tired."

"If you had a problem you'd tell me, wouldn't you? You know you're like a son to me. . ."

For no clear reason, Cristian felt he had to defend himself against this show of affection. "My father's dead," he stated, drawing back from Mimmíu.

"I know that, you young brat, I know that only too well." Mimmíu's tone suddenly became cutting. "It was I who found him. And you aren't even worth as much as his finger-nail."

"Public acclaim and money, that's all that interests you," Cristian hit back, staring him in the face.

Mimmíu held his gaze, then shook his head. "You overgrown baby, you dickhead," he said. "Do you need a cause? Can't you accept the fact that things haven't gone the way you'd have liked them to go? Is that a reason to wreck everything? Have you any idea how many people like you I demolish every day? You may take me for an idiot, but that's one thing I'm not. You may be able to fool Domenico, but I know what's going on in your head. And I'm telling you to watch it. Be very careful. Because if things are the way I think they are, and I'm not talking about the business now, then I'll show you . . ."

"And what will you show me?" Cristian was getting agitated, and could not control himself.

Mimmíu held his gaze without even getting to his feet.

Marianna chose that moment to appear. "Your room is ready," she said, then squared up to the two men and asked them what was going on.

"We've had a talk," Mimmíu told her. "Man to man."

"Go and rest," Marianna said to Cristian in that particular tone of hers that was just a millimetre from issuing a command.

"Yes," Mimmíu agreed. "Rest is what you need. A good sleep's better than any medicine."

"What wisdom," Cristian commented, heading for his room.

It had stopped raining. The streets were as slippery as the backs of eels, the sky over Núoro a dripping sponge. A troubled breath emanated from the trees and surrounding hills. The world seemed to have stopped weeping as if for an indefinite period, like the final sob after a crisis, but a spasmodic wind had arisen from the whirlpool of time to mould the clouds into a purple ring, and among them a few unusually bright stars stood out. Something to replace disaster with hope. One may never take much notice of words, but if one is aware of one's surroundings, the quality of that darkness and the absence of stars that accompanied it may give some idea of the meaning of the word disaster.

Cristian slept fitfully.

But he dreamed he was a child hearing his grandfather Luigi Ippolito describing how he came to meet his grandmother Erminia.

. . . There was that matter of keeping absolutely still: Corporal Sanseverino had often told them the only way to avoid being seen in the dark was not to move. Which was why they were waiting at the foot of Monte Santo, scarcely breathing and not making the slightest movement.

"You know how it happens, don't you?" his young, uniformed, grandfather said.

Cristian indicated he didn't.

Luigi Ippolito gave a light laugh: no, of course you don't, he thought, seeing that his grandson against all expectation was saying nothing and waiting for him to carry on.

A light wind rose, adding pungency to the air. Now, when you breathed, you could taste the impending night. Luigi Ippolito unbuttoned his jacket to feel the air on his chest, exposing his white shirt and welcoming the relief he felt with a half-smile.

"Well," he continued eventually, "the thing was not to be seen. We had been pretty lucky up to then: a thick fog had suddenly come down from nowhere. It was December, as I told you."

Cristian nodded, his grandfather had indeed already said it was December. And it must have been a relatively mild December; not too cold, but maintaining the same temperature, like an obstinate fragment of autumn determined to continue for ever.

"It was nearly Christmas, our first Christmas as soldiers," his grandfather went on. "Everything we normally did then at home, like our expedition to see Don Cabiddu to be given parts in the pageant, or clearing snow from the yard in front of the forge with Gavino, or eating whole slices of *sebada filante* without even waiting for it to cool; these things suddenly seemed unbelievably far away. It felt as if we had moved on several millennia in just a few years. But that's not what we were talking about . . ."

Cristian studied his grandfather more closely: there was something uncorrupted about him as if, sixty years after his death, he had managed to preserve a stubborn youthfulness. But that's what dreams are like, isn't it? We can talk to someone who has been dead for decades as if they were contemporary with us, and understand things that cannot normally be understood. And some dreams can be tenacious.

"It was December . . ." Cristian prompted, so his grandfather would not stop telling the story.

Luigi Ippolito quietly resumed: "A beautiful December," he continued. "The summer here is certainly endless, and the little bit of winter that survives has a melancholy sort of sweetness."

Cristian was well able to understand that melancholy; for him winter on the island was motionless in time. And it was precisely that motionless time that made him wish to escape and travel as far away as possible.

Luigi Ippolito started again. "There had been a rather animated discussion between the lads in the platoon, because some thought it was worth leaving it to the friars to find the right moment to signal the surrender, while others argued we must act at once and organise a pre-emptive lightning strike under cover of the absolute darkness . . . Remember, there were fifty-seven of us in all, and we did not yet know what we would learn an hour or two later, that eighty Austrian soldiers were barricaded inside the Church of Monte Santo . . . either we were really lucky, or perhaps it was just that during that December of 1915 even the seasons had grown tired of fighting, and were sliding into one another in a sleepy sequence."

"I don't understand," his grandson interrupted. "Did you want to capture the church?"

He waited for his grandfather to confirm this, which he did.

"And then the whole mountain?"

"The one involved the other . . . Aren't you sleepy?"

Cristian was indeed sleepy; he was back in the room where he had slept as a child, which accounted for it.

"You said you'd tell me how you met grandmother . . ." the boy insisted.

"Would you mind if we continued tomorrow?" Luigi Ippolito now said, without even waiting for a negative response.

Cristian agreed that would be alright, but in fact this was not quite true.

"Tomorrow" was his next dream.

This involved great-uncle Gavino, who died at sea.

Massed together with more than four hundred prisoners in the hold of a cruise-ship acting as a prison, in the real sense of the word. Because he was an Italian in England when we passed from allies to enemies of the English. Here was yet another Chironi who found himself in the wrong place at the wrong time. In fact, in the belly of the *Arandora Star* when she left Liverpool for a prisoner-of-war camp in Australia. To Gavino, that voyage beyond Britain's shores should have saved him from the Fascists who had tried to crush him to teach him a lesson, never mind that he happened also to be a Chironi.

Cristian knew only one photo of that great-uncle, when he was very young at the seaside . . .

He had always thought people were exaggerating when they insisted that he and Gavino looked like one another. From the black-and-white photograph it was impossible to see clearly if Gavino's hair had been the same colour as his, as Marianna claimed.

But as he was dreaming, perhaps he could have used his own eyes to decide whether the colour was identical or not. Can you dream in colour?

Crossing the sea did not save Gavino. In the case of his brother Luigi Ippolito, on the other hand, leaving for the war as a volunteer had saved him from himself. For him literature had been more important than life. He believed all you had to do was tell a story for the story to come true. He believed in a Biblical breath that could transform words into flesh. So he had written a fanciful story describing the origin of the Chironi family, which in fact had never had any real origin . . .

"Tomorrow" was his next dream.

On December 23, 1915, at the foot of Monte Santo, a platoon

of fifty-two men were in sight of the church on the summit.

Not that he could say it with certainty, because neither he nor his fellow-soldiers as they waited for orders could claim they had been able to see much. Though in fact the pitch darkness surrounding them was occasionally lit by flashes, like when two metals scraping against one another produce sparks. And they were aware of mines which seemed to explode in the sky but were in fact exploding on the highest crest of the mountain, next to the sanctuary.

It was there, while they were waiting, that Corporal Sanseverino, whom Luigi Ippolito had first met at the clearing station, had produced his theory that in such circumstances, the less you moved, the less likely you were to attract attention. He had insisted that with the light behind them they must squat and stay motionless, disobeying nature which was urging them to run for their lives.

"When the order comes," he said, "advance calmly: one step, then stop and wait, then another step."

In photographs taken from airships, the summit of the mountain looked like a sea-horse or, to anyone with more imagination, a hammerhead shark.

Long ago, during the night of time, the sea had gently caressed the shores of the Dolomites, but there had been more recent moments, even just a few millennia ago, when these shores had been eroded by roaring waves that had drawn back after carving the valley. The very same valley where five infantrymen on reconnaissance had allowed themselves to be swallowed up.

Suddenly from the summit came a signal of surrender: three white rockets like when the fireworks begin after the Madonna has been put back in her alcove. When the godless follows the holy.

No sooner had these five foot-soldiers started their climb than they realised that the slopes of the mountain were more densely inhabited than they had suspected. Mostly by groups of shepherds or foresters and their families.

"They suddenly gave us the order to advance." Cristian made himself comfortable while Luigi Ippolito continued his story: "They told us to advance and make a lot of noise. So we ran and shouted like when, as boys on horses in full harness, at a carnival, we wanted to impress the women we were attracted to . . ."

"But you, didn't you ever want to come back here, I mean back home to the island?" Cristian asked suddenly.

The answer was simple, but his grandfather took time over it. "Yes, I did," he said eventually, "and I did come back, didn't I?"

They looked at each other like people in the know. The grandson looking for a supporting hand or authorisation, the older man wanting to give body to his absence.

"So you ran with the others towards the summit," Cristian said bluntly.

"Together with everyone else," his grandfather agreed. "It was strange, treading that ground. It was completely dark because there was no source of light; and the few inhabitants left had been hit hard by war and retreated in good time. Yet suddenly, at nightfall, it all changed, and every light was forbidden . . . everyone did their best to be self-sufficient. The mountain folk even ate small shelled creatures straight from the rocks. As soon as we started climbing we could hear the noise of people coming towards us waving torches and a few gaslights: 'Here,' they were crying out. 'Here!' Women, most of them. And children."

"Grandmother too?" Cristian asked, point-blank.

Luigi Ippolito shook his head. "Not yet," he said, "Not grand-mother."

So they ran on towards the sanctuary, aiming to add a further handkerchief of ground in the absurd land-registry of that war . . . they could sense the spikiness of the mountain beneath their boots, as if releasing smells as they stepped. Then within the darkness they became aware of land like a sumptuous draped material, a piece of rustic cloth carelessly folded or thrown aside, as the backwash of repeated cold winds had reshaped the rock. Over-come by weariness the mountain had found a form for itself, adapting to the currents, yielding so as not to succumb, crumbling at the edges like crisp delicate cakes fresh from the oven. What was left was an area of high ground, the spine of a whale or dolphin, that had crumbled over successive millennia to achieve the quality of dry land, a place where the righteous would have been able to find refuge from the surrounding floods.

Sometimes they ran for a little, then kept still for a little, waiting in the way Corporal Sanseverino had told them to. They dispersed at the edges of sheep tracks, resting in the folds of rocky wall, and dissolving into the density of the earth.

Luigi Ippolito would not even have been aware that he was climbing, had it not been for a slight shortness of breath as he went up and up. Down below, in the valley, mines were flashing as they exploded into the air, and those momentary flashes of light showed him that he was utterly alone. Shots skimmed past him and went on to smash into the rock. He touched his chest to make sure he had not been wounded. Splinters flew so fast that he did not notice when they pierced his khaki uniform and cotton shirt to bury themselves in his flesh and cause light bleeding. He had not been wounded, but in that total darkness without stars or moon, he felt lost. Until, from the valley below, or from the side of a nearby mountain, a cone of more persistent light came to illuminate him, infiltrating the purple night; a luminous track that set on fire some sleeping shrub of artemisia or holly, producing a shining pollen that was blown into infinity above the honeysuckles.

It was then that he saw her before him. Erminia Sut. In dreams you can recognise people's first names and surnames before they even say them. Erminia was standing there, frozen, as if she too had heard the order to save herself and stayed put. Her eyes, in the light of an explosion, reflected a calm curiosity, like animals who have not yet learned to distrust humans.

She did not run away, nor did he. Luigi Ippolito was able to say with certainty, with a confident perception that came before all other forms of awareness, that he knew the woman standing before him, and had never been aware of perfection in nature until he saw that absolute evidence of it. The strip of light moved downward to lick the earth, as if to illuminate the path behind her. And still she did not move, knowing that from the same gorge from which Luigi Ippolito Chironi had suddenly appeared (she too, incredibly, in Cristian's dream knew things it was impossible for her to have known before), the Virgin Mary had appeared centuries earlier to a shepherd girl called Orsola Ferligoi. Erminia knew no harm could come to her from this armed man . . .

*

84

Was that how it happened? Was that how Luigi Ippolito Chironi from Núoro met Erminia Sut da Cormons? In Cristian's dream that was how it was.

Luigi Ippolito finished his story: "In the end, thanks to the darkness, we captured the mountain." He again felt the precise sadness that assailed him whenever he thought back to the first time he had seen the woman of his life. The anguish that had driven him mad. There he had been, running and exhausting himself, full of doubts before the beam of light lit her, before she stretched out her hand to lead him to himself; before she revealed that he was exactly where he must be. And even now that they were both dead, after such a short breath of life together, she seemed to stand motionless before him in Cristian's broken dream to show him the path he must travel to reach her. Beautiful . . .

HE WOKE WITH A START TO SOUNDS FROM THE KITCHEN. Marianna was making breakfast.

"Did you sleep here?" Cristian asked.

"No," she said. "At home." By home Marianna meant the house at San Pietro. "But this morning I woke early, and told myself that if no-one made breakfast for you, you would start on an empty stomach. Eating a good breakfast is vital."

"I would have gone to the bar." There was a basket of fragrant ring-shaped buns in the centre of the table, and Cristian nibbled at one while waiting for hot coffee and milk.

"Exactly," Marianna said. "I've seen the sort of muck they sell at the bar . . ."

"I dreamed about grandfather. His face was just like in the photos." Cristian hesitated, anxious to report his dream without losing a single detail.

Marianna placed a steaming jug of milk on the table silently so as not to disturb her nephew's effort to remember.

"I dreamed I saw my grandmother for the first time." He poured milk into his cup.

"Your grandmother? The girl from Friuli? She must be on her way to the Day of Judgement by now," Marianna said, unable to stop laughing. "But how can you have dreamed of her? No-one ever saw her, I don't think there's even a photograph . . ." Marianna's comment seemed a simple statement of fact.

Cristian shrugged. "I don't know, we can't control our dreams, can we? Uncle Gavino was there too . . ." he added, but as if speaking of something that was retreating from him, inexorably fading away.

The only thing he didn't say was that in his dream his grandmother, the unknown woman from Friuli, had Maddalena's face.

Strange days followed, like the aftershocks of an earthquake. Cristian worked on building sites, Domenico mainly in the office, summarising the essential difference between them. Among other things, they were busy refurbishing a house on Corso Garibaldi: a family home, which in defiance of building regulations was being increased to three times its previous size.

The Chironi were now no longer restricted to working only with iron, and the Guiso family, in addition to simple decoration, were now having to look after fundamental structural work as well. Obtaining permits and navigating the corridors of power was perhaps beginning to become more important than knowing how to do things well. When the communal engineer, the particular assessor of the moment, chose to close one or both eyes even if no walls had yet been erected, the house was virtually built. This was where what Domenico Guiso defined as "respectability" came in. And recently sparks from the economic boom had reached Barbagia like a flame that must be kept alight at all costs. An ugly fake city was taking the place of the earlier bucolic aesthetic, aping the unfounded provincialism of a different and distant world. Any such change should have taken decades, but the initial jump had already been taken. Permission had been given without rhyme or reason to build in completely illegal places. People wanted large houses with no expense spared. Houses several storeys high that would equally well suit elderly couples or young newly-weds. Enormous houses to satisfy the egos this new fortress was cultivating. Egos being ignorantly encouraged as progress. Overseas, entry into the club of the great of the earth was being founded in blood, but in Sardinia, in Barbagia, after an initial cannibal stage of anonymous banditry followed by a decade of delay, a sense of entry into the powerhouses of the world was developing. Even delinquency had developed into what had come to be accepted as collusion between common bandits and terrorist cells. Which as usual was like becoming more Catholic than the Pope – if you can't beat them join them. This meant that the old romantic refrain about redistribution of wealth was being replaced by a spirit of business, of confiscating or plundering so as to finance terrorist groups. It had always been easy to confuse these two levels of activity in this part of the world, where the concept of delinquency had never had any exact meaning or consistency. But as always, whatever was needed sprang from induced needs.

To Cristian, plying his trade involved understanding this only too well. He accepted dissident groups until they justified violence. But to Domenico such people were simply delinquents. He was terrified at the thought that Cristian, even if only superficially, might consider any of their theories worth discussing. By the late 1970s Núoro was troubled and turbulent, like the younger sons of certain families who imagine they have received less love than they have actually been given. Cynical but not sceptical. Intelligent but unsophisticated. Cunning but superficial. Convinced that they have everything under control, but incapable of distinguishing the beginning from the end.

Anyone who had seen Mimmíu's smile as he handed a coffee to the head of the municipal technical office, would have clearly understood that in that sealed garden, for the moment at least, a few plants already extinct elsewhere were still flourishing.

But the building to end all buildings, on which every effort was concentrated, was to be the new multipurpose community centre planned to replace the demolished Rotonda, the obsolete nineteenth-century prison. This new centre was, with the Cathedral, intended to be the most impressive building in the city. And certain materials needed to be researched and percentages to be calculated, together with quantities of cement and bricks, numbers of working hours, and how many men would be required to do the work.

For this purpose it was now necessary to arrange a trip to Carrara in Tuscany, to fetch samples of the top-quality marble that was to embellish this new public building.

"What are you crying about now?" Domenico asked Maddalena.

She was not crying, she had simply started breathing more heavily the moment he released her and pulled away. "I'm not crying," she said. But she could not reveal to him that this kind of sob was the aftermath of her orgasm, because then she would have had to explain that she would have appreciated it if he had continued to hold her in his arms rather than withdrawing the moment he had ejaculated. You could describe Domenico as having an innate sense of duty. And also say that once he had done his duty, he could hardly wait to get back to the next item on his list of things awaiting his attention.

"Is everything alright?" he asked, but naively enough, for the question seemed not to require any assessment of the act he had just completed.

Maddalena studied his broad shoulders and the remarkably childlike luminosity of his skin. The very opposite of Cristian, whom you could fairly describe as a child with the instincts of a man of the world. She felt a strange tenderness for this simple-minded man who now turned to smile at her. She vowed only to deceive him as far as might be necessary to preserve the illusion that she loved him. But she admitted to herself that living such a lie might not in fact be unbearable with him. His sweetness of character was dangerous, because he had never been able to love anyone unconditionally except Cristian and herself. In that order – an order Maddalena could well understand.

"What are you thinking about?" he persisted, reaching out to stroke her face.

"That what we have done was not very clever. Doing it just like that, without taking any precautions."

Domenico stretched out on his back and crossed his forearms over his brow. "What does it matter?" he reflected. "If anything happens, we'll take care of it. I have no intention of dishonouring you." Maddalena, out of his sight, smiled because what Domenico had just said might have seemed ironic or even sarcastic, coming from anyone else, but not from him. "As far as I'm concerned, we're already married," he pointed out.

Maddalena rested her head on his chest. She could hear the

strong thump of his heart beating and feel the damp warmth of his smooth skin. Shutting her eyes, she thought of the creature she knew she was carrying in her belly. She had known about it ever since her first morning sickness.

They lay without moving or speaking, in the absolute calm of a silence as strong as a thread of tensed steel. Prolonging that silence was the only way to salvation, she told herself. She brushed his chest with half-open lips. Domenico opened his mouth.

When the telephone rang he disentangled himself to go and answer it, dragging the sheet with him to cover himself. Maddalena saw him listen intently, then mutter with resignation before replacing the receiver.

"My father," he announced, putting on his socks. "He says I must go to Carrara with Cristian, because we have to get used to working together to learn the difference between just being friends, and working together as colleagues and so on . . . I have to go now, my love –" He pronounced "my love" as if he had been practising the words in front of a mirror.

Maddalena kept her eyes closed. "Fine," she answered from behind shut lids. "Don't make yourself late." But it was like talking to herself.

Domenico stopped buttoning his shirt. "I'll stay, if you'd like me to," he said. "What's the matter?"

"Nothing, really." This was a lie, but not a major one, because suddenly she had felt a sharp twinge of pain, as if from certainty that within the darkness she was building inside herself, nothing good would grow.

"This big contract is driving him mad." Domenico sighed, referring to Mimmíu, who was more nervous now that the contract had been signed, than he had been before, when its outcome had still not been decided.

"Is the contract the only thing that's driving him mad?" Maddalena gave a malicious smile.

Domenico smiled back. "I know," he agreed. "When is my father ever not nervous? He's become fixated on the idea that Cristian will somehow lose us the job . . . Those two aren't getting on at the moment, and I end up in the middle between them."

Mimmíu put two hundred thousand lire on the table in banknotes, not even hidden in an envelope. The notes came straight from his wallet and he had placed them beside the glass of wine the boy had just emptied. Raimondo Bardi's face lit up. "Easy work and well paid," Mimmíu explained, "and you'll get a free trip to the mainland out of it. You do have a driving licence, I suppose?"

"Of course." In his clothes Raimondo seemed bigger.

"You board ship from Olbia to Livorno, then go to Carrara and back, he explained. Your job is to do the driving and make sure no problem arises between the other two. Is that clear?"

Yes, quite clear, Raimondo agreed. The Chironi and Guiso families were operating cautiously, given their status and wealth. "And I've got something that may be useful in an emergency," he added, miming a pistol with his index finger pointing forwards and his thumb pointing up.

Mimmíu nodded.

"Thank you," Raimondo added with unexpected politeness. "Thank you for thinking of me." He pocketed the banknotes. "I know Cristian, so at least we won't get bored," he added enthusiastically.

"Which is why I thought of you." Mimmíu held out the keys of a Ford Transit. "The very reason."

If Raimondo Bardi had been dressed in what the local big shots would have called "traditional clothes", he would have been perfectly happy. No need to ask why. He felt secure in coarse woollen fabric or *orbace*, as it was called in Núoro, and his stocky hairy body even became beautiful, encased in such a sheath.

And beyond that he had a further source of pride. Dressed like his shepherd ancestors, Raimondo Bardi felt himself more valuable, and his voice more powerful. So once his shift on the building site was finished, he could not wait to go home and change his clothes. Naked he was nothing more than an anthropological specimen. But in his white pleated shirt, he was the embodiment of his culture.

Wearing that shirt defined him. Bardi Raimondo Pietro Serafino, son of Dionigi and Pasqua. And in gaiters he became "de Sos de Tauledda". But it was his *"chintorja"* or belt of worked leather that lent him the final touch, transforming him beyond all possible doubt into Remundu or Mundeddu . . .

"SEE? THE DEVIL IS PLUCKING THE FEATHERS OF CELESTIAL *pigeons. And creating a snowstorm,*" Cristian muttered, leaning back to rest his head in the Ford Transit (second series).

They had reached the road to Marreri, which God willing would soon be reduced to a mere memory once the new junction to the 131 highway from Prato Sardo was opened. But for the moment there the old road still was, curve after curve of it, meandering between oak trees, holly and asphodel. The granite rocks, on that particular slope of Monte Orthobène, had put on moss for the winter, as if the very stone were feeling cold.

Raimondo had asked for a car with radio and cassette-player. He had brought his own music with him, and now he was tackling the curves sustained by "Us and Them" at full blast. "Did you say something?" he asked Cristian, turning the sound down. Cristian gestured that he had said nothing. Outside the car the weather grew ever more grim.

"Did you say it was snowing?" Raimondo asked, as if grasping, after some delay, what his passenger had been saying a little earlier.

Cristian raised his eyebrows, without worrying that his companion, intent on driving, could not see him. But Raimondo was in some way aware of his response: "I'm sure it will snow," he said, and turned the music back up full volume.

They raced on through the unchanging countryside. Thanks to the odd breath of wind, it was able to greet them as if with a light wave of the hand, but nothing more. Occasionally a crow, at home in the cold, protested against the glassy silence. Flocks of stunned sheep parted like the waters of the Red Sea to make room for the occasional passing car. One could imagine being the only person who had ever seen the original dough from which the world had first been formed as it clumped together. A few cutting blades on Monte Corrasi revealed traces of steel that defined the very genesis of the mountains, like walls that had absorbed divine light at the very moment when it had first come into existence. A few plants: turpentine trees, spiny acacias and sambucus – profiteers by nature – exhaled a primordial stench that was rising from the depths.

Meanwhile Pink Floyd were at their dirty work of making everything trivial seem important, and everything ugly seem beautiful.

Raimondo began to sniffle. "This is stronger than me," he said to justify himself. "This song makes me cry . . . Here, at this point! What does it mean?" He grew more excited as the song got louder.

"That everything's just empty and goes round and round, just words," Cristian summarised. Outside the Ford Transit, the Siniscola sand-pit welcomed them. From then on it was a matter of passing small coastal villages that would soon be seen as the humble sisters of other much better-known localities. The sea was quietly singing a solo of its own.

"Yes," Raimondo agreed passionately. "That's just how it is, going round in circles, like donkeys." Then switching on his right indicator, he signalled he was about to pull over.

"What's the matter?" Cristian asked.

"Nothing. Just desperate for a piss."

Like the peasant poet, they pissed against the moon.

They only realised at the last moment that Domenico had decided not to come with them.

At Olbia they had to wait for all the non-commercial cars to embark before they were allowed on board the ferry. It was as if they were being swallowed up by an enormous metallic whale. And the ship stank like a whale, too. Cristian couldn't bear it. Every time he made the crossing he cursed the fact that he lived on an island. This seemed not to affect Raimondo; in fact, apart from his emotion in the car a little earlier, he seemed not to be suffering from anything at all.

They found their twin-berth cabin, then went to eat in the dreadful restaurant with its hospital pasta, gummy cutlets and potatoes, and extremely greasy fried calamari, with a few pieces of seasonal fruit, stale bread and cheap wine. Although the ship was half empty, the self-service was chock-full. It was a time of year when many lorry-drivers were travelling, together with people heading abroad to work, plus a few haggard winter tourists. And the occasional family, off to who knows where to see sick relatives or fathers who had emigrated . . .

Towards midnight the ferry began to vibrate, then half an hour later to roll gently, and at about two in the morning, to pitch violently. With Raimondo snoring, Cristian decided to force himself to sleep and must somehow have succeeded because he began to imagine himself standing on a station platform waiting for a train that was late. He was expecting someone: a woman he loved, or a friend, or a close relative; someone who had promised to come but had not yet arrived. He had certainly come in good time to meet the train; he hated keeping other people waiting, or even spending much time waiting himself. He had got ready with meticulous care, because he believed that preparing himself properly was essential when meeting people. He had bought wild flowers for the woman he loved, had a smile and handshake ready for his friend, and had prepared a clean bedroom for his much-loved relative. When the train finally appeared round the final curve in the track, he held his breath. And when it stopped, he looked anxiously over the shoulders of the passengers who were crowding the platform.

Of course, this was what he dreamed life would be like, full of apprehension and a certain anxiety about what he might be able to achieve, as he worried about the imminent meeting. But the woman did not appear. Nor did the friend or the relative, either. The platform emptied in a moment, leaving him alone with his wild flowers and clumsy composure, and realising he had point-lessly made up a bed with fresh linen for someone who would never come. The imperceptible moment before everything vanished had taken him back to that station platform as if he were still obstinately hoping to greet Life rather than Death.

Black.

"Everything OK?" Raimondo asked.

Cristian stared, recognising their cabin, and the constant rolling of the ship. "What's the matter?" he asked.

"You were shouting out. I was quite scared."

"What do you mean, I was shouting out?" Cristian was getting nervous. "I couldn't sleep because you were snoring so loudly."

He was still conscious of the sadness of his long and fruitless wait on the platform.

For a while neither spoke.

Then Raimondo asked, "Are you still asleep?"

Cristian was not asleep, but did not answer.

At dawn someone knocked on the door to tell them they must leave so attendants could clean their cabin while the ship was unloading. The strangeness of the morning somehow hushed the noise of the port. To Cristian, Livorno seemed the colour of a bun or cake, but that may have been because he was hungry. When they got into the Transit, Raimondo lit a cigarette, explaining he had not smoked in the cabin not out of consideration for Cristian, but because he had left his cigarettes in the car, and after their meal had not been allowed to fetch them. Cristian opened the car window, and said, "The first bar we come to outside the port, stop."

"Just give me a shout," Raimondo answered, half-singing the words.

The salt air filling the Transit had a foreign quality, and even the light was different.

A few metres after they exited the port, a patrol car with three uniformed carabinieri signalled at them to pull over, which Raimondo did. The maresciallo, complete with bullet-proof vest and machine gun, asked for their licence and registration papers and told them to get out of the car. The other two policemen looked at each other as Raimondo and Cristian got out.

"Where are you headed?" the maresciallo asked.

"Carrara." Cristian was doing his best to seem calm.

"Work?"

"I have to get some marble for my firm."

"I see," the carabiniere commented without taking his eyes off Cristian. "We'd like to check your luggage," he added, pretending this was not an order.

Raimondo looked at Cristian as if to remind him that if he had anything to declare, this was the moment to do it. Meanwhile the other two carabinieri had opened the back door of the Transit and noted that the space was empty. This was followed by long minutes of absolute silence during which the two junior carabinieri mysteriously continued to rummage in the back of the vehicle, until eventually one of them shouted, "Weapons!"

"Weapons? What weapons?" was Cristian's reaction.

"If you are referring to my pistol it is officially registered, and I can show you the licence," Raimondo said. But that was not what they had in mind; they had found a dozen small machine guns and ammunition stowed under a hidden floor in the back of the Transit.

"They've deliberately tricked us," Raimondo muttered.

Meanwhile the maresciallo waved his weapon at his colleagues to signal that they should handcuff the boys, and said the tip-off had been entirely justified.

The air was different, the light was entirely different, the sounds were all different, absolutely everything was different.

Like a fearless soldier advancing into the mouth of a cannon, Cristian lunged forward. He noticed Raimondo saying something to him. But everything was too different, and he continued to advance on the armed carabiniere who, utterly astonished at his madness, even made as if to get out of the way. So Cristian started running, on what he was aware was entirely unfamiliar ground. It was as if he had suddenly remembered something that needed immediate attention. He caught a glimpse of Raimondo who, dragged to the ground, was struggling to wriggle free. Then bullets hissed near his right thigh and neck, followed by a sharp pain by his ear like the slash of a razor. He saw there was no longer land beneath him but still ran on.

. . . It was as though he had been watching a wave forming on the horizon. A loose crest of black earth accelerated towards him like a stormy ocean, though it was too viscous for him to be able to run fast, and too slimy to surprise him. All he could do was stay by the shore and wait calmly for the the waves to hit him. Then he threw himself in, feeling a cold shock as the water swallowed him up. He felt as if he was continuing to wait while at the same time watching himself wait, as if the primary object of that incredibly slow impact were not himself but somebody else identical to him.

Once in the sea he was vaguely aware of the whine of more bullets being fired from the quay . . . everything was so different.

He could see himself waiting for his own death, a spectator in the delirious theatre of the sleep of reason.

There was a burst of fire, but too far away to seem dangerous.

Like a rumble originating in the entrails of the ocean and inexorably finding expression in a mountain of self-propelled water.

Like a gigantic ploughshare that, cutting deep into the sods, forces strips of land to twist in search of more space.

He felt himself suffocating, because he was neither swimming nor floating. Simply fleeing.

Black . . .

*

Those on the quayside saw him disappear below the surface of the water, which was barely disturbed. The current took him further out. The maresciallo ran to the patrol car to alert the coastguards.

He came to the surface again, and for a moment was able to breathe . . .

It was as if he had exhausted himself through sheer obstinacy. By keeping awake to receive a delivery, by working all night with a plane or a chisel. Or being forced to close his eyes because he was concentrating so fiercely . . .

Black . . .

Raimondo was shouting at them to do something, that Cristian was still alive . . . But the carabinieri did nothing, what happened in the sea was not their concern.

It was like surrendering to sleep. And once asleep, he remembered everything . . .

He remembered harvests like oceans, infinite seas that rose and fell, fluctuating against the sun at its peak. He remembered huge curves pierced by red-hot rays sweeping between ears of corn with the fury of scythes. He remembered the changing scales of fish which he had caught in stream or lake or river before flinging them down on rocks or sand or grassy banks to suffer death in the air. And he remembered his farewell at the hospital to his mother: her watery eyes, and how she had stayed with him to the end, afraid he would fear death more than she would . . . He remembered everything minutely: every second, every moment, the wordlessness preceding tears like a cough held back. And the unbelievable dissolution of every certainty, like a mouse escaping from a trap. And the sweaty smell of disturbed earth, almost as though the soil were regurgitating blood after swallowing litres of it. He remembered everything. The month and the year, the town hall where he had been registered, the church where he had been baptised, Maddalena kissing him, and even the kiss he had given Domenico. The teacher who had punished him, the parish priest and the great-grandfather who had reprimanded him, the friend who had smiled at him and the one who had betrayed him. The plants he remembered, the smell of hot bread and milk, the fragrance of cakes fresh from the oven, boiling wine with cloves, brandy for toothache, and the still-warm liver of a slaughtered pig, fine wool newly shorn from a sheep's back, and the sliminess of cows' teats.

Everything, he remembered everything, now that he was drowning . . . His great-uncle who had also died at sea. Maddalena's curls. The wild jasmine in Aunt Marianna's yard.

Everything, except his name.

That he could not remember.

Black.

THE PROFOUND WORD

Núoro, April 1979

SHE WAS CERTAIN IT HAD BEEN ENOUGH FOR GOD, THE
Ancient of Days, to generate the Flood by placing the palm of his
hand on the frozen crust of the earth. And, for this reason, she
thought her every creative act of her own must have derived from
concealment rather than revelation. Each time He turned His back
on His creation, man had tried to imitate Him, and had evolved,
had managed to progress. But when on the contrary He had
revealed Himself and looked His creation in the face, that creation
had not been able to hold His gaze and had regressed thousands
of years to being a stuttering cave-dweller. Humanity was just a
small immature child, to be put up with in his excessive presump-
tion and punished when necessary. That was the Creation as
Marianna understood it. To her the fact that Cristian was dead
made no difference at all. It was just the way things were. She did
not weep. But she was furiously angry. And she was angry simply
because she could not understand at what point the clear presenti-
ment of Cristian's death could have escaped her. She placed her
throbbing hand on the surface of the table and held it there until
she could feel the chill of the marble running up her forearm.

Mimmíu thought for a moment that Marianna was about to
reach for the paper and pen he had put in front of her. But he was

wrong, because she seemed not to have even seen them. Her wide-open eyes were not focused on anything, as if she had died without anyone having had the grace to close her eyes.

Cristian dead? Fair enough. Just one more Chironi gone ahead of her, and yet another not ready to lie in a grave, like her mother Mercede, who had vanished long ago into the otherworldly emptiness of madness, as impenetrable as the solidity of the ravines; and like her brother Gavino, another who had also met a liquid death, his body too never recovered. So this death came as no particular surprise. The darkness of Cristian's death made sense, a matter of continuity and stubbornness. Like the compulsive repeating of the endless battering ironsmiths needed to control and work their metal.

All she needed was to keep her eyes open, to accustom them to the darkness; not to give in, to hold her gaze with unhesitating firmness, never backing away.

The Ancient of Days was standing before her. "Sit down," Marianna whispered.

Mimmíu was quite certain the command had not been directed at him though they were alone together in the room. Even so, he sat down at the other end of the table. Then, indicating the paper and the pen, he attempted a smile. "It's only a power of attorney," he said, taking care not to seem too anxious.

Marianna made a brief movement, like someone waking to a feeling of stiffness after several hours in an uncomfortable position; the muscles of her shoulder and neck seeking to relax the fierce tension that had enabled her to keep her head up. "What you are is what you remain," she hissed.

Mimmíu agreed. "Of course," he said. "But don't imagine people are queuing up to become Chironis."

This produced a genuine laugh from Marianna. One had to know how to laugh in the face of the Ancient of Days, she thought, because she did not believe she was so resigned as not to react at all. The game had been won: Cristian was dead, and she was the last survivor; after her there was no-one else. And no matter how hard Mimmíu tried, he would always remain what he was.

"Why did you send Cristian off by himself?" Her woman's voice was becoming shrill with energy, so that it could only with difficulty still be considered human.

"Where?" Mimmíu managed to ask, surprised that Marianna seemed to be speaking to him in such direct detail.

"Where you made up your mind to send him." Her explanation made nothing any clearer.

"It was part of his job and he wasn't alone." Mimmíu was desperately trying to sound as casual as possible.

"I have the impression it was not just an ordinary journey," she said.

Mimmíu's lower lip trembled: how could she talk to him like that? Cristian had been like a son to him, and only God could know what he had felt deep inside at that death, at the way things had turned out . . . How could she? The old witch, he thought. "It was a job of work," was all he replied.

Marianna gave him a long look.

Mimmíu dropped his eyes. "Domenico is unrecognisable," he announced.

Marianna sniffed and looked away. Long ago, as a girl, she had seen a demonstration of hypnotism. A ridiculous figure in oriental dress had called for a volunteer to join him on the stage and forced him to behave in a comic way without him being aware of it, then woke him out of the trance so that everyone laughed at his bewilderment. This was how she now felt inside herself. Suddenly the reality round her seemed tangible: the kitchen, the garden beyond the French window, the characteristic smell of the fireplace, Mimmíu sitting there before her. Now that she had recovered control she looked around as if it was only now that she could make sense of the man, the surface of the table, the sheet of paper and the pen. "I'm not signing anything."

Mimmíu went home with the unsigned power of attorney in his pocket. He was gripped by the powerful though temperamental April wind, and by a thought. Around him houses and people seemed to have become fluid, as if liquified by the boiling gaze of an infuriated divinity. He told himself that what had to be done, had been done. And the way it had happened could not in any way have been avoided. And when the time came for explanations, he would be able to supply them. He had defended Domenico's life as well as his own.

The quality of the light, suddenly turning brown, convinced him of his good faith. A warm fragrant amber protected him from himself as he passed in front of the Church of the Rosary without glancing at the door or crossing himself. He hoped to be able to close his eyes and sleep without being tormented by the image of Cristian drowning. But it was not for him to claim peace, that he knew. So he paused to get his breath back, breathing as deeply as he needed, taking in long steady draughts of air, as rhythmically as a long wave.

The weather that season remained inconclusive; it refused to return to winter but had no wish to move forward to spring either, despite the fact that, in sheltered gardens, everything was flowering in harmony with the metabolism of the earth. In any case, the insistent north wind discouraged any expectation of warmth, forcing people to cover themselves at dusk. Even longer drawn-out winters had been known: Mimmíu could remember years when it had been necessary to keep the fire burning until May.

What had happened at Livorno was clear to him, and it was equally clear that he would never have any opportunity to make up for it in this life. As for Domenico's bitter grief, he had taken that into account. It would pass, in the way that all things passed.

In the month that followed Cristian's disappearance, Domenico hardly spoke. He seemed to need all his concentration to continue to exist. On the surface his life had not changed: he still got up at the same time and went to bed at the same time . . . He went to the building sites and replied monosyllabically to anyone who asked what he had seen on the local television news. Sometimes people asked him about Cristian as if expecting that he must know more than they did. But for him all this was a break in reality. But to those who asked about Cristian, or simply took the trouble to enquire how he himself was keeping, he would have claimed he couldn't say for sure. Domenico was a young man unable to talk in metaphors, which in these particular circumstances might have helped him. To describe the chasm, the absence, the emotional paralysis that had overwhelmed him; this would have meant being able to react and pull himself together. And he could not react or recover. People close to him said that time, that gentleman, would rub away the stain that cut the daylight out, and replace his exposed wound with a scar. But he well knew it was not like that. Cristian was dead and could never live again. The situation was irreversible. An unbearable certainty. And he, Domenico, well understood the furious justice that prevented him weeping for the man who had been both his friend and his brother. He could not imagine himself outside that grief but only totally inside it, like another Domenico hiding behind a sheath of normality, whereas the fact was nothing would ever be normal for him again, or even in any way like the time when Cristian still existed. Not even Maddalena.

Suddenly he was sorry he had not responded to the kiss his friend had given him at via Deffenu during the engagement party, or rather he cursed himself for having shrunk away from it. It was the curse of having committed an irreparable error, because he had refused to accept something that he understood perfectly well. Like everyone else, he wanted a calm life, but he knew that was something he could not have, and that the best he could achieve would be an appearance of tranquillity, though never the substance of it. So, buried in his own silence at the building sites, or walking around with Maddalena on his arm, he never stopped asking himself how he was able to carry on despite everything. He imagined a night full of stars, like when as a child he had imagined the sky like a sort of photograph album where your affections are stuck in after you are dead, too far away to be recognisable but still bright and active. In the brilliant chaos where people dear to him ended up, there was the consolation of not being left alone. So Cristian must be there, but how was it possible for him to realise this and still find no peace? It must be the strangeness of imagining death, that must be what it was. So much so that sometimes Domenico had a precise feeling that he himself must be the one who had died while Cristian, still in the world of the living, must be weeping for him.

Even so, to look at him, you would have been convinced that Domenico Guiso had reacted to the news of Cristian Chironi's death with great fortitude.

News that had been given to him by his own appalled father. Who found it hard to forgive himself for not having intervened when Cristian had started keeping dangerous company, in such dangerous times. But to Domenico, such reasoning seemed suddenly pointless. In fact he was aware that his father had not been deeply upset in giving him this terrible news, but had admitted that it was something he had expected to happen. And this was someone who in the course of his sixty or more years, had had to pass on such news to people more than once, but in this case, as absorbed by the distorted feelings of Domenico, the news seemed to have been conveyed with a touch of voluptuous pleasure.

Just a few days before the engagement party, Maddalena had realised she was pregnant. Something she knew before her body revealed it to her. Possibly from the very moment it happened. Which is why she acted in the way she did. Now that Cristian was dead she knew she must provide a father for the creature growing inside her. It did occur to her to have an abortion, certainly. But she considered this without believing in it, as though it was right to mention the possibility, while knowing perfectly well that she would never carry it out. The facts had already taught her that, beyond any feeling she might have for Cristian as the creature's father, or for Domenico as her future husband, it was important to restore order in the chaos she had just experienced. To know how to grade the revelations she might or might not make. To control time to the second. Not to give way to uncontrolled reactions.To survive. In a very short time her condition would become obvious, and she needed to know how to react.

Cristian's death had bequeathed her a strange bitterness, a sort of annoyance, something that had prevented her appearing to be affected, despite Domenico's sharp pain. He was so consumed by his own anguish that he never even noticed her coldness. And Maddalena knew that would always be the case. Because Domenico was only capable of loving her superficially. Especially because Domenico had loved Cristian much more than he would ever have been able to love or even known how to love her. So they were equal. Both at exactly the same level: the one an orphan and a widower, the other a wife and a lover by proxy. It would have been a perfect marriage, she told herself, had it not been for the illusion that it was a marriage at all.

When she went to look for Domenico at the building site, she found him assessing a plan; his eyes apparently unfocused. At first, he did not even notice that she was there. Then suddenly raising his head, he saw her. He smiled, something he knew how to do well. Maddalena immediately noticed how much weight he had lost, much improving his looks. Getting up, he put his arms round her. Every time he embraced her now, he seemed to be searching for an unattainable consolation, a man trying to overwhelm her with affection.

"I need to speak to you," she said as he caressed her neck.

"Yes," Domenico answered, but as if understanding nothing at all. In fact, he sat down again and continued studying the plans spread out on his work table. "This is the new cultural centre on via Roma," he told her without looking at her. "Sit down, sit down . . ." He gestured at a small armchair facing the table.

Maddalena sat down. Neither said anything until the sound of a small revved-up scooter came from the road. Then she said clearly, "I'm going to have a baby."

It took Domenico a few seconds to react. "A baby?" he repeated, as if articulating an unknown word.

Maddalena looked at him, confirming the words with a movement of her brows. Now that she had pronounced the unpronounceable, there was no way back.

Domenico closed his eyes as if unable to take in any good news that might distract him from his grief.

"You don't sound pleased," she said.

He started, as though he had not understood what little there had been to understand before that moment. Getting to his feet he looked around as if to make sure he really was exactly where he thought he was. "No, I'm not displeased," he protested. He had been afraid he would never again be able to speak to anybody, and now here was Maddalena telling him he was going to be a father, and he had only managed to say, "No, I'm not displeased." It was as though he were talking about something else. A tear he could not hold back escaped from the corner of his eye. He sniffed, as if pretending some irritation as an excuse to wipe his cheek.

Maddalena smiled at him and stood up so as to be able to reach him from the other side of the table. She put her arms round his neck and Domenico put his round her hips and laid his ear against her belly as if to listen to where the new life must be feverishly forming. He burst into a fierce fit of weeping.

For the Chironi family, empty coffins were nothing new. And for Marianna it merely meant that things were doggedly repeating themselves. When she had buried her mother, all she had been able to think of putting into the coffin had been her mother's traditional formal dress, her filigree jewels and her shoes. Everything except her mother's body, because that had been absent after Mercede had gone to die heaven knew where, and searching the surrounding countryside had not helped in any way. Proof that she had known how to disappear despite the fact that no-one had thought her particularly self-aware; she had preserved a flicker of efficiency when it came to dying in her own way, slipping out of the house without anyone noticing, like stale air escaping from a half-open window. She had crossed the courtyard barefoot in her nightdress with her hair loose, then followed the lanes that led from the edge of the city straight into the country and let herself drown in the surrounding green, as if she had finally reached the open sea. The wildness of Nature had welcomed her with ravenous enthusiasm. Neither sniffing dogs nor searching hands could discover anything at all: Mercede had simply disintegrated. But how could her human body have passed through the land of the living without even being seen? It was impossible to retrace her steps because no-one had seen her. An elderly woman, with loose hair as wild as the Furies, barefoot like a penitent and dressed in a nightdress like a concubine. Possessed like a pagan Goddess, but a wife and mother devoted to the Heavenly God. It was enough to drive one mad, beyond all reason, and her husband Michele Angelo could only cling to the idea that she had never died at all. He had given up every other occupation to wait for her. And had continued to wait until the day he died himself at the ripe old age of a hundred and one, in the bed where he had slept, loved and suffered with his wife.

It had been left to Marianna to keep the terrible score, after so many of the Chironi family had succumbed to the ugly vice of dying senselessly. And when she tried to define "senseless" she decided that what she meant was "not long enough for them to claim that they had really lived". Her brother Gavino, for instance was another who had never come home; in his coffin too she had only put good clothes, and the pocket watch he had been given on his twenty-first birthday. He too had suffered the burden of uncertainty and had tried to find justification for his existence in times that did not lend themselves to it. He had been like a vanguard, a beautiful but sad young man swept away by a burst of fire before he could even take two steps towards the enemy trench. Gavino dealt a particular blow to the heart because he summed up so many tragedies in himself that seemed theatre but were, quite simply, life.

Marianna could not account for all the others whose bodies they had been able to bury. They had been just that. Certain character traits are revealed over time, and Marianna had turned out to be a person who lived longer than others. It was not so much that she had to accept this, more that she had no way of refusing it.

The name of Cristian was not even spoken. Whoever arranged his funeral must have done a good job, or so people said. It was not Marianna who arranged it, because she would never have attended another funeral, would never have conveyed more condolences to anyone, would never have again knelt before a priest, visited a cemetery, admitted to any future life, accepted any earthly consolation, thought of herself as privileged, felt any affection, or believed in any future whatsoever . . .

After her nephew's death her face changed somehow, as if

each new tragedy made her more beautiful. She was seventy-seven years old now and, if she could trust numbers, she had already survived long enough to expect to be allowed to step aside. But no; her body was still proud and upright, and her forehead still as smooth as it had been at forty. Everyone said she had reached perfection in maturity. She had never been thought beautiful as a girl, but she had grown into a beautiful woman, and retained her beauty into old age.

There was always something needing attention in her garden, and in this way days would pass. And years. And centuries.

Someone was knocking at her door.

"You talk so much because you've never had to sweat for any of the things you have," Mimmíu shouted.

Domenico decided he had to give Mimmíu a chance to let off steam. That was the way to deal with his father, who was an irritable type who liked to speak first and think later. So it was best to give him time to mull over what he had said.

"You're quite right," Domenico said finally.

Mimmíu, as expected, pulled himself together. "Bloody hell!" he hissed without conviction.

Domenico waited a moment longer. "I don't understand why it's so urgent," he said. "Let me say something."

Mimmíu seemed to accept this. "Go on," he said.

"I'll have a word with Aunt Marianna and get her to sign the power of attorney. And meanwhile let's get on with the jobs we're already working on . . . Plenty needs to be done."

"Certainly. But what if she won't sign for you either?"

"She will." Domenico was reassuring. "But there's something

else I have to tell you," he added. Mimmíu waited for his son to go on. "Maddalena's pregnant."

Mimmíu showed no surprise. He took an embarrassed step towards Domenico, mimed an embrace, and seeing that Domenico did not draw back, completed the gesture. "At last," he whispered in his son's ear.

"No-one else knows about it yet," Domenico said.

His father nodded. "We must arrange the wedding."

"Something simple . . . No point in making a fuss."

"I know, I understand," Mimmíu agreed, having seemingly entirely lost his previous irritation. "But it must be done properly, with all the sacraments. Not like this modern stuff."

"Alright," His son smiled. "No modern stuff."

Mimmíu looked at him, thinking that, to all intents and purposes, the boy seemed to have grown into a man. Grief had made him thoughtful.

"I'll take care of it," Domenico added after a long silence. His father looked puzzled. "I'll go myself and talk to Aunt Marianna, I'll use the wedding as an excuse to discuss everything . . . You'll see, she'll listen to me."

"I know you're not in the mood for such things at the moment, Mimmíu said patiently, "but even you know how it works . . ."

"I've told you I'll talk to her, haven't I?"

"Yes, yes," Mimmíu agreed, but not without a certain anxiety. He concentrated on the new creases running between the base of Domenico's nose and the corners of his mouth. Signs of exhaustion as well as strength. People had always considered Domenico the essence of gentleness. But those who believed that had not yet observed him as his father was able to see him at that moment.

115

"Aunt Marianna will talk to me," the young man promised, staring strangely at his father.

"What's the matter?" his father asked, not quite sure he wanted to hear the answer.

"Nothing," Domenico said. "I'm just looking at you, what's wrong with that?"

Mimmíu lowered his head. He was conscious of the sadness of a king who has abdicated in favour of his son, but who at the same time wants to conceal his satisfaction at having achieved his aim of passing on the throne. Years had passed since Mimmíu had been a man whose only creed was to maintain everything himself. He now had no gods to appeal to anymore, and no graces to claim. He had Domenico. Who was now about to become a father in his turn. Which would lend meaning to all the actions, good or bad, that had brought Mimmíu to the point he had now reached.

"I did it for us," Mimmíu said. He seemed about to go on, but added nothing more.

Domenico raised his chin as though looking for a space in his head into which to insert what his father had just said.

"You'll understand too when your child is born," he went on after a very long pause, as if wanting to counter an objection. But Domenico said nothing, and made no sign of wanting to know anything more than necessary.

"It would have ruined us, in fact it was ruining us," Mimmíu insisted.

Domenico held his breath, opened his mouth, swelled his chest, and bit his lower lip until he could taste blood. He did not want to weep; he had done enough of that.

*

What Marianna insisted on describing to herself as "Cristian's funeral" was in fact nothing more than a hasty commemoration. In fact, two days after the event, the carabinieri knocked on the door of the Chironi home to assure themselves that the missing nephew had not returned to his great-aunt and guardian.

All Marianna asked of the officer who showed her the search-warrant was that he and the two others who came with him should not cause too much upset in the house. Then she went into the courtyard to wait until they had finished. They did not take long, because it was quickly apparent that the boy had never come back.

Though before they left they warned her that if her nephew did reappear, it would be her duty to report the fact to the police. In other words, she would be wrong to think she was protecting him if she kept quiet, that would only get him into more trouble. So "Chironi Cristian" remained officially missing and a fugitive from justice, which seemed to Marianna the only good news she had had so far. The sergeant didn't quite understand what the old woman had found to smile about, but he was experienced enough to realise that she was not being arrogant or sarcastic.

As soon as the carabinieri had gone, Marianna re-examined her house: kitchen, corridors, bedrooms, bathrooms. Even the great disused workshop. Everything.

These were not good times, and she was not sure there had ever been any. It was a horrible season of reckoning.

The house seemed unusually large, with some corners in it she scarcely recognised, and others she remembered only too well. Between the kitchen and the larder was a little recess where as a child she had hidden to listen to her parents talking. It was here she had heard for the first time the terrible story of her twin brothers Pietro and Paolo, killed when ten years old, and their torn bodies left for wild boars to eat. And from there too she had adored, unseen, her brothers Gavino and Luigi Ippolito, listening to them whispering in front of the fire, the one so fragile and the other so determined. Form and act, poetry and prose.

Marianna understood that she must control every memory to prevent the memories controlling her. She was pedantic in her careful domination of these memories because that was how she wanted it to be. Her capacity to remember had made her what she was, sharpening for her the torment of reality.

Outside, April was predicting warmth to come. Though inside the sepulchre in which she had entombed herself the ice would be eternal. She arranged a shawl across her shoulders to give this thought physical reality. She had insisted she would be fine on her own and, already sealed into her tomb, would end her days on this earth without anyone noticing. She switched on the television, something she had not done for months. She stood in front of it, waiting for the moving images to greet her. A huge rainy city was being filmed from above, with enormous buildings wrapped in greasy fog and a huge number of people milling about far below like ants. Marianna Chironi knew nothing of the outside world, but she was cursed enough to know that no amount of knowledge could save her from herself. She was one of those women who are born experienced, with an innate talent for understanding the ways of the world.

She had understood Mimmíu's embarrassment. And had figured out that the death of Cristian had lifted him, even though he had taken refuge in dejection. She did not know how she had intuited this, but knew it is always easy to slip into negative thoughts. Meanwhile there, on the screen, was a city of the future, where the rich lived up in the sky and the poor down in an underground hell – just the opposite of the Gospel. The television remained fixed in a single, ongoing, infinite season, while outside, beyond the French window, April was slowly giving way.

There was a knock at the door.

Domenico did not wait for a sign from Marianna. She seemed so absorbed that for a moment he wondered whether he should not go in. In the short time it had taken him to cross the courtyard, he had rehearsed a short speech with two fixed points: one, not to raise, unless by accident, the issue of signing the power of attorney and the other, to make it clear that he was making a courtesy visit as a relative, or as someone who considered himself a relative, to an extremely important person who was very dear to him, to inform her about an extraordinary event. But reaching the French window to the kitchen, he knocked.

Marianna, keeping her eyes fixed on the television screen, made a brief gesture with her hand. Domenico tried to come in with as little noise as possible, as if entering a hospital ward where a patient was resting. Then he waited.

"The things that exist in this world. It is really hard to believe . . ." Marianna remarked, showing no sign of having seen him come in.

"Good evening," Domenico murmured.

"Good evening," Marianna replied after a pause. "Please do sit down." It was as if she had suddenly lost interest in the television programme that, only a moment before, seemed to have completely absorbed her attention. "Have you eaten?" she asked.

"No," Domenico answered hurriedly, "but if you yourself were just about to eat, pay no attention to me."

Marianna shrugged. "I'm in no hurry," she said. "But you look exhausted."

"As you know, this hasn't exactly been the best of times for me," he admitted, trying not to sound pathetic.

"The times are what they are," Marianna commented, turning the television off. She almost seemed to have understood Domenico's sensitive approach and determined to counteract it. "What difference do you think one death more or one less can make to me at my age?" she asked, not expecting an answer. "Soon, if it's God's will, you'll be counting me among the dead as well."

"Don't say that," Domenico said.

"But in any case, what use am I now?"

"Well, for a start, you are safeguarding things you have made sacrifices to achieve."

It seemed to take a long time for Marianna to work out what she thought about that conclusion. Then, almost imperceptibly, she nodded. As Domenico saw it, it was quite clear that she had survived to nourish the Chironi plant which was otherwise threatening to collapse or permanently wither. Or worse still, dissolve in silent oblivion. What the boy had in mind was to offer himself as a substitute Chironi. Mimmíu and Domenico were clearly moving by opposite paths towards the same goal.

"Have you brought that document with you?"

Marianna's question took Domenico by surprise. "No . . ." he stammered. "Er . . . I mean yes." He patted his jacket pocket. "But that's not what I came about . . ."

". . . No?" the old woman interrupted. Since Domenico said nothing more, she took the initiative: "Then what have you come about? Just to tell me that life goes on? Or to explain that worse things can happen than being forced to watch your whole family die out . . . well? Let's hear it."

"No, it's just that . . ." the boy babbled. "It's just that I couldn't bear it that Cristian was no longer here in this house. Look, if the truth be told, I didn't even come here for you. I just needed to understand what things would be like from now on . . ."

Marianna stuck out her chin, as if this incongruous reply was entirely legitimate to her. She knew well the vague confusion Domenico was referring to, what it was to breathe in a house progressively losing its essence, growing emptier with no clear sense of ever expecting anyone else to arrive, or worrying about someone suffering, or preparing a good breakfast for them. "Nothing will happen from now on, really nothing. But sit down," she commanded. "Will you have some coffee?"

Domenico did not want to sit down and did not want coffee, but he did sit and accepted the coffee. Marianna now seemed suddenly to grow calm as if rejuvenated. He could not say how this happened, perhaps the skin on her brow and cheekbones became smoother, or perhaps it was just the dying light at dusk. The days were getting longer, as were the hours when one could look other people in the eye.

"What do you think we should do?" Domenico began with renewed boldness. "Tell me. Shall we jettison everything? I'm ready to do that. And start again from the beginning. To you what is due to the Chironi, and the rest to us. And you can have the accounts checked by anyone you like. As for myself, I only want what is due to me . . . and to my family," he added firmly.

"I don't think that's what we are talking about," Marianna said without even turning round, as she made the coffee.

"On the contrary, it is exactly what we are talking about."

"You've become a man overnight," Marianna stated as she lighted the little stove. And if you have, you will understand that the point is never what you ask, but how you ask it."

"I must get married," Domenico declared.

"Must?" Marianna asked sharply.

"Must and want to," he confirmed, adding, "Maddalena is pregnant."

This statement seemed to have little effect on the old woman. To her it was just one more of those things that people try to pass off as exceptional, but which in reality happen all the time. "So that's what it was," she said after a pause, putting a steaming cup on the table.

"You seem different too," Domenico said, barely sipping his coffee. "It's good. The coffee has always been so good here."

Marianna thrust this aside, to all appearances playing at being a young girl once more. "Oh no," she protested coquettishly. "You should have heard what my babbo used to say . . . you really should. My mamma would say, 'Get your father to make the coffee, men do it better because they are not stingy like women.' Then she would always add, 'Never be economical when you make coffee or tomato sauce.'"

"I remember great-grandfather Michele Angelo," Domenico said, with a touch of emotion.

"So now you are going to be a father too," Marianna burbled on. "It seems only yesterday you were playing in the yard out here . . ."

"Oh," said Domenico, like a child caught at something he shouldn't have been doing. "We haven't told anyone yet."

Marianna stared at her own reflection on the blank television screen, almost as if afraid that from somewhere, perhaps from the next world, someone may have been watching her. "No need to worry about me," she assured him.

Domenico nodded. "Of course, Aunt Marià, I know that . . ."

She interrupted him. "Well then, show me where on that document I need to sign?"

Domenico, genuinely embarrassed, pulled the power of attorney from his pocket and placed it on the marble table top. "But that's not what I came for," he whispered, watching Marianna sign beside her name.

She pushed the paper back to him. "Wait here," she said, and crossed the corridor that led from the big kitchen to the bedrooms.

In less than a few minutes she was back, with what looked like a very fragile package. A tiny bundle wrapped in tissue paper that to Domenico, as he took it, seemed as sweet-scented as a meringue.

"What is it?" he asked, noticing how very little it weighed.

"A little thought for the mother-to-be and a viaticum for the new child . . . women's business. Maddalena will tell you what it is."

Domenico held the package as delicately as if it had been a little chick. "Thank you for everything," he said.

"Yes, yes . . . please. You know the way out," Marianna said briskly, as if suddenly reverting to her usual self.

SHE SAW AN IMMACULATE EXPANSE IN FRONT OF HER. SHE was not sure whether it was agricultural land or the far edge of a great city. There was a snow-covered plain with very few trees, marked by the tracks of vehicle wheels. She felt very cold, as if an animal had bitten into her back. The house, as simple as the countryside, was as white as a sheet of paper. She realised she could see herself both inside and outside it. She noticed a pile of firewood, a little enclosure for chickens, and the outline of a small kitchen-garden under the blanket of snow. But the house was warm, a simple space, furnished with a collection of furniture that did not match, synthetic table-cloths with ethnic patterns, and small couches. She saw herself rummaging in a drawer and coming on a very old photograph of a man with a serene expression, a dark pullover with a high collar and a tight jacket, apparently immersed in an oily atmosphere, as if something to do with the emulsion had not taken properly and the photograph had developed an icy surface with a corpse swimming under water. Now she was outside the house again in a smell of iron and vanilla. The white expanse was enclosed by the dry beards of trees. She told herself that was nothing special, yet she was certain that this very ordinary countryside was completely unknown to her. She could see little bodies, small trunks, dried flowers, tiny creatures, imprisoned in the frozen surface of a river like insects in amber. It was extraordinary to realise she could concentrate on details so deep down within her. In her convulsive coming and going, all she had to do was to imagine returning inside this house for this to happen. Here she was moving about in an empty room, possibly a living room. The wall in front of her was hung with an enormous green carpet like a tapestry. The windows were hidden by white curtains and blinds the colour of fuchsia. She asked herself where on earth she could be, but she was not anxious. The man in the photo, printed in the glassy abyss of his own image, was able to speak and said *Es esmu šeit*. And she, for some unknown reason, understood he was trying to reassure her, but at the same time to warn her.

Maddalena opened her eyes.

The first thing she saw was the white packet Domenico had brought her the previous evening and which, for no known reason, she had not wanted to open. Her future husband had returned reassured from his visit to Marianna, bringing her this gift, but she had not taken it well. Though there was no obvious reason for this as everyone present had noted, being pregnant could justify anything. The simple fact was, she had left the packet unopened.

As often recently, she had had a slight attack of nausea like nothing more than a small mouse imprisoned in her stomach crossing her oesophagus in a bid for freedom. But she told herself the feeling was likely to get worse.

It was enough for her to sit on the bed to forget almost everything she had dreamed, leaving nothing but a subtle yet precise hint of alarm. The creature growing inside her was helping her perfect her intuitions and Maddalena had learned, without anyone having to teach her, that the only course open to her was to trust those intuitions blindly. Thus, despite Domenico's good humour, she could not see Marianna's apparent friendliness in a positive light. And it would have been enough for the old woman to have looked into her eyes to understand that.

She leaped to her feet because her nausea was always followed by a need to urinate. Her mother met her in the corridor. The evening before, Domenico and Maddalena had decided the moment had come to make an official announcement even though everyone was already aware of their situation. Certain expressions had immediately changed at home, as if she were being congratulated and criticised at the same time. At least, that was how Maddalena interpreted some unusually nervous behaviour on the part of her father, who up to this point had always been calm.

A little before they made their announcement, Domenico had gone to see Mimmíu to give him the counter-signed power of attorney. Father and son had just looked at each other without further explanation. They had agreed to meet again in the Pes home, where all sat down after supper to share the good news. The result was a comedy of congratulations followed by a melodrama of negotiations. Once married, Maddalena and Domenico would be representatives of a new, progressive generation, one gifted a fortune that had perhaps cost more than it had yielded. As a married couple they would live in a house of their own, in every respect worthy of the social status bequeathed to them by earlier generations. The time had come to make public what had remained hidden for too long.

Mimmíu would have preferred, if it could have been agreed, that after appropriate adjustments and modernisation, the two young people could move into the house on via Deffenu where they had celebrated their engagement. Maddalena imagined Cristian must have been born there. This gave her a jolt, as if some submerged memory had suddenly surfaced, and she shuddered. Domenico, embracing her, asked about the little packet he had brought. She had to admit she had still not opened it. He imagined this must be a mere whim, since of course women in her condition were allowed liberties not otherwise acceptable in everyday life.

This was the first properly warm evening of an unusually inclement April. Far away from them, the nation was still in the midst of a bloody uncertainty that, if one thought about it, was not that different from the recently ended local battles. Domenico had begun to think that his own miraculous childhood, seen from the outside, might appear to have been some sort of hell. He had lived through a terrible period of banditry and kidnappings: and, like most other children of his age throughout the land, had gone to school with his hair in a quiff and his satchel on his back, but with the difference that for him the journey between home and school had been paved with ransoms. Ten million alive or dead. Yet even the barbaric Wild West, reconsidered at a later age without any tinge of innocence, could be seen to have been an age of adventure. In fact, he had often felt like one of the heroes in the "Intrepido" adventure comic, a boy strengthened by endurance like a cowboy.

But now his childhood was past; all it had taken was for him to turn round and be distracted a moment and it was all gone, his eyes had less wonder in them, his voice had grown gravelly, and his body tougher. Stamina, forbearance, patience, staying power, resistance, perseverance; these had become his permanent companions. Or aspects of his curse. Or the names of chains that restricted him. The frenzy of duty that had made him what he was, viewing the world from a synthesis of conformity and from a practical point of view. Certainly he was on the way to becoming a humdrum adult like his father, since fruit can never fall very far from the tree it has grown on. So when Maddalena told him she had not even opened Marianna's packet, he made no objection, apart from warning her to watch out for a possible negative response from Marianna.

He often thought about Cristian. He had even thought of him that very evening, imagining him sitting with the rest of them to hear the news of the forthcoming marriage and the child on the way. He had imagined Cristian cheerful, happy for them both, happy about everything. Because Cristian had had a remarkable capacity to appear calm and sometimes even happy whether he felt it or not. Then Domenico stopped thinking about this, because he sensed that too much dwelling on it would merely make things look darker. So he hugged Maddalena so hard she complained he was hurting her. She asked him what was the matter and he forced himself to banish the cloud that had formed before his eyes, telling her it was nothing, maybe just a touch of sadness . . .

So she promised she would open the present first thing next morning.

She had gone to bed quite early because she felt extremely tired; and immediately, perhaps even before she closed her eyes, had found herself immersed in the total whiteness of a threshing-floor covered with snow where a white dog was running about. She recognised everything at once: it really was a threshing-floor, the big white dog was called Tatra, and only a few steps away, past the rusty carcass of an old tanker lorry, you could skate on the frozen loop of a river. She knew every inch of that house though she had never seen it. She was certain she recognised every corner, and every trinket displayed on the sideboard in the big room. She knew that only a few steps away from the little path at the front door, bordered by two lines of evergreen dwarf thuja trees, there was the entrance to a great stall. And the pile of manure at the back whose smell permeated the cold air did not even seem to have an unpleasant odour, because it was as if paralysed by the frost . . .

When Maddalena opened her eyes the first thing she saw was Marianna's present.

On her way back from the bathroom, having met and reassured her mother who had also been unable to sleep, she decided the moment had come. Taking the little package very carefully in her hand, she tried to open it without tearing the tissue-paper, not so much from caution, but as to delay her discovery of its contents.

Which turned out to be a little silk garment, a baby's christening robe. On the chest, embroidered white on white, were the initials LIC. "Luigi Ippolito Chironi", Maddalena instantly realised. This must be the garment Cristian's grandfather had been baptised in: Marianna's favourite brother, even though Maddalena might not like to acknowledge the fact. It had already been clear to her before she opened it what this present could mean. The package also contained an envelope holding five one-hundred-thousand-lire banknotes and a handwritten message: *I wish you and your child all the happiness you deserve. Marianna Chironi.* Maddalena gritted her teeth so as not to scream.

*

For the whole of that day she remained in a state that could be defined as concentration, as if doing a difficult sum in her head and afraid to lose count. One might describe this as distraction, but not absent-mindedness. If anyone asked her anything, she said she had slept badly. And in fact, with all that ice and snow, she could not claim to have slept well. But what filled her mind was how to resist the look she knew she would see on Marianna's face. There was an answer somewhere, she knew that. And she knew it would be more effective if she herself could discover this answer. She could not turn to anyone else for help.

At lunch she picked at her food, claiming she was unusually tired so they would let her retire to her room. When Domenico telephoned, she told him to stay at his own home or go out with friends for the evening: she just needed a good rest. And when he protested she told him not to worry. She needed time, she needed to be alone to think. It was clear that Marianna knew everything, and it was equally clear that she could not bring her child into the world hampered by such a curse.

Nevina Pes could not believe her eyes when she saw her daughter leave her room dressed and wearing make-up. It was just before five. Maddalena gave herself a final check in the hall mirror, then picked up her bag and announced, "I'm going out."

"What shall I tell Domenico if he calls?" her mother said.

"That I've gone out," said Maddalena, without giving her time to say more.

The weather seemed to grow suddenly worse. Mimmíu's Fiat 127 swerved up to Predas Arbas, a little way beyond the city. He reached an unfinished stretch of residential housing, and came out onto a white road leading to an as yet unbuilt site covered with weeds. He parked and left the car.

He spent a few minutes examining the plot. It was larger than the others near it, surrounded by iron tubes and yellow and black plastic ribbon. This arbitrarily selected agricultural land was now almost ready for construction to begin. The local elections were not far off, and suitable building sites and votes were nothing if not interconnected.

You could say anything of Mimmíu Guiso, so long as you did not claim he had no intimate knowledge of the small world in which he had been placed. He had always been shrewd, with the sort of far-sighted shrewdness that makes certain kinds of education seem pointless. Though he had been unhappy studying arithmetic at school, he never had any problems doing accounts. He was a disaster when it came to the Italian language, yet had no need of dictionaries when he needed to explain himself. Nevertheless, with the extraordinary nature of his own qualities so obvious to him, he expected Domenico to go to school and have no difficulty coming near the top of the class. Because he told himself that two strokes of such good fortune in one family were impossible, or at least extremely unlikely. In fact, Domenico was different from him in every way, except that both were convinced that they belonged together, completely and proudly. And he would have done anything – or nearly anything – for his son, who was sensitive, studious and thoughtful where he himself was cynical, ignorant and instinctive.

Distant thunder could be heard. When Mimmíu looked up at the sky, he saw big purple clouds gathering beyond the hill. But it could not be about to rain, he told himself; this seemed to be thunder without conviction, like thunder in a theatre that makes a lot of noise but little else. And he knew never to fear noise, but only silence. That above all.

He looked at his wristwatch. Another clap of thunder, even further off, was followed by the clear sound of a small motorbike struggling up the hill. This carried a boy of twenty at most, so tall that to prevent his feet touching the ground he was forced to lift his knees against his chest. The boy braked, raising a cloud of dust, and dismounted. He held out his hand to a puzzled Mimmíu.

"Babbo has had problems," he said as if to explain himself.

Mimmíu surveyed him from top to toe: this boy was a good twenty centimetres taller than himself. "Well?" he said.

"This is the site in question," the boy said.

"And you are?"

"Nicola."

"Nicola, I would never have recognised you . . . You've grown so tall."

The boy lowered his chin and raised his shoulders. "Babbo and Leonardo have had to go to Cala Liberotto, to finish a house there," he explained. "But as you see this site here is a good one, it's one of the bigger ones and there's no doubt the house will be able to be built, so much so that Babbo says you may as well go ahead and lay the foundations.

All of which Mimmíu was perfectly aware of. "Yes," he said. "But the fact remains that this plot is not enough to repay what he owes me."

"Babbo says if you can wait a little longer, things on the coast are settling down and we'll soon be fine."

"Soon be fine," Mimmíu repeated sceptically. "On the coast where?"

"Near Agrustos . . . Ottiolu . . ."

"Yes, yes . . . the tourist harbour," Mimmíu added to show he was perfectly well aware of what they were discussing.

"They are contracting out the work for a tourist village down at the port."

"Nicò. . ." Mimmíu interrupted. "Tell your father I've already bought six of those plots at Ottiolu. One more won't help me." He waited for the boy to grasp the full import of what he was saying, then continued, "Your babbo knows quite well which plot interests me, and that's the one that will keep us even."

"That's what babbo told me to tell you," the young man said stiffly.

"Well, you give him my answer. It would be good if he could prepare the papers and everything for this site; but as far as the other plot is concerned, tell him not to try anything funny. He and I talked of Cala Girgolu but certainly not of Ottiolu."

The boy opened his very dark eyes, the eyes of a calf, as wide as he could. He knew the land Mimmíu was referring to was much more valuable than the land he and his father were offering. "The land at Cala Girgolu is all rocks, and in any case we can't be sure if they will allow us to build there, or when," he ventured.

"Then tell your babbo he will lose nothing if he gives it away. I'm taking that risk myself. That settles the matter." Mimmíu could make his voice sound terrible, especially when he was stating an indisputable fact. The boy knew there was nothing else he could say by way of argument.

133

"OK," he said and spread his arms wide. "I'll tell him. Keep well, Uncle Mimmí." He took his leave, resuming his acrobatic position astride the motorbike.

Mimmíu waved him away, like an elderly Indian chief dismissing a Yankee soldier after a negotiation.

Above him, through a gap in the clouds, a shaft of cinematographic light struck the earth just as on one of those old colour prints about the creation of man used for catechism lessons, or on a Jehovah's Witnesses' pamphlet. But it was not about to rain. He had been right about that.

The firm footsteps of Maddalena Pes echoed through the evening. Everyone who saw her pass, caressed by the fading light, reflected on nature's brilliant talent for making pregnant women look beautiful, walk elegantly, and smile sweetly . . .

Maddalena was talking to herself as she walked. She was preparing to outmanoeuvre any cunning ruse, lie, or deceit that Marianna might think up. She had thought of one solution, an extremely simple one. It had cost her a night's sleep, but it had been worth it. She was about to prove how determined an expectant mother could be.

Thunder could be heard in the distance, and it occurred to Maddalena that in her rush to leave the house she had forgotten to bring her umbrella. A sinkhole had opened in via Roma, where the massive structure of the Rotonda had recently stood, the nineteenth-century prison, a Bastille that had survived revolutions only to be destroyed by futile efforts at preservation by local politicians. She walked confidently past the Fascist structure of the Teatro Eliseo, which in more recent times had been home to the city's last cinema. Then she climbed via Ballero, on her way up to the old quarter of San Pietro.

By the time she reached the Chironi house she was out of breath, and before facing the gate and the courtyard, she sat down on a block of granite and leaned against the surrounding wall. She needed to get her breath back and calm down. The thunder had led nowhere, merely an empty menace. A few shafts of light pierced the dark clouds . . . Maddalena was so wrapped up in her own thoughts that she did not notice Marianna approach, carrying several shopping baskets. She had seen the young woman sitting in front of her house, and assumed that, not finding her in Maddalena must be waiting for her.

"If you'd told me you were coming, I'd have made sure I was at home."

Maddalena, deep in her thoughts, started at the unexpected sight of the old woman. "Oh God!" she exclaimed.

Marianna gave a strange smile. "Did I scare you?"

"You took me by surprise . . . I thought you were in the house. I must speak to you . . ." Maddalena stammered.

"But I was out. Are you coming in?"

Maddalena nodded, but did not move. She seemed to be concentrating so fiercely as to be almost incapable of raising her head. Marianna put down her baskets, careful not to let their contents spill. "I had nothing left to eat and I don't like having my shopping done by strangers . . . If I want things done properly I have to do them myself."

"Look, I'm not going to dress my child in this stuff," Maddalena whispered out of the blue, still staring at her own feet. Marianna saw her rummage in her bag for the little package, rewrapped to

135

the best of her ability, that Marianna had sent her with Domenico. "I don't even want this stuff in my house." She held out the package.

"Are you coming in?" Marianna repeated.

She went ahead into the yard. Maddalena waited a few seconds more, then followed. When she reached the kitchen, Marianna was already unpacking her shopping onto the dresser, and into the wall units above the sink and the refrigerator. Something in the smell of the room reminded her of Cristian, possibly a combination of biscuit and jasmine, or perhaps because it was just that the room contained so many things that he had touched: his cup on the draining-board, his beaver jacket hanging in the corridor, and his hairbrush on the bathroom shelf. Or perhaps it was just that it was impossible for her to forget him.

"So you don't like the present I gave you." Marianna was provocative.

"I don't want it."

"Why not? Do sit down." Marianna seemed to be enjoying the discussion.

"I think you know very well why not . . ." Maddalena refused to let herself be provoked by the old woman's tone. Marianna curled her lip, a sign she was trying to look sincere. Maddalena laughed. "This creature has done nothing to you," she said, her hand on her belly. "You, who know so well what it is to suffer, should not wish suffering on other people, least of all on my child."

Marianna took this in. "How many weeks are you now?" she asked unexpectedly.

Maddalena hesitated as though making a careful calculation. "Five, five and a half," she mumbled.

Marianna looked doubtful. "Maybe Domenico can believe that."

"Domenico believes everything, even that your generosity is sincere."

"Then tell me. Whose child are you carrying?"

Maddalena shook her head, as though suddenly deciding not to be beaten. "But even if it were as you think, would it not be even worse if you had tried to put a curse on this creature?"

"If that creature is a Chironi, he or she is already cursed before birth. No-one can force me to love yet another Chironi. God willing, we shall soon all be gone from the face of this earth once and for all."

"No," Maddalena objected. "Not my child!" She finally sat down. "I didn't come here just to give you back that garment, but to tell you that, even if you didn't mean it, you have given me the answer I was looking for. I didn't want to discuss it with Domenico before speaking to you, but I have decided what I shall call the child whether a boy or a girl . . ." She stopped, waiting for Marianna's face to darken. "Don't you want to know?"

The old woman replied with an amiably disinterested look, as she had first learned to do when forced to reconcile herself to the death of her only daughter who had been called . . .

Maddalena cut in. "Mercede. Mercede if it's a girl. Luigi Ippolito if it's a boy," she added, seeing Marianna had been rendered speechless.

A new era had come, a time when children would mercilessly devour their parents.

Now Maddalena's only thought was to get out of the house as quickly as possible. Getting up, she walked over to the French

137

window that led to the courtyard and through that to the rest of the world.

Marianna said nothing, making no attempt to explain or even to stop her. She only blamed herself for having been a poor hostess because she had not offered her guest anything. She gently stroked the little silk christening robe, enjoying the feel of the embroidery against the ball of her thumb. Taking the five one-hundred-thousand-lire banknotes out of the envelope, she dropped them into a tin marked ROCK SALT which she then replaced on the worktop behind her.

CERTAINLY THEIR LIFE BEFORE WAS NOT THE BEST POSSIBLE, but it was what fate had allotted to them. These were days during which they began to be aware of the infinite layers of reality. Accessing other people's lives by merely pressing a switch had transformed survival into something much less heroic: on the screen millions led identically depressing lives and others were even worse off. But then there were also some who were better off. Being aware of this changed things. Because abandoning the world of conjecture for a world of proof meant giving up on the poetry of needing to create one's own bespoke existence.

What Mimmíu thought of as modernity was translated in his head into a practical sense that you no longer had to seek knowledge but could have it brought right into your home for a monthly fee. If one knew how to make the most of these developments, one could conceive of a new world, ignore the rules, and embrace a different and more fitting morality. Mimmíu knew this perfectly well even though he did not know it. Now that he was about to become a grandfather he could visualise himself as a boy at the very beginning of everything. In the workplace, for example, if anyone protested that something was new, or that some particular thing had never been known before, or that certain materials hadn't been used in their part of the world before, he would argue that things previously unbelievable were now employed everywhere. If you knew how, you could now get improved results at half the cost. The country might be in funereal mode, but he was happy. He knew that even if happiness was never infinite, unhappiness was never infinite either; the difference being that though you might never get used to the first, you could easily get used to the second. From his point of view, they had experienced enough unhappiness. From his point of view the last three seasons of the Seventies had brought about a genetic mutation. Like when after a long convalescence you realise that the moment to start running again has finally come.

That was how he saw his own immediate future, and that of his son and his grandchild: as an enormous manufactured article, like a gigantic children's game. Feast and famine would always alternate, you just had to be wise and adapt. This was how it had always been and there was no brand of modernity, real or presumed, that would ever be able to change it.

To people who asked him why he held certain convictions, he would say "because I know". This was no vague answer. In fact, it was the only meaningful response possible. Because Mimmíu knew, and the fact of his knowing prevented any imagined atonement for the facts. It was not that he had deliberately changed himself, but he had evolved. Breathing deeply, he had struggled to the top, and now was determined to enjoy being there before letting himself fall, precipitously, without a care. He felt he would need a decade at the top, to enjoy the illusion of being there permanently before his descent began. Not everyone had understood this, but Mimmíu had. This was exactly what had made him who he was.

He realised that he despised those who made a show of working hard, simply because he himself was present at the building site. "Slackers," he would tell himself, "– just look at them pretending to work." He would gesture to the foreman, who would immediately stop whatever he might be doing and go over to him.

"I think we're seriously behind," he would say without putting any special stress on the words "I think".

"It's not that we're behind," the foreman would venture. "But we hit water while digging for the foundations. With all due respect, no proper geological survey was done here." He would think this an acceptably neutral observation.

But Mimmíu would not bat an eyelid. "These fucking surveys cost us money and time. What is there for us to survey, eh? Just a little water, and we can pump that away. Bachí, Bachisio!" he would call out to a plump workman who happened to be passing. "What the fuck have you been doing with that mixture?"

The man came over. "What mixture?"

"The mixture for the containing wall," Mimmíu said.

"Sorry?" The workman looked at the foreman. "We haven't been doing anything with it. What do you mean, Uncle Mimmí?"

"Nothing. I'm just saying there's been a lot of waste. Too much cement and too much water . . . What was it I told you?" he asked Bachisio.

"This is the way we've always done it," the foreman said.

Mimmíu glared at him as though he had spoken out of turn. "You should be more careful not to be so wasteful."

The other two exchanged glances, determined not to reply; in any case, when the boss had made up his mind to be awkward, there was nothing to be done. And what with all the trouble he'd

141

had at home, with Cristian Chironi shot dead in the port at Livorno, one could understand.

"If that's the way you've always done it, you've always done it wrong," Mimmíu said. "Things change."

"Some things don't," the foreman replied.

"Meaning?" Mimmíu roared.

"Meaning," the man said, "that as long as I'm the one who signs the official papers, the relationship between water and cement cannot change. We apply the law here."

"Bachí, excuse us a moment, I have something private to say to the foreman."

Bachisio happily rejoined the rest of his colleagues who were preparing a cast.

When they were alone Mimmíu took the foreman by the arm in order to force him to look him in the eye.

"Well, Mister Lawyer, when is it you come up for retirement?" Mimmí was whispering so near his face that the other man could smell his breath. "I know everything, both what's in your pay packet and the black part of your earnings as well."

"What's that got to do with anything?" the other man protested.

"What it's got to do with anything, is that if we're going to apply the law, we must apply it the same all round. Don't you agree?"

The foreman gave an almost imperceptible nod.

NOW SHE WAS ABLE TO LOOK MORE CAREFULLY AT IT, SHE noticed the house was not white as she had previously thought, but a very pale blue. And even the snow was not really quite white, but also verged on blue. She was beginning to understand, for example, why she was not feeling the cold despite the fact that she was only wearing a slip and was barefoot in the middle of a snowbound waste. Which, considered from a different point of view, could mean that she was in the midst of a rather unimaginative dream. The image in front of her could not even answer straightforward questions, like was she dreaming in colour or not? And is white verging on blue a colour? The white dog ran towards her. She heard the word "Tatra!" spoken behind her. Turning, she saw a tall young man with fair hair and a beard. He was standing at the entrance to the blue house, his fists on his hips like a proprietor waiting outside his premises for customers. He too seemed aware that her clothing was inadequate. He, on the other hand, was well covered, in a tight jacket that made him look like a teenager who had grown too quickly. "Tatra!", he called again in a strangely metallic voice. The dog turned and looked at him, almost as if wanting to make sure who he was, then launched itself at him. Careful to prepare himself for the impact, the man welcomed the

143

animal. They ran into each other's embrace in the dazzling whiteness. The man's laughter reached Maddalena like a hiss of wind. She watched them, enchanted by the love revealed in their encounter. She took a step towards them. The snow felt tepid to her bare feet. The man had reached a group of skeletal birches between the farmhouse and the frozen loop of the river, and for a moment the big dog seemed to lose sight of him. The man was slim and agile in his shabby threadbare jacket, and from its shrunken sleeves also emerged stretches of the sleeves of his jumper. Yet at the same time he was elegant, with the elegance of an intrepid traveller setting out in tweeds and balaclava to reach the North Pole early in the twentieth century. The dog propped itself up on its front legs to look about itself. The frosty air gave substance to smells of peat, dung and vinegar. *"Esmu šeit!"* was suddenly heard from the brushwood in the wooded area. The dog, like a tightly wound spring, threw itself towards the voice, reaching the man in the dense shrubbery. They vanished from her sight, though she could still imagine them there. Then someone touched her with a very cold hand. She was about to turn to see who it was, but woke up.

Her mother Nevina was at her bedside. "Maddalé, hurry up, if we don't get a move on we'll be late . . . Everyone else is nearly ready."

The girl shot up. "What's the time? Why didn't you wake me sooner?"

"It's alright." Nevina felt a need to reassure her. "If you hurry we'll be fine."

"Why didn't you wake me sooner?" Maddalena repeated.

"You were sleeping so peacefully. In any case, the rest of us had to get ready too . . ."

Maddalena shook her head the way she had seen the big white dog shake its head in her dream. She stood up. Her wedding dress had been laid out over the armchair. Absolutely perfect given the circumstances.

"Isn't it too white?" Nevina said, more afraid of its inadequacy than the poverty it hinted at.

"It isn't white," Maddalena protested, "It's a blueish off-white."

"Yes," her mother cut her short. "But get a move on, the hairdresser will be here in half an hour."

Maddalena disappeared into the bathroom. Her mother looked around for her. "Where are you?"

"I'm here," Maddalena answered before turning on the shower. Peppino Pes and his son Roberto were waiting on the sofa in the small dining room, both dressed exactly as they had been for the engagement ceremony. But not Nevina. She, as mother of the bride, had had to fork out for another outfit, a tasteful three-piece suit in soft periwinkle blue that had to be worn with nice shoes and a matching handbag.

"Yes, that's right, you two, just sit there like that and never mind creasing your trousers," she said as she came into the room. The two men jumped to their feet and patted their legs. Nevina went up to her husband as if she were about to whisper a secret, and beckoned to Roberto to join them. "If she asks you, say her dress is pale blue, is that clear?" Father and son nodded in unison.

Shortly after this Maddalena came in with a big towel round her shoulders to protect the dress from her wet hair. "Both of you, what colour is this dress?" she asked the men.

Peppino squared up to her and looked at her intently. "Pale blue," he stated confidently. "Robé, it is pale blue, isn't it?"

Roberto said neither yes nor no, merely lifting his eyebrows. Maddalena looked at her mother, who met her gaze with the hint of a smile.

The bell rang. Nevina ran to open the door to the hairdresser.

That Mimmíu Guiso counted for something in Núoro could be judged from the fact that it had only taken him a few hours to have the little church of the Redeemer at the top of Monte Orthobène opened up for Domenico and Maddalena's wedding. A wedding requiring a certain haste and not at all as everyone had expected it to be, but still needing an exclusive setting. There were very few invited guests. Marianna, realising she had only been included because it would have been impossible to ignore her, did not appear.

She had something else on her mind that Ascension Day morning. The weather, at last, was warm and windless. After she had watered the plants in the courtyard, she took a hot bath. Then, without even dressing, she went into the room that had once belonged to her brothers, then to Vincenzo, and finally, for a long period, to Cristian.

That was the room with the writing-desk, and in a drawer, sheets of white paper. She took out some paper, found a pen, and began to write:

I the undersigned Chironi Marianna, formerly Serra-Pintus,

being in the full possession of my faculties, wish the following instructions to be carried out after my death, which I hope will occur quite soon:

that all my earthly possessions, both movable and unmovable, shall go to the child about to be born to Guiso Domenico son of Guiso Giovannimaria, and Pes Maddalena daughter of Pes Giuseppe known as Peppino;

that this bequest shall apply equally whether the child is a boy or a girl;

that the possessions referred to shall be administered by the legitimate father of the child until he or she reaches the age of twenty-one years;

and that at my death be consigned to Pes Maddalena, the envelope containing the story of the Chironi family as written in his own hand by my older brother the late Chironi Luigi Ippolito son of Chironi Michele Angelo.

Written on the sixth day of May in the year Nineteen Hundred and Seventy-Nine,

In witness thereof I sign myself,
Chironi Marianna, formerly Serra-Pintus

Outside the church, after the wedding, some twenty carefully selected guests greeted the bridal pair. Most of them, having previously been present at Maddalena and Domenico's engagement party, were aware how similar to a wedding that ceremony had been, while the event they had just witnessed had seemed more like something semi-clandestine.

A lunch was organised at premises just outside Núoro. And

by three in the afternoon, everyone was back at home, while the newly-weds took possession of the apartment Mimmíu Guiso had given them. Maddalena did not like it, and particularly disliked the furnishings her father-in-law had personally chosen for their love-nest. It was a large, even perfect residence, and you certainly could not dismiss it as ugly. But to Maddalena it seemed more like a cold suite in a luxury hotel, aggressively new like a car on display at a motor show.

"You don't like it," Domenico commented, helping her out of her coat.

Maddalena used her toes to push her shoes off her heels. "It's not that I don't like it . . ." she said, to gain time. "It has everything." Meanwhile Domenico, still holding her coat in his hand, was looking for somewhere to hang it.

According to Nevina's enthusiastic accounts to her neighbours, the new flat had everything: two bathrooms each with its own dressing room, three television sets, two telephones and even a dishwasher of the sort you only ever saw in films. There were pictures already on the walls, and complete sets of plates and glasses in the sideboard. Definitely a noble wedding present!

"I know it lacks the feminine touch, but you needn't accept anything you don't like . . ."

"That picture," Maddalena said, pointing to a sort of weeping clown over a shelf, "and that lamp . . . and, for heaven's sake, those curtains," she went on in a rising voice.

Domenico dropped her overcoat over a fake-antique armchair. "I did tell him it wouldn't be a good idea, but nobody ever listens to me."

Maddalena looked at him, tempted for a moment to comfort

148

him, but she felt too tired. "It doesn't matter," she murmured.

Domenico sat down beside her and reached for her hand. "We don't have to stay here if you don't like it."

"Don't make me out to be utterly capricious, Domé."

"You know what Babbo's like. It hasn't been easy for him, and he's had to do everything himself . . ." He stopped, aware that Maddalena was pulling away from him.

"Alright, that's enough," she said. "It's you I married, Domenico. Is that quite clear?"

There was no need for anything else to be said, so they said nothing more, and in the silence it seemed that the alienation emanating from their surroundings had exploded so violently that even Domenico was able to feel it and grasp its absurd intensity. Emotionally, it was as if they had taken over someone else's house, a dolls' house even. The whole place was a toy, a home someone had imagined for people with no will or taste of their own.

Maddalena felt she was being overcome by a subtle understated affliction, like being consoled in advance of inevitable despair.

When the telephone rang, Domenico jumped. He took a couple of steps towards it as though to convince it to stop ringing: he knew it would be Mimmíu calling. He turned to look at his wife who was doing her best to avoid encouraging him to answer it. The ringing continued obstinately. Maddalena did not move from the sofa. Domenico, standing with his hand on the receiver, did not move either.

When the phone stopped ringing, the two continued looking at each other for a while without saying a word, afraid anything they said would underline the embarrassment they both felt. Then the ringing began again.

"Let's go," he suggested.

"Where?" she asked. But in a tone of voice that at last showed some interest.

"What does it matter where? Let's get into the car, and head for the coast. Take a ship? Go to Rome?" Domenico sounded increasingly enthusiastic.

Maddalena realised that every time he yielded to the illusion he could put things right, she felt a tenderness towards him.

"When my mother died I became aware that . . ." Domenico suddenly began. "I have no idea why this came into my mind at this particular moment," he added immediately to excuse himself for mentioning it. Maddalena waited for him to go on. "Perhaps because I never again felt quite the same, till now." He stopped again. His wife held out her hand to invite him to join her on the dreadful Las Vegas-style sofa. He sat down.

"I swear I was aware of it," he continued without looking at her. "But I pretended otherwise. Because I imagined if all those around me thought I had not realised what had happened, it must mean that it could not be so bad, even that it had not in fact happened. And now it's the same thing: Cristian dying in the way he did, and then the two of us, the baby on the way, this marriage . . ."

"Who could have stopped it happening?" Maddalena asked, stroking his hand. "Who could have done that?"

Domenico turned to look at her, his mouth trembling. "I could," he confessed. "I was not even able to stop all this." He indicated the room with a wide sweep of his arm. "Just like that day when my father insisted on saying, 'Everything will be fine, you and I will make it, we don't need anything else,' and I wanted to say no, that nothing was fine, that my mother was dead . . . But

I was afraid. Afraid. Like now . . ." Domenico put his hands to his head.

"What are you afraid of?" Maddalena asked, stroking his neck.

"Of you realising you made the wrong choice."

"What are you saying?" The conversation had taken an unexpected turn; Maddalena was trying to speak with forced detachment. "You said yourself it wasn't the end of the world, didn't you? What am I saying? That I don't like this place. Let's find somewhere that really suits us . . . Alright?" She was trying to reassure him, but Domenico did not seem comforted. "We won't let anyone else make decisions for us. Agreed?" Domenico took a breath as if about to reply, but she got in first. "Not anyone else, agreed?"

"Not anyone else," he repeated.

It was only then they realised the telephone had long ago stopped ringing.

Mimmíu put the phone down at his end, struggling with a mixture of irritation and disappointment. He had expected thanks, but understood that for two newly-weds entering their new home for the first time, feeling grateful to the person who had provided it was not likely to be their first thought.

Yet at the same time he knew what that silence meant. The moment had come to rethink everything. To take a new look at things from every angle. He became aware of something he had never really thought of before: that what he had unquestionably gained now, was a chance to be on his own.

The thought had come into his mind just like that, suddenly complete and precise, as if till now he had only been thinking in bits and pieces. He confessed this freely to himself in silence but, being in an empty room, he could equally well have shouted it out because no-one else would have heard him.

He sat down, looking towards Domenico's former room. Then, going back to the nothingness that was bothering him, he told himself he had done everything possible to ensure he could remain on his own.

He remembered a morning many years before, when he had waited impatiently for people to load the boot of his car with the last things still left after a ceremony at the priory of San Francesco di Lula. After which they told him there was still one more charitable act required of him, which was to give a stranger a lift to Núoro in his car. That person had been Vincenzo Chironi. So he had driven Vincenzo to find his relatives in Núoro.

Mimmíu wondered why on earth that memory should come back to him now, but eventually he understood that some people, of whom Vincenzo Chironi was one, had their destiny clearly written on their faces. And it also occurred to him to wonder if anyone looking at him, at Mimmíu Guiso, at that moment when Vincenzo had first got into his car, would have been able to understand terrible things about him. For example, how it would have been possible to push him, Mimmíu, into depriving Vincenzo of everything. As soon as he was sitting in the car Vincenzo had given a faint smile as though already recognising him as indebted, before pushing his quiff of black hair back out of his eyes. Vincenzo had barely been able to cram his long legs into the limited space in front of his seat, though he had not seemed in any way awkward or clumsy when he sat down. Then, once the car had started, he had revealed his Chironi profile. And at that moment, Mimmíu had experienced a feeling of acidity in his mouth, as though forced to swallow a bitter fruit.

That was the absolute truth. And now that there was no-one with him anymore, Mimmíu was able to whisper to the wall in front of him that he had always envied Vincenzo Chironi. It was later, only later, that he understood that the most effective way of giving expression to that feeling, realising the opposite would come to pass, was to load the man with unconditional love.

Now that he had done what he had done, Mimmíu was able to acknowledge the combination of anguish and relief he had felt when he found Vincenzo hanging from the grille on the office window. Everything had been summed up in that moment: he had not been able to avoid envying Vincenzo, but had also not been able not to love him. He had tried with all his might, though unsuccessfully, to be indifferent to Vincenzo's fate, but Vincenzo had a way of coming back. He always came back. Even after his death.

At this very moment, Mimmíu could sense Vincenzo sitting beside him. Vincenzo had something to say to him, something that sounded like an auto-da-fé: "Just wait and see, my friend, you have abandoned me, and my son will very soon abandon me too."

Though he would never have mentioned Cristian because what happened to Cristian was a fact whose importance he had not yet fully grasped. In any case, Vincenzo had never met his son Cristian. Not in this life, so . . .

Mimmíu shook his head in the way people do when they would rather not believe something.

Now he could understand clearly what it meant to lose a son. A simple event like that failure to answer his phone call had flung him into depths of anger, into the obscure void inside him. And he could imagine that his whole life, from that moment on, would be a life of expiation. Because he knew only too well what human beings are capable of doing even to people they think they love.

And children. They repay everything to you, both the good and the bad.

The local TV channel was transmitting an investigation like those broadcast on national television. Documentaries founded on fact, but narrated sensationally with plenty of suspense. Did viewers remember the Priamo Camboni case of 1970? Mimmíu nodded at the screen: he certainly could, but he had never really understood it . . .

At all times of the year, Priamo Camboni's house had always been warm. This was because his wife Gessica, who had suffered badly from the cold during the poverty of her childhood and adolescence, was now determined, after making an excellent marriage, never to suffer from the cold again. How much she may have sacrificed to achieve that marriage it was impossible to say, because Gessica was beautiful while Priamo could not be described as good-looking. But he was rich.

Gessica had been barely fourteen when she fell in love with a handsome but very poor seventeen-year-old, who had taken her virginity in Núoro bus station when they were both bunking off school. The coincidence that they were both local and poor, and had both chosen the same day to shelter in the bus-station waiting room rather than go to school, had inevitably led to a kiss, after which they had moved to the toilets near the waiting room. They had not said much, just looked at each other and kissed, and then gone further, and at the time she had not even known the boy's name.

A little later Gessica had seen a photo of him on the front page of the local daily and discovered that he was called Emanuele Sias. A fine name, Gessica thought. And she also thought that even that grainy newspaper photograph proved how good-looking he was. The newspaper was reporting that Emanuele had been accused of robbing and murdering a Núoro jeweller. The story was that two days earlier, at about eleven in the morning, he had stuck a gun into the stomach of the jeweller Gilberto Arru, 53, a father of four. When his victim refused to hand over the day's takings, Sias had shot him on the spot, and left with some 200,000 lire's worth of cheap jewellery.

That night, faced with Emanuele's newspaper photo, Gessica could not shut her eyes, but she was sure the boy could not have done what he was accused of. Just before eleven in the morning, two days before, she had been with him in the bus-station toilets. And she was certain of that, because at the very moment when she realised she had lost her virginity, the clock in the toilet where all this was happening had shown exactly eleven o'clock.

The following day, Sias claimed in the paper that he was innocent because he had been somewhere else on the day of the murder. The article revealed no more than that. At table, Gessica's father referred to the story, adding general comments to the effect that a youth who refused to take responsibility for his actions deserved no consideration whatever. Gessica lowered her eyes.

Two months later, the case of Sias Emanuele came up for trial. By now nearly everyone except Gessica had forgotten the unfortunate crime.

She had a particular reason for remembering it, because she had been suffering from morning sickness for several weeks.

She needed to think, and to think long and hard. The son of the Camboni family had been looking at her, and since the day when she lost her virginity, she had come to understand the precise nature of that look on his face. Local people described him as a dimwit, and it was true that his expression revealed no particular intelligence. But it occurred to Gessica that the only way out of her dilemma was to exploit that look on Priamo Camboni's face.

So she seduced him the second time they went out together, and a month later told him she was pregnant.

On the day of her marriage to Priamo Camboni, Gessica heard that Emanuele Sias, sentenced to life imprisonment for the murder of the jeweller Gilberto Arru, had hanged himself in prison. She fainted when she heard about it, but everyone attributed this to her interesting physical condition. The female wedding guests slapped her to bring her round, while she complained of feeling cold despite the fact that it was now high summer.

Her daughter Emanuela Camboni was officially judged to have been a seven-month baby, if an exceptionally large one. But not even the birth of her child could cure the mother of feeling cold.

As everyone expected, Priamo did not prove to be a good husband. He happened to be one of those who, precisely because they initially seem stupid and unaggressive, paradoxically turn out to be exceptionally violent. For fourteen years he brutally abused his wife, while doting on his daughter. At home the only person able to control the fury of this otherwise ineffective and idle if wealthy man, was his daughter Emanuela. She meanwhile had grown beautiful, much more beautiful than her mother.

One August evening, Priamo, coming home drunk, as usual

started shouting at his wife. From her room, Emanuela heard them quarrelling – a terrible battle on this particular occasion.

Then the whole house fell silent. Gessica looked into Emanuela's room and told her daughter that Priamo had fallen and knocked himself out, and with any luck was dead. We must call the police, she added, and told her daughter that if she could tell them that she saw her father fall, no-one would suspect anything, and that would be the end of the matter and the great wealth of the Camboni family would be theirs.

Emanuela smiled, but it was not a reassuring smile. In fact, when the police arrived she told them that her mother had killed her father by pushing him over.

So Gessica, the black widow, was arrested, and on reaching the age of eighteen, Emanuela inherited her father's fortune.

That's children for you.

Mimmíu switched off the television.

It was a lovely story he had never previously understood, but now he understood it only too well.

It took the whole of the next morning for the weather to improve. May was struggling to establish itself. It was not till about two that afternoon that the battle against the wind, which was shifting the clouds and turning the sky grey, was won. Blue impregnated entire areas previously green and grey, spreading above the trees and granite. The dead season had been smothered by the season of the living as if to confirm the regularity with which the ages follow one another, in spite of those who claim the opposite. Some were forced to accept their mortality that day, and others to leave the comfortable warmth inside their mother's body. It was a day for remembering beginnings and endings. As is always the case, but this time it brought a new degree of clarity. Mimmíu had been aware of the uncertain light at dawn. Then of the opening wide of a shameless afternoon, too luminous for its late arrival, when the wind had suddenly dropped and given way to silence. Although he had not slept well, he was not feeling tired, not as tired as he should have been. For Mimmíu rest was nothing more than a ceasing of thought. It meant nothing to him if his sleep was short or long, the important thing was that it silenced his mind.

When the telephone rang, he went calmly to answer it.

It was Domenico, who sounded embarrassed. "Excuse me for not calling earlier," he said.

Mimmíu cleared his throat and took his time. "You've had other things to think about. How's the house? Do you like it, the two of you?"

Domenico skated round this. "Yes, the house, we'll come to that later . . . Haven't you heard anything?"

Mimmíu made a gesture to indicate no, as if his son could see him. "No, what should I have heard?"

MARIANNA CHIRONI, FORMERLY SERRA-PINTUS, KNEW HER last day had come. She understood this without any shadow of doubt from the fact that there was such a crowd of people in the kitchen. And not just anyone: Babbo and Mamma were there, and Gavino. And the young twins Pietro and Paolo. Franceschina and Giovanni Maria too. And Luigi Ippolito with Vincenzo. Dina was there and also Cecilia; and even Biagio. Giuseppe Mundula was there. And others she did not remember ever having met.

All this made it very clear to her that this must be the last day of her life. She understood that this uncertain month of May must have been specially chosen for her. She would have preferred a luminous May, with days full of porous light and teeming with pollen. When, that is to say, the emptiness is filled with a substance even if not a compact one, rather than an immaterial Nothing. And indeed, even being able to assist at the miracle of a nothing that can be filled with something at the same time as it remains nothing, would seem to be a suitable termination for a very long life.

Luigi Ippolito shrugged because, having had an education, he knew that there is no miracle in the fact that pollen invades every pocket of air we breathe; even if only perhaps as a shaft of light

159

slipping through a half-closed Venetian blind, and that this teeming substance becomes visible in penumbra despite its apparent non-existence.

Marianna nodded, because there can be no doubt that knowing things makes them more familiar, less surprising. And she may even have been thinking that it might be possible to know so much. And that knowing so much could mean losing all capacity for astonishment.

In any case, she had to make do with that pale, wan May day.

I'm dying, she told herself, but without gloating over the fact for fear that her delight might be repaid by the annoyance of doubt. So, pretending it was nothing, she sat down on her usual chair by the fireplace, pretending to ignore all these people who had so suddenly crowded into the house. She looked out through the French window at the courtyard; it was grey and windy, just like the morning of her wedding day. She was tempted to turn towards her mother Mercede to ask her whether she felt the same about it. And whether she too had been upset, when she got up that morning, to see how uncertain the weather was, just when all the guests were beginning to arrive. Marianna had always thought of her own wedding as if it had been another woman's wedding. As far as she was concerned, she had always been either single or a widow, and hardly remembered anything at all of her brief period as a wife. Even her experience of motherhood had always seemed so short that it scarcely counted. Everything she had learned had come to her through a process of subtraction. It had been a very hard school, always kneeling humiliated on chickpea husks in the corner of the stable reserved for donkeys. But this had saved her from harbouring too many illusions, and she had been able to catch things as they flew past. Now she was dying. She knew it and was not afraid. Everyone was there with her in the kitchen. She expected to be called from one moment to the next. It was becoming ever more difficult to pretend otherwise.

Luigi Ippolito was the first to speak, looking exactly as he had in front of the little church of San Spiridione, Trieste, in 1917, shortly before his own death.

He wanted to make sure that, as Marianna's favourite brother, he would be the first expected to speak. He waited for a moment or two: but no-one, among all those present, dared to interrupt; since they all knew how much that sister had loved him, so that there there was little or no reason for anyone to object.

"The Word is profound, dear sister," Luigi Ippolito began. His voice had the soft but firm quality of one who had never known the slow gnawing of age. And his face had never had time to develop wrinkles. He had the mobile gaze of one who has not experienced the patience that age brings. "The Word is profound," he repeated, then went on, "like a stone falling to the bottom of the pool and disturbing the mud. The Word is breath taking concrete form, giving substance to what would otherwise have no body."

"Yes," she murmured. "I know what you mean. And I have never wasted a single word."

"The Word sanctifies everything that it represents. You have only ever said what you thought would deserve to be remembered. You do know that, don't you?"

"I know, I know . . . That's why you're here, isn't it?" she said, passing her hand between her nose and mouth, as if to brush away a fly.

"And so here we all are." Luigi Ippolito waited ceremoniously for Cecilia and the twins, Babbo and Mamma, Gavino and Dina, Biagio, Giuseppe, Franceschina, including all the others either born dead or never born at all, to approve. They all nodded. Except Vincenzo, who seemed on the point of tears.

"You've all come," Marianna confirmed, smiling at her favourite brother, before turning to her reticent nephew.

Then, when Vincenzo, after a great effort, also approved, she continued. "You are all here to breathe the breath that generates stories."

Luigi Ippolito agreed, sadly this time. "After you, dear sister, we shall have to depend on our memories, I think." He was the only one who spoke, but he was also speaking on behalf of the others who again nodded. Except Vincenzo, who still seemed lost.

Thus it was quite clear that 7 May 1979 would not be a day just like any other for Marianna Chironi, the ultimate widow and orphan.

"Good, then let's start from the beginning again," she said, turning to those present. "Michele Angelo and Mercede begat Pietro and Paolo, Giovanni Maria and Franceschina, Luigi Ippolito, Gavino and Marianna; Marianna and Biagio begat Mercede known as Dina; Luigi Ippolito and Erminia begat Vincenzo; Vincenzo and Cecilia begat Cristian; Cristian and Maddalena begat Luigi Ippolito . . .

Those dead and alive all kept count on their fingers.

*

Luigi Ippolito was sitting in the precise pose in which he had always been familiar to her; you could not call it stiff, nor relaxed either. In Marianna's personal catalogue he came first, as Arcesilaus had been first for Homer. Marianna remembered every detail of him; the slight trembling of his lip just before he left to start school at the *liceo*; and from the period when he had been concentrating on writing, she remembered his lowered head and the lock of black hair nearly touching the page, as he created his narrative of the Chironi family, a story that had never in fact existed, but as he had said, if no-one takes the trouble to write it or tell it, a story can never come into existence at all. And she remembered how at the end of 1915, he had pinched the air with his fingers as he looked for words to tell them that he was going to volunteer for the Carso front; and how he had returned home from there sealed in a coffin. And she could remember his exact smell, like a scent of wafer and warm bread; and how his clothes would still be clean even after he had been wearing them for a whole day, and how every smallest part of his body from his hair to his toenails seemed to have been specially finished or chiselled. And how she had loved him with a furious, blind love, much more than she had ever loved herself.

Marianna turned to look at Vincenzo, then turned back to Luigi Ippolito. The two were so alike, but if you studied them carefully you could detect small differences between father and son; the line of their eyebrows, for instance, formed a sharp curve in her brother, while in her nephew the curve was slenderer and almost straight, and then ran along his temples. And the brilliant whiteness of their skin was opaque in the father, and tended more to reflect light in the son. And their ankles were very fine in the father, thicker and more solid in the son. She had kept a careful record of all these subtle differences, because she knew well that these details contained the significance of her own existence.

Now, in harmony with this, Vincenzo appeared behind her in the blue suit he had worn at his wedding. He still looked starved of love, just like his father, together with his subtle and languorous silence and his melancholy knowledge of symmetry. He was the second, undoubtedly, because Marianna had been in love with him even before she knew of his existence, every time she had imagined the return from the war of her favourite brother; after which she had had to make do with this previously unknown nephew, born to start everything off again before dying to bring it to another end. This was why her mouth trembled, because Vincenzo's story had twisted her heart from the very moment he had set out to battle locusts and mosquitoes.

Oh, Gavino . . . And Mamma Mercede and Babbo Michele Angelo, together . . .

"HOW DID SHE DIE? MIMMÍU ASKED, ALMOST AS IF HE had been told something impossible.

"The fact is, she's dead," Domenico said. "A heart attack, it seems. The cleaner found her not long ago."

"It doesn't seem possible," Mimmíu exclaimed. "It doesn't seem possible. It doesn't seem possible . . ."

"As for the funeral and everything, we'll have to see to that ourselves. There's no-one else to do it."

From Domenico's tone of voice, Mimmíu understood there could no longer be any doubt that Marianna was dead, and that his son was now a real adult. "Yes, yes, of course," he hurriedly confirmed. "I do seem to have realised it somehow, I never closed my eyes last night."

So, with the help of female neighbours, they moved Marianna Chironi's body from the kitchen to her bedroom to wash it and lay it out. They wept to see a soul leave its body in this way. But they had no idea how happy she must have been.

Only Maddalena could imagine that, no-one else could. Although the others tried to excuse Maddalena from the duty of laying out the body, she refused to be pushed aside. She insisted on looking into the dead woman's face to understand exactly how

165

departing from life can produce an automatic, almost physical serenity.

Marianna certainly looked rejuvenated, but it was not her own death that had caused this, Maddalena was thinking, so much as the death of Cristian. She knew that between them there had been an unwritten pact, an agreement of intentions that had come from opposite aims. Is that not how it happens? People come together both wanting the same thing, by no matter what path. Maddalena wanted to give her child a father, and Marianna wanted to live long enough to see the final chapter of the Chironi family in this world.

Which is why what remains unspoken does not exist at all, Maddalena decided, as she held Marianna's body upright so one of the women could comb her hair. No breath means no existence. It's as simple as that.

That night for the first time she noticed a movement in her belly: nothing more than a gurgle, but precise and unfamiliar, like an unknown signal from another world. She told herself it was nothing negative, but simply life bubbling up again, desperate to regenerate what everyone had so desperately tried to eliminate. A local woman now expecting her fourteenth child, had told her it was enough not to want children for them to arrive anyway. There was a certain logic to that: once children have been conceived, it is sufficient not to want them for them to arrive. You must never show yourself desperate to have children, as had happened with the Chironi women.

Domenico was watching Maddalena. "You were restless in your sleep," he said.

"I can't remember what I was dreaming about at all." She was lying to some extent, because though she thought she could remember a dream, in fact she couldn't.

And that was all. They got ready for their appointment with the notary Sini, who had important things to tell them about the estate of the late Chironi Marianna, widow Serra-Pintus.

"Have you spoken to your father?" Maddalena asked Domenico as she straightened his tie. "Because when you do speak to him, I don't want to be there. Is that clear?"

"You've seen for yourself how things have been lately, Maddalé! Have a little patience, it's not as if you were living in a hovel . . ."

"That's not the point . . ."

"The point is that you are making it a question of principle," Domenico objected.

This didn't seem to worry Maddalena. "Exactly, it's a question of principle," she agreed.

They spent the next few minutes, the time they needed to finish getting ready, in silence.

"But do you know whether Cristian could swim?" she asked suddenly.

Domenico's face darkened slightly."Why are you asking me that?"

"Just because." She dismissed his question. "It's just something I asked myself, that's all."

"That's all," Domenico repeated, as if playing the irritating children's game of repeating other people's exact words. "No, he didn't swim much." He moved to be able to see himself in the mirror. "I'd say it was more a question with him of trying to keep afloat. But how come you were suddenly thinking about that?"

"No special reason." Maddalena seemed to be groping in the dark. "Something I dreamed, I suppose."

"You've been dreaming about Cristian?" Domenico was strangely calm as if anxious not to reveal any interest in the matter.

"I don't know," she repeated, feeling the full weight of a burden that had only left a subtle trace. "You know how when you're asleep you say you won't forget something but then you do forget it?"

Domenico agreed. "That can happen when you're awake too," he said firmly, opening the hall door and standing aside to let his wife pass.

Notary Sini's office smelled of secrets. Full of the deceptions of people forced to continue living together. And in his files continued to fester the bodies of the dead who had entrusted him with their final papers and wishes. Final wishes determined not to fade away but rather to endure, to condition the lives of those who remained.

"Wills," Sini mumbled, a tall thin man drenched in perfume, "are acts of survival; in their wills those dear to us address us directly." He turned to his secretary to complete the formalities.

Only Domenico and Maddalena were present.

Mimmíu had been asked to wait outside.

With studied deliberation, the secretary opened a sealed and countersigned envelope and took out what looked like a page from an exercise book with closely written lines of text, which he handed to the notary after muttering something to confirm that the envelope had not been tampered with in any way. Marianna's handwriting stood out beautifully clear on the front of the envelope: *For Pes Maddalena and Guiso Domenico* – the names set out in that order, as if in her infinite wisdom of the ways of the world, she had wanted to make the precedence absolutely clear.

The notary opened the document with a certain ceremonious flourish, and proceeded to read out a very short text, which for Maddalena and Domenico boiled down to: She has left Everything to Us.

Sini then made clear that a share of the estate was due in law to Chironi Cristian presumed dead, but that in his case the concept of *habeas corpus* would apply, at least for the ten years required by the law.

He also explained that after the termination of those ten years, which would be the length of time required to establish the legitimacy of the beneficiary (son or daughter, whichever he or she might turn out to be), the will could be considered definitely valid beyond any possibility of challenge.

The notary then asked Maddalena and Domenico if all this was clear and they agreed it was. Sini looked at them as if they were yet more swine being fed pearls from heaven, before turning to his secretary and pointing to some bookshelves behind him. The secretary looked annoyed as this required him to get to his feet, but he nonetheless took a couple of steps towards the precise spot indicated, and turned back with the required file in his hands. He put this on the table. The notary checked that it actually was the file mentioned in the will before handing it directly to Maddalena. She took it, hesitating slightly as she did so, and looked at Domenico. They then left the room.

Everything they had heard and signed for seemed logical, but they were nonetheless aware of a vague sense of disquiet, as if behind this unexpected fortune must lie a hidden sorrow.

Mimmíu was now called in separately, to be told that it was the last wish of Chironi Marianna (formerly Serra-Pintus) for a gravestone to be arranged for her according to the agreement that Guiso Giovannimaria (known as Mimmíu) had signed, and that otherwise she had left all her personal effects without exception to Guiso Domenico, exactly as set out in her will.

No-one spoke outside the notary's office. Domenico and Maddalena walked a few steps ahead, followed by Mimmíu, his thoughts weighing heavily on his shoulders.

Domenico slowed down for a moment to allow his father to catch up, while Maddalena continued to walk ahead. "What's the matter?" he asked his father, without taking his eyes off his wife.

His father sighed. "Nothing." The word broke from his mouth as if in fragments.

Domenico took a few more steps in silence. The city all round seemed to be inviting them to run away. As in ancient times, detail was more important than size. They must glorify brickwork and venerate the incomplete. Filling every space to avoid the horror of emptiness. The Guiso family had contributed in no small degree to the spread of this pervasive pettiness, but now seemed oblivious of it.

"She has left us everything, hasn't she?" Domenico exclaimed, peering sideways at his father.

Mimmíu didn't answer at once; perhaps tempted to try and alter with his eyes the surrounding abomination of blocks and bricks, which some might call progressive building, but he could not. "She has left us everything and taken everything away," he said.

"What has she taken away?" Domenico asked.

"Our peace . . . everything . . ." Mimmíu explained, clearly following his own thought and not even facing the fact that what he was saying might not make sense to others.

"Peace?" Domenico repeated, almost as if in some hidden corner of his mind he had at least grasped the basic sense of the word his father had just pronounced. But instead he just said, "I don't understand. Nothing whatsoever has changed."

A mirthless laugh burst from Mimmíu. "Just ask your wife what has changed and then we'll see."

"It's not what you think," Domenico said, shaking his head. Yet at the same time he knew his father was not wrong. The universal heir in Maddalena's belly made her sit up straight at the table at every negotiation from which Mimmíu had been excluded, Domenico did understand that, and while he did feel confident in assuring his father that nothing had changed, he could not guarantee the same for his wife. He sighed bitterly. "Aunt Marianna thought it through," he was forced to admit. "But it's not as if we need all that money, is it?"

Mimmíu gave him a crushing look. "We don't need the money, but we do need freedom to dispose of it as we think best. We are in a tricky position with the banks, and our credit depends on them accepting my signature. But now, with all these inheritance restrictions . . ."

"I'm its guardian." Domenico shouted because the only thing he had understood in what his father had been saying, was that the problem was the passage to himself of the guardianship of the estate.

"You have not understood," Mimmíu interrupted. "It's not

you I'm afraid of. Not you." He looked ahead at Maddalena's shoulders, moving quietly two paces ahead of them.

"I'm sure we can come to an agreement." Domenico was trying to speak calmly.

"You have no idea what parents can do for their children." Mimmíu's tone was suddenly no longer resentful, even peaceful. He was remembering a story his father had told him a thousand times about an old man forced to eat on the floor in a corner of the house. His meals were served to him in a wooden bowl by his daughter and her husband, who found it irritating that the old man was a noisy eater. A few days later their young son placed two other empty bowls on the floor beside his grandfather's bowl. When his parents asked him why, the boy said he was preparing bowls for when his parents themselves became old . . .

"Well, maybe I don't understand that now, but five months from now I will," Domenico answered, heading towards his wife.

"Marianna knew I would be the perfect diet for the woodworm she was inserting," Mimmíu muttered to no-one in particular, as he watched his son move away.

Summer thrust its nose from behind the long-closed curtain of sky, and a strange light began to spread over that corner of the world.

That night there was thunder, and a violent wind began whirling in the violet darkness, which lit up at intervals like full day.

The flashes came like phosphorescent discharges from huge electric fish in the depths of the sea. Anyone who believed that earth and sky were interchangeable would not have been surprised to find sea monsters foraging for food as confidently in the firmament as in the ocean. Now that waves from the sky were smashing themselves against the inviolate realms of the galaxies, one could hear Nordic giants thundering on timpani, with the bone castanets of tall ships sucked into whirlpools of sky. With the moans of dying sailors, dispersed in the void, reeling in terror, and abandoned to drown in the luminous hydrogen of the salty and ferrous ocean of the sky. Almost tempted by the inevitable, but still undefeated. So long as a thread of life survived.

Lightning struck a few steps from the Chironi courtyard.

Domenico, in bed, opened his eyes wide. He placed a hand on his chest to make sure he was still alive and touched between his thighs to be certain he was still a tangible part of the universe. Finally he turned onto his side. Maddalena was sleeping peacefully.

And so . . . There was no more snow. Perhaps this was how August was in those distant lands. Very hot summer weather that ended every night, never lasting longer than ten or twelve hours at the most.

The man in the tight jacket, who I now know to be called Juris, looks me in the eyes. His expression is full of curiosity but not hostility. No-one is hostile in this part of the world.

"*Zivs*", they say to me.

That must be my name, I am sure.

"*Zivs*", I repeat, and Juris has a good laugh, because it is possible, if not certain, that I must be pronouncing the word wrong.

We communicate in gestures when he wants to give me a drink, something that happens all the time, as he carefully holds an invisible small glass between his fingers. I mime an invisible watch on my wrist, as if to tell him it is too early for drinking, and that this is the hot part of the day. Juris continues to smile at me and tries saying something in Russian, because ever since childhood he has been used to thinking that everyone in the world must be able to speak Russian.

"*Zivs*" he says again, miming a fish. He points at me, "*Zivs*", and says the word again.

So I am a fish.

When it begins to snow it means summer is over with no possibility of any autumn. Juris and I are finally beginning to understand each other.

When Tatra, with swinging gait and dangling tongue, comes up to me, I know Juris must be near.

"*Esmu izsalcis,*" I say. He smiles in admiration, and takes bread, dried meat, boiled potatoes and gherkins from his bag. And vodka. "*Vēlos strādāt,*" I say.

This time Juris is struck. "*Drīz!*" he cuts in.

"What do you mean, it's too early? I'm fine," I protest. "I want to work," I repeat. But it is only at that moment that I realise I am in a bed and cannot get out . . .

"Maddalé, wake up . . ." She half-opened her eyes as Domenico's voice tickled her ear. She was at home now. "I was beginning to get worried," he murmured.

"What's the time?" Maddalena sounded hesitant, as if she was afraid she would not be able to find words for what she was thinking.

"More bad dreams?" Domenico asked.

Maddalena shook her head. But she touched her belly because

now the feeling inside her was so vivid it could have been real. Then she reached between her thighs with the usual fear of discovering some kind of loss. "Are you going out?" she asked, noticing Domenico was fully dressed.

He nodded. "I'm popping over to see Babbo. Yesterday he didn't seem right at all."

Now he was about to do it, Mimmíu understood how important it was to concentrate properly. And by "concentrate", he meant that particular condition in which a whole life, however twisted it might have been, can suddenly smooth itself out. "Imminent death produces clarity," he told himself, "especially if voluntary."

It had taken him hours to get everything ready despite the fact that all he needed was some strong cord and a suitable beam. He remembered Vincenzo Chironi, who had already crossed that particular bridge. Who knows if it had been equally difficult for him to gauge the strength of the rope and the exact point from which to hang himself. Or whether he had done everything instinctively, without a thought . . .

The storm, which had shattered the mirror of that May night, had finally convinced him to take stock of his life, including the evidence of his bankruptcy. He had grown up in uncertainty, and prospered in envy. Because whenever he looked beyond himself, all he had ever discovered was an open wound. And these open wounds had grown more numerous with time despite the goals he had achieved. Giovannimaria, before everyone started calling him Mimmíu, had never had any real childhood. He had been the youngest of four children born to a mother who had not survived his birth and a father who never had the faintest conception of family life. Then they had been cut down further, with two of his brothers dying of Spanish flu while he, though frequently under-nourished, totally neglected and entirely left to his own devices, survived. Then his father, on a farm where he had been working, was found dead from alcohol poisoning. And finally his eldest brother was spared by illness only to be killed in war. He had never really known his brothers, had Mimmíu. Nor what his father's face had looked like, nor if there had ever been any single precise moment when he had imagined that he loved his father. In fact, he was sure that there never had been such a moment, and that his own obstinate insistence on staying alive had been nothing but an admission of guilt. Certainly there had been a period he had defined as "happy". But that had consisted of no more than a passing incursion of normality into his life. He had turned eighteen in that season in which everything seemed possible, like a wild beast surviving then all the stages from infancy to puberty, simply because he had never had any childhood. And he had known from the start that choosing the right home is what allows a parasite to flourish. He knew nothing and yet he knew everything. His entire existence could have been a blank page waiting to be written. During military service he had learned to drive better and faster than all his fellows, confirmation that his mind had some-how been trained to learn faster. Growing up in other people's care had made him attentive to small details, voracious and imitative like a young employee in a hurry to oust his master, or a young actor eager to take on lead roles. Spontaneous and cynical, he had intuited that imitation was the route to perfection. He had forced himself to read unlikely things so long as they could at least provide him with language, the right words for the right moment, as he

176

had noticed was the case with people who came out on top, as winners did. Indeed, Vincenzo had been the prime example of this type of fascination for him. Not in any sense a physical fascination, but something more like a mirror attraction. Mimmíu had seen himself as an exact copy of Vincenzo, sensing perfection when able to see himself in the other man. Not because Vincenzo was so good-looking, or at least it was not only in appearance that Vincenzo corresponded exactly to Mimmíu's model of perfection. His life had changed the very moment when Vincenzo Chironi, absent-minded and dressed in shabby but respectable clothes, had climbed into his car precisely so that he, Giovannimaria Guiso known as Mimmíu, could give him a lift to Núoro. And you could perhaps state that, in some sense, this was the only occasion he could remember unquestionably falling in love.

After that it had been left to him to try out this new, silent happiness which had depended on the fact that he had discovered his ideal model. Vincenzo's life had contained certainty, genuine words and genuine actions. After that, all Mimmíu could do was return to the volatility of his previous life in which he could only create meaning from one day to the next, without hope of stability.

By hanging himself, Vincenzo had betrayed him, had thrown him back into instability. This despite the fact that he had also made a new man of him, an expert entrepreneur and the father of a family. And the fact that destiny had mocked him to the extent that it had been he, himself, who had found Vincenzo hanged, said a great deal about the secret connections that underlie what we often, and often erroneously, believe to be imponderable. He was like a father who, while claiming he wants to teach his son to ride a bicycle, lets go of the saddle before he is sure the boy is able to keep his balance. So that the child, in falling, learns that fathers are capable of making mistakes, but also that making mistakes is part of life. A combination of recognition and delusion. Warning and instruction rolled into one.

Now that he was about to do it, Mimmíu was able to think of many thousands of other things he had said he wanted to do and had not done. He had grown up accustomed to inadequacy, but had never dared admit it until Vincenzo had been there to live for him.

In fact, the happy period of his life had not been short. It had lasted from 1943 to 1959. From the moment he had offered a ride to that returning Chironi until the moment he had found him dead. All he remembered of that first journey was that after five kilometres of curves it had been necessary to stop because Vincenzo, stuck in a deep contemplative silence, was showing clear signs of car-sickness. Above all he remembered being certain that Vincenzo, in his absolute way, was at his ease even with this problem, since, although he had no idea what it might yet mean, Vincenzo had himself done nothing to become a Chironi; he just happened to be a Chironi and that's all there was to it. With time Mimmíu's awareness of this had attained a precise consistency, as precise as his anxiety to be like Vincenzo in every respect. Even though he had understood that the surface that reflected him like a mirror, was in no sense clear and limpid but but always clouded over at the slightest shock.

Vincenzo had been a quick learner. It had not taken him long to realise that he could even curse and squander the good fortune that had come to him. A fortune that had consisted not so much in finding himself rich as finding himself loved. And by his side was Guiso Giovannimaria who had never been loved. It was now clear to Mimmíu how long one could brood over an affection with one's face twisted with resentment. And now, when he was about to commit this act, he could also stop lying to himself. Admit the subtle pleasure he had derived from any bad news about the person he had claimed to love: for example when Cecilia, Vincenzo's wife, had her third miscarriage. Or when Vincenzo took to drink for no clear reason, just to fill a need, because of a lack of feeling. He was able to understand this and to see how he was anxious, involved and worried about what was happening to his friend and model, but also at the same time happy about it. Now he could even admit that aloud. And he himself had married for no good reason, just to have a child of his own in contrast to Vincenzo and Cecilia who despite repeated efforts had failed to produce any. And so Domenico had been born.

Then everyone started rumours that Cecilia had not been impregnated by Vincenzo, but by Mimmíu. And he had denied this without denying it, in the way only he knew how. With that exaggerated uneasiness that made people believe the very opposite of what he was saying.

Cristian's appearance, from the moment he was born, removed all doubt about who his father had been. The genetic force of those damned Chironi was extreme and unmistakable.

Even so, in the absence of Vincenzo he could imagine himself a second Vincenzo, and indeed that was how many people saw him. Though Marianna was certainly not among them; all she had to do was look at him for him to find himself exposed as the honourable parasite he really was.

He could not explain this to Domenico. Nor could everything else be explained, either. The sense of liberation he felt when his wife died, for example. And his furious, almost erotic urge to use money to rule other people's lives, the only thing that seemed to have any real meaning to him. He knew love could be bought, but this was not a wisdom he could transfer to others, it was a wisdom that had to be suppressed and concealed even when faced with the reality of basic truths. He had done terrible things, but only in defending what belonged to him.

And now Marianna Chironi, the damned witch who had seemed to have left him everything, had in effect taken everything away from him.

So he needed to take time to choose the best place to do what he now had to do, especially since it would most likely be Domenico who discovered his body. He found this reassuring rather than disturbing. He did not know exactly why, but the fact was that it excited him physically. He decided on the larder in the cellar, a place where hooks were fixed in the ceiling for hanging cold cuts of meat and cheeses. He needed to free one of those hooks. He chose one in a slightly concealed position, in a corner to the right of the entrance. The chimney was on the right, so he would not at first be seen by whoever came in. He liked the idea that for the first few seconds after they came in, it could still seem possible that whatever they may have feared had not actually happened.

The cord seemed strong enough and the knot held. He passed one end over the hook and calculated the distance. Who knows if Vincenzo Chironi had been so accurate. Or whether so determined.

Once he had adjusted the noose he fastened the free end to the hook, then checked it for weight by pulling it towards the floor and dangling from it with his arms in the air like a bell-ringer. Finally he positioned a chair and stood on it . . .

. . . But he would have liked to write something before hanging himself. A simple message for his son. Mimmíu was someone who did not know how to put his thoughts into words, but he did have thoughts. For a moment, balancing carefully on the chair before kicking it away, he was regretting that he had no talent for writing. There was something he wanted to say to Domenico, to warn him not to become like himself. A single line would have been enough, something like "Dear son, I have done what I have done to give you a chance to do better than me."

. . . But he put the noose round his neck and kicked the chair away.

He had never travelled by train, never flown in an aeroplane, never eaten truffles or quails' eggs, never seen an opera, never drunk champagne, never been to the circus, never stepped inside a theatre, never worn a pair of jeans, never learned to dance, and never set eyes on Venice except on television. Was that enough? No it wasn't. He had never planned a holiday and never really wept . . . Never . . .

Domenico rang the bell three times before using his keys to open the door. He found the house in a strange disorder, as though after various ineffective attempts, his father had altogether given up trying to sleep and had decided to go out, and walk away the night while waiting for dawn. Though given the recent terrible storm that destroyed any semblance of peace, this was unlikely to have been the case.

Domenico called out twice, "Babbo? Bà?"

No answer.

The house seemed temporarily abandoned, as if some sudden urgency had interrupted the owner's daily routine. A noise from the larder in the cellar made Domenico direct his steps down to the basement.

The door had been closed from the inside. He knocked.

"Babbo?" he called again, realising that for no apparent reason his voice had become shrill, almost as if his throat was aware of a danger that his mind had not yet analysed. He tried the handle to test whether the door had been properly closed, then began to push it, hoping that increasing persistence might make his attempt to open it more effective. But the door held firm: it was locked. He threw his shoulder at it, though still without result, hearing ever more clearly a strange sound like the squeaking of a cable when a boat is berthed.

The space on his side of the door was limited, so it took time and strength for him to force the door. But in the end it flew open, hit the wall behind and recoiled, striking him on the shoulder. Now the noise was sharper and more precise, like the swinging of a large tyre dangling on a rope from a tree.

Mimmíu was still kicking when Domenico thoughtlessly threw himself onto his father. Holding him tightly round the legs, he lifted him to slacken the tension of the knot. His father's feet struck his chest repeatedly. He could feel himself wet with urine and smell the stinking creamy quality of shit. This did not worry him, as he told himself that lifting his father higher would enable him to begin breathing again as the rope slackened, and once laid down on the floor he would be able to explain what had happened. But now Mimmíu stopped kicking and no longer responded. And by the time Domenico decided to loosen his grip, half an hour had flown away.

The emergency team found him exhausted, with painful arms and shoulders but no tears.

The corpse, swollen and disfigured, was not something to look at.

They kept Maddalena away until the shapeless mass had been sealed in lead inside its coffin. But in any case she had made no effort to see it. She knew this death had been aimed among other things at herself, and to anyone who tried to sympathise she simply said, "Let's be silent."

Domenico did everything to protect her, insisting, "Leave her alone."

They remained silent for several days, only going so far as to agree that Mimmíu should be buried in the great Chironi vault where both the dead and undead of that family rested, and where he would lie beside Marianna.

So in his eternal resting-place, Mimmíu achieved in death what he had never managed to achieve in life.

A time of confusion followed.

After a respectful lull for mourning, Mimmíu's creditors came to see Domenico, while those who owed him money made themselves scarce, hoping that his father had not recorded their debts in writing. But in fact he had left proof, and in considerable detail. Thus Domenico discovered that for many years his father had been a loanshark, demanding valuable land from those who could not pay what they owed, and exploiting his position as administrator of the Chironi estate to obtain credit from banks. Domenico discovered how they had acquired the land at Cala Girgolu and how construction work on a tourist village in the San Teodoro area had suffered delays that had prevented the repayment of bank credits by the agreed deadlines. This now required extended contracts with participants who could offer guarantees. The Chironi estate was accepted as an adequate guarantee, but Domenico was forced to take risks in order to salvage pending business, and to make personal contact with local functionaries who had profited from their relations with Mimmíu.

Maddalena well knew that the general inheritance must unfold in its inevitable way, but told herself she would intervene at once if the specific inheritance of her unborn child was threatened. From her point of view anything intended for Cristian must be preserved untouched and complete for her son or daughter, whichever the child turned out to be.

When she judged the right moment had arrived, she decided to tackle her husband over the question of names, Luigi Ippolito or Mercede.

Domenico, needless to say, took this discussion badly. That Maddalena should have already come to a decision of her own did not please him at all. The only other serious talk they had had since their wedding had been about the horrible house Maddalena was so keen to leave.

"One thing at a time, for goodness sake," Domenico begged, reflecting that though when a house collapses it is usually the consequence of long and gradual disintegration, such things may sometimes happen very suddenly. Which may seem a contradiction but actually is not, since a building's collapse may be caused not so much by lack of understanding on the part of those living in it, as by their neglect of warning signs.

Domenico had indeed realised his father had been on the point of collapse, but had pretended not to notice. And now he felt like Percy in Shakespeare's *Henry IV*, the part he had played at school as a child, who despite extreme self-confidence, allows himself to be worsted by the apparently dissolute Prince of Wales. Too much trust in words and appearances can also often lead to the collapse of a house.

Waiting for him to speak, Maddalena noticed he was lost in his own thoughts, as if acute pain had permeated his whole being and knocked him senseless. "I don't want to put pressure on you," she said gently, "but you must realise how important it is. How do we want this child to come into the world?"

To Domenico, Maddalena seemed to be talking of a parallel universe. "Do you know what I was thinking about when I was on the way to Babbo's house?" he said. She shook her head. "I was thinking I'd get him to watch the match with me: Argentina versus Holland, can you imagine? And I was still thinking of that afterwards . . . how stupid can you get?"

"There's nothing stupid about that," Maddalena said, waving her hand as though to say he should not imagine such things.

"I was telling myself everything would be fine. But now I'm afraid of everything . . ." He gripped the base of his nose between finger and thumb as he struggled to hold back his tears.

"How do you mean, you're afraid of everything?" Maddalena asked calmly, if with emphasis.

"Everything," Domenico repeated. "This house and you not

wanting it . . . and how could I disagree with you? And this creature about to be born . . . and I'm afraid –" he was still holding back tears – ". . . I'm afraid you might leave me."

Maddalena moved closer to be able to take him in her arms. Now it was she who was holding back tears. "We'll survive," she said. "It's hell at the moment but we'll survive. We just have to do what has to be done, Domé."

He buried his face in her breast. "Yes, yes," he agreed. It was as if from somewhere high up in a ship, a lifebelt had suddenly landed on him as he was drowning in the open sea. "But what will people think if we give our child Chironi names?"

Maddalena did not answer immediately. "I know we can't change the past . . ." A note of determination entered her voice. "It's more to honour our dearest friends. Just that."

Neither said any more.

Suddenly one evening June arrived, burnished and fragrant, as if cooked in a hot oven.

A month later, on July 5, when the necessary work had been done on it, Domenico and Maddalena moved into the house in via Deffenu.

She was now six months pregnant and no longer dreaming, or at least no longer remembering her dreams. Meanwhile, day-to-day business completely absorbed Domenico, who was showing unexpected good sense. As a businessman, he seemed less reckless than his father, an attitude some people mistook for weakness. These were destructive times; times of infinite present, without past or future.

No-one could claim that Domenico Guiso had his father's

instincts or his ability to think quickly. But when the owners tried to re-negotiate contracts for the land at Cala Girgolu, Domenico refused to give way to them. People had felt that, with Mimmíu dead, they would be able to extract less demanding terms, but the young man wouldn't have it. He said he needed the land for his son, just as his father had needed it for him.

FOR MANY NIGHTS, ONCE THE NOOSE FROM WHICH HE WAS suspended had been removed, and despite his son's attempts to keep him alive, Mimmíu always fell to the floor. Dead.

For some time now circumstances had changed, so that Domenico had been able to watch him preparing the rope, soaping it the way people did it in films, and making sure the chair was in the right position. Then came the moment when, with aching shoulders and his clothes soiled with his father's piss and shit, he lost his grip and the body was dragged down with such force of gravity that the vertebrae of the neck could be heard cracking. Sometimes the rope snapped, dropping Domenico to the floor with a thud, though he could never be sure that this had happened. It was like watching a distant film, or following Mass from a pew at the back of a church.

But sometimes Mimmíu did not die. Resting his hands on his son's shoulders, he would free his neck from the noose, start breathing again and, clearly sapped of energy, suck in as much air as he could.

At first he did not speak, nor did Domenico expect him to. Then he would suddenly look his son in the eye with a strange diffidence, as if unable to recognise his own boy. Who was after all no longer a boy now, but in every respect a man.

"Where's that document?" Mimmíu would ask.

"Here, I've got it here with me . . . Babbo, I never thought I'd hear your voice again."

"Why such a hurry to step into my shoes? Silly boy! You won't have to wait long anyway," the old man threatened, tearing the power of attorney from his son's hand. "This is hardly more than scrap paper now. This whole inheritance, which you imagine to be so secure, is held together by nothing and a mere puff of wind will blow it away. You could not wait to see me dead. Your whole life proves you never loved me!"

On that particular night Domenico's eyes streamed with tears. "Here's your document, Babbo," he said anxiously. "Enjoy it, and live to be a hundred or more . . . The only reason I took it was to keep it from the hands of strangers. Just now, when I came in here, I thought you were dead, and God strike me down if that is not the truth. I decided I had to protect you from those who are determined to ruin you."

At those words Mimmíu seemed to soften. He was wearing a black corduroy suit and a white shirt, just as he had at the lavish engagement party, and at Domenico and Maddalena's hasty wedding. He gave an unexpectedly warm smile.

"A good answer, son. Come and sit here beside me. Now listen carefully." Mimmíu waited a moment before adding, "This is my last bit of advice. God only knows how much it cost me to lay my hands on everything we own. Only I know how many nights I spent worrying about it. I don't want the same thing to happen to you. Everyone has always dismissed what I've done as a mere gift from someone else. You've no idea how they hold it against me, how false their greetings are. But when I'm dead, because I

189

have to die, what was due to me will come to you. But only if you can get on with those who are still friends of mine. And be shrewd enough not to make enemies of my enemies." Then he began to cough. "I'm out of breath. You must do better than me."

Suddenly, by some trick of perspective, almost an optical illusion, Domenico was able to see himself in the whole scene, as in a vortex returned to its primary state. He found himself trying to hold his father up by the legs. The only difference was that now Maddalena, not far away, was watching them without moving. And she was crying. And calling him, "Domenico, Domé!"

Domenico, when she touched him, gave a start; Maddalena was standing, leaning over his side of the bed. "My waters," she said, without any particular anxiety. "I think this is it."

KNIGHT TO F6

Núoro, October 1979

AT 4.50 A.M. ON OCTOBER 12, 1979, FOUR HUNDRED AND eighty-seven years after the discovery of America, at the San Francesco Hospital in Núoro, Luigi Ippolito Giuseppe Guiso was born. It was a long and exceptionally difficult birth. So much so that after twelve hours of labour, they decided on a Caesarean. Maddalena was prepared, but no sooner were they about to go ahead than her contractions got so violent that the baby's head appeared with a jerk that nearly made her faint. Even so, impelled by a kind of overriding power and torn by pain which was reaching unimaginable peaks, she pushed with barely concealed hatred to free herself of this fiercely resented foreign body. The new-born child instantly opened his eyes and puckered lips still crammed with amniotic fluid, mucus and blood, before emitting a short whine as if of boredom. That was all. Thus he was born. And began dying.

Domenico filled the room with flowers. He had paid for a private room at the hospital, as rich folk do. The nurses saw him as a resplendent knight and Maddalena as the luckiest of damsels. But their admiration changed to irritation whenever it occurred to them, as it often did, that fate had blessed this local Núoro couple with a substantial fortune they had done nothing whatever to earn. A couple born with silver spoons in their mouths, they whispered: the son of a father who had amassed wealth and never spent any of it, and the daughter of a mere nobody who had happened to meet the right man.

In the house in via Deffenu, Luigi Ippolito Giuseppe was given the room that had once belonged to little Dina, Marianna's daughter dead before her time, and more recently to Cristian. It was as though the Guiso family had now decided to become Chironi. To the neighbours this seemed like a swing of the pendulum, a counterweight to what should have been, and they all crossed themselves and thanked heaven that Marianna had died before she could witness such a farce.

It really was an age of farces. The generations no longer followed each other in a natural order, but could now be eliminated at random. Such chasms had developed between fathers and their sons that one would have imagined them separated by centuries rather than belonging to successive generations. As always this particular tiny corner of the world had to make do with scraps left over from the rest of the country. A pregnant period of heroic delinquency had passed discontinuously to an age of openly common delinquency, and then to the ignominy of a political mask. At which point all these tendencies coalesced into one: ambiguous, many-headed and deceptive, in which the generations were able to express themselves through every possible deformity and call it freedom. It was like saying that words and concepts could be ingested like junk food, capable of nourishing a bodily need but certainly not the imagination and the brain – like empty vases created for non-existent contents. Maddalena and Domenico had no idea, they could not even conceive, how terrible and complicated being parents in that terrible era would be. Because when one is living inside a particular age all seasons seem possible, and the fact that one is ignorant of better or worse times is one's only consolation. Memory comes at a cost. It requires skill. Or sensitivity if one has been born unlucky. If Maddalena and Domenico had known this they would have prayed for that child to be born into another world or another age, or (as Marianna had hoped) not to be born at all.

But Luigi Ippolito Giuseppe Chironi had been born on the cusp of the Eighties, which was like offering live flesh pulsing with blood to a cannibal god.

Domenico's affairs became a sort of waiting game and that didn't bode well. Two dockyards on the coast were closed, and the third, the most important one, was still waiting for official planning permission from the local administration, so that houses, some of them already finished, continued to remain vacant. Meanwhile in Núoro, work on the new multipurpose centre intended to replace the old prison building was grinding to a halt. And despite Mimmíu's assurances, the contract for the fixings and window and door frames for the new hospital had gone to a firm on the mainland.

Domenico either did not know or did not want to know if all this could be explained by his new role as a father, for fear the baby could be blamed as a bringer of misfortune. In fact, Mimmíu's death had brought many circumstances to a head and Domenico had done his best to juggle them all. It was he who had to fight off the violent backlash Mimmíu's sudden death had caused.

But for Maddalena all this was simply another stage on her road to autonomy. For her the child was the incarnation of a new world. Mimmíu's suicide had been a sort of blackmail. She was waiting for Domenico, once the period of stress was over, to show what he was made of once and for all.

Luigi Ippolito Giuseppe immediately proved himself a difficult baby. He cried often, slept little, and there seemed no way to interest him in Maddalena's breast. Whenever he was offered the nipple he shut his mouth in a definite gesture of refusal. "There, he doesn't love me, he knows everything," Maddalena concluded. He was a lazy child, the local women decided; most of them had given birth to at least five children, and they judged him lazy, like all first-born sons, who imagine the world was created especially for them and for them alone. Mother and son looked at each other in a strange way as though what they were sharing was not so much love, as a pact of non-belligerence, a pact the child constantly broke. Maddalena spent months trying to attach her son to her breast without much success, so that most of his meals came to consist of artificial powdered milk.

Then one night something unexpected happened. Luigi Ippolito was sleeping beside his mother in the double bed, while Domenico had retired temporarily to the guest room. This at least ensured him a few hours of uninterrupted sleep. He found himself dreaming of a house in snow and a white dog, everything utterly strange and yet at the same time curiously familiar, as happens in dreams. In the house, food was being prepared, including platefuls of stewed sauerkraut and pork with gherkins in vinegar and beetroot soup with sour cream. Domenico had never eaten any of these things, but in the context of his dream, they all seemed utterly familiar. He was aware of the pungent smell of caraway cheese on the table, but where had that come from? Now that he was standing in that strange yet familiar kitchen, he was able to observe the way things were being set out with the curiosity of someone who discovers something unfamiliar in what is before his eyes every day. "What an incredible dream", he told himself while he was dreaming it. Then he turned his head the better to hear sounds coming from outside. The dog was running and treading the fresh, crackling snow. Then it whimpered and, unbelievably, moaned like a child. Then he saw someone in the kitchen had eaten the food set out on the table without him noticing. But who? Domenico was dreaming and at the same time wondering, yet again, how what must be impossible could seem so real. Because one thing was clear: someone had emptied the plates which a moment earlier had been piled with food. And though he had not let the table out of his sight for an instant, he had not been aware of this happening.

Then he realised he was sweating.

His journey back to reality was slower than usual, because despite the fact that he knew he was now awake, Domenico could not see the room in which he had fallen asleep, but only the simple kitchen and table from his dream. And he could still hear small moans from the bedroom where Luigi Ippolito and Maddalena were sleeping. Moans and whimpers as of lovers hoping not to be overheard during sex.

Domenico felt an urge to get up and surprise these secret lovers in the midst of their embraces. This impulse woke him completely and he got to his feet. Despite a feeling that he must have gone to lie down many hours earlier, no more than two hours had passed. Without turning on the light, he groped his way into the bedroom. Now the sounds were clearer.

"Look," Maddalena murmured, inviting her husband to join her. She had one breast free and Luigi Ippolito was happily sucking at it in his sleep.

Domenico continued to watch them until, getting used to the half-darkness, he could not help noticing that the baby was watching him without letting go of Maddalena's nipple.

He knew then that he had welcomed an enemy into his home.

He asked himself whether all new fathers experienced such a sudden fall from their initial exaltation when they assume that birth must be the beginning of everything. Because he, and as he realised everyone else, understood almost instantly that such exaltation was utterly unjustified. Because birth was really the end of everything. But now, at last, Maddalena seemed satisfied. Living in the house she had always wanted, together with that child with his unusual name, she seemed to have achieved complete serenity. She had put on a few kilos during her pregnancy and, despite the long labour which had left her exhausted for ten days after the birth, she now looked calm and glowing. Domenico sat down on the bed. The baby stopped sucking, and started whining again, as usual when he was awake.

"There," Maddalena said, "you've interrupted his feeding." But there was no reproach in her voice and this made Domenico feel even more at fault.

"I'm sorry." He jumped to his feet.

Maddalena laughed. "Don't be silly. This is your bed."

Domenico nodded, then shook his head as though accepting what a fool he was. "I feel nervous about sleeping here with the two of you because as you know I'm a restless sleeper and I'm afraid I could smother the child."

His common sense touched Maddalena deeply, as if Domenico had decided to play at being equal to the child. "I knew in the end I'd end up with two children, not just one," she whispered. "Come here, you can't smother him; nature wouldn't let you do that." She patted the empty side of the bed.

Domenico obeyed; wishing he could share Maddalena's faith in the power of nature. As he saw it, this was nothing but instinct, and he knew how much harm that could do. But Maddalena, being a woman and a mother, insisted the opposite was true, believing in the existence of a feeling more fundamental than reason, as though there is a sentinel in our hearts to keep us in check.

So he did what she asked, but to be absolutely sure, lay down on the extreme far edge of the mattress, rolling back every time the baby moved between them. Maddalena reached for his shoulder. "Don't worry," she said.

But he was not sure which of the two she was speaking to.

Six months passed before they went back to sleeping together without the child in the bed. In some way, it was like starting again from scratch. In matters of sex, that is, as Maddalena, after a couple of unsuccessful attempts when she noticed Domenico was tense and embarrassed when he touched her, put a pillow under her hips and looked at him as if to say, "If you start something you should finish it."

As for him, he felt as though the past was over and the present was revealing entirely new and unfamiliar features. He had been waiting impatiently for that moment, but it now seemed she did not understand how much she meant to him. That was the point, it seemed no-one understood that as much as he did.

Not even Cristian had shown any great consideration for her, even though he had shown more need for her than anyone else ever had. Domenico's love had always seemed committed but subdued, as though he were a butler waiting for orders behind a closed door, the sort who occasionally dozes off, especially when most needed, so that although constantly available, he is remembered only for his rare failures.

In other words, people were always aware of the rare occasions when Domenico was not available and never noticed the countless times when he was ready but silent.

That was how it was now when she scolded him, however mildly, for not being sufficiently uninhibited in expressing his desires.

"I went too far," he told her firmly, pulling on his shirt.

She buttoned her blouse without another word, thinking it was obvious he did not desire her enough. Men with hang-ups like Domenico, she decided, are always on edge, always unreliable.

"I've been waiting a long time for this moment," he added.

"You seemed so distant," she answered, almost as if she had decided to put into words a tiny bit of what had only been hinted at up to that point. She felt irritated to be feeling so irritated. Any woman in the world would have given anything to have a man as sensitive as Domenico. But at the same time, due to some uncontrollable primitive urge, the same woman would have also wanted to experience moments of savagery, a ferocity that challenged her desires and his fundamental needs. A nuance that would never have escaped Cristian, or so Maddalena believed.

Domenico stood up to fasten his trousers. He urgently needed to get out of the room, to get away from her delusion. But she wasn't even deluded.

"I wasn't expecting anything different," he ventured without even turning to look at her.

"I know. You said that before."

Domenico nodded in agreement. For an instant he felt like a young boy again.

But once outside the house, he felt reassured. A gentle but steady wind was filling the lanes with a foretaste of spring, while a moderate sun offered porous light. A twittering scattered among the trees encouraged his light-heartedness. Convinced by this classic choreography and symphony, he decided not to take the car but to walk. And on his way, bathing in the scent of freesias and gillyflowers, he felt filled with an impetuous enthusiasm. Realising how lucky he was, he was now able to understand the nature of happiness and how to find it. Thus he felt happy, despite what he was about to do. Or, maybe, precisely because of it.

In the summer of 1972, when Domenico had been fourteen years old, everyone had gone crazy for chess, while Fischer kept Spassky waiting until the last possible moment. Cristian had been there with Domenico, in front of the television screen. They immediately took opposite sides because the Russian, silent and formal, was so much like Domenico. While the American, restless and suspicious, was a hundred-per-cent Chironi.

So, in Reykjavik, for a long time Domenico waited for Cristian to come. Then at a sign from the international judges Domenico began the dance: white pawn to B4. A calm, prudent, predictable move. Typical of him. But that first move enabled them to start the timer for his opponent.

Like Cristian, Bobby Fischer almost reached his time limit before moving: knight to F6. An opening that made everyone jump. Knight to F6 seemed like the end of the world. Everyone had been waiting for hours for Fischer, while Spassky with his unemphatic punctuality had begun to seem invisible.

Fischer, distracted, was not on form. While Spassky stayed concentrated, organised and perfectly calm. Neither made any mistake, though everyone was waiting for Fischer to move just to see how he would get the measure of his opponent. This is what always happens: humanity has a propensity to prefer those who are unreliable. And perhaps it is a fact that stories, all stories, are nothing if not tales that involve unreliable types. When Fischer had arrived, he had looked around as if blaming traffic problems, just as Cristian had done on the day of the engagement. Then he made his move: knight to F6, initiating an action that seemed light, ethereal, even distracted, as if to emphasise that it didn't even require much concentration for him to get the better of the calm, reliable opponent who was facing him. It had been that precise form of unreliability that Domenico had aspired to with all his being on that July day in 1972. Despite his being only fourteen it was clear to him that Cristian, at twelve, already knew far more than he himself would ever learn. And perhaps he had said, or simply hoped, that Cristian would one day have to pay for his know-how. And death had been a sufficient payment.

When still a few steps from the house where he was heading, Domenico understood everything with a clarity that would never come to him again. He understood, for example, that there was no virtue in his rectitude, because it was the consequence of a permanent but hidden propensity: a lack of impulse and courage, something that would always prevent him from making astute decisions, those that required walking a fine line or simply accepting the error of his ways. The sort of decisions that had ensured and were still ensuring that Cristian, despite everything, had always been so wholeheartedly alive.

Before ringing the doorbell, Domenico took a few seconds to come to the conclusion that up to that moment he had spent half his life doing things that were good and just, and the other half regretting them, while Cristian had spent half his time making mistakes, and the other half chiselling such errors into meaningful shape.

Then he rang the bell.

The smell of the apartment disgusted him at the same time as it excited him. It was as if the windows had been sealed for years, preventing the escape of the slightest odour, human or non-human. A smell of walls steeped in cigarette smoke, and of old food in refrigerator, pail or dustbin. A smell of sweat from old armchairs and used bedclothes, and from the folds of seemingly clean towels. The woman of the house was no different; not dirty, but like the den in which she lived, giving off a smell of hasty hygiene, an atmosphere of rapidly achieved order, as if in anticipation of unexpected guests.

From a portable cassette player the Bee Gees, like cats on heat, were yelling out "Tragedy". There was much to discourage Domenico, but in fact this manifest discomfort helped him to feel he was in the right place. The woman received him just as she had repeatedly during the previous four months, pretending she was seeing him for the first time and acting surprised that such a fashionable young man as himself had come deliberately to find her.

Domenico placed a fifty-thousand-lire banknote on the table in the middle of what was quite a large bed-sit, then added another ten-thousand note separately, so that she could not fail to notice it. When she did so, she reacted with a sly smile communicating neither tenderness nor recognition. She had understood a few basic facts about this man who had come to see her so regularly over the last few months. One of which was that she should never be unduly familiar with him: he liked to start from the beginning each time with the same embarrassment as on the first occasion. When, that first time, she had started to unbutton his trousers, he had grabbed her wrists as if to say that was something he could do for himself, and had then pulled off his belt and laid it on a chair like the skin of a snake. Then, without even looking at her, he had stripped calmly until entirely naked, then picked up the belt and offered it to her. She had shown signs of wanting to strip too, but he clearly didn't want that. The important thing was for her to take the belt and thrash him while he stood with his feet slightly apart, fists clenched and the hint of an erection, waiting for her blows. The first blow had made everything clear to him; a pain very different from what he had expected, more all-embracing, like a glorification of punishment itself. By the third stroke she had gained in confidence. Domenico felt this with absolute precision: a powerful stinging stripe running from the back of his neck to his left hip.

"Again!" he commanded in a changed voice.

She understood very clearly that when he said "again" he meant "on that precise spot again". So she waited for him to clench his fists, then repeated the previous stroke, this time penetrating his skin to draw blood and serum.

Then she lowered her arm, breathing heavily and letting the dark tongue of the belt lick the floor.

Domenico clenched his jaws so hard he was afraid of breaking his teeth. "Again!" he repeated.

The woman wrapped the belt round her hand, and struck him sharply between lower back and buttocks.

Domenico held back his tears as long as he could, then turned and held up his hand. The woman understood this to mean the session was over.

They repeated this ritual, at least once a week, for four months. The punishment gained power from the fact that it was always repeated in exactly the same way.

But on this particular occasion Domenico had felt a need to vary the routine, convincing himself that this was because he had decided to walk instead of taking the car, and that he had underestimated how important memories were.

Oh, that summer of 1972, in front of the television with Cristian playing Bobby Fischer, while he himself had been left to take on the more modest role of the imperturbable Boris Spassky. Everyone had been waiting for the genius, who was late, while the worker had made his move and started the timer. Then, almost at the last moment, the other had arrived and grabbed his knight, as if to mark a distance, even from a choreographic point of view, between the modest action of the Russian and his own more daring move. White pawn to B4 followed by black knight to F6. Then, during the course of the match, at the twenty-ninth move to be precise, Fischer had got it all wrong, allowing his bishop to be taken, and from that moment for him the match was lost. The rest of the action had been pointless.

But no-one remembers Spassky's first win; what everyone remembers is that Fischer was defeated. And Domenico could understand it for other reasons. Which was why, when he arrived at the woman's place that day and placed his usual banknote on the table, he had added an extra ten thousand lire before taking his clothes off. And when she picked up his belt, Domenico had turned, looked her in the eye, and said, "Knight to F6."

Not knowing what to answer she had looked at him suspiciously, then switched on the particular smile she used to mask any awkwardness. "You've been a really bad boy," she told him. "But I'm here." Then she raised her arm to strike the first blow.

Domenico looked her in the eye again. "Knight to F6," he repeated. "Not the usual pawn. Hit me with the buckle," he ordered. And clenched his fists.

DEATH, THE MOST TERRIBLE OF ILLS, CANNOT EXIST FOR US.
For when we are alive there can be no death, and once death has come for us we are gone.

This was how, with a note scribbled in pencil on an orange folder, the story of the Chironi family began. This was what Marianna had left for Maddalena Pes: a hundred or so pages handwritten in a sharp, clear script. Something that only a few years earlier would have been described simply as "calligraphy" without the tautological word "beautiful", which people in these miserable times insist on adding. The word "calligraphy" includes the idea of "beautiful", so insisting on "beautiful calligraphy" is like saying "beautiful beautiful writing". As the methodical old schoolteacher Olla would have pointed out, who though he taught at elementary level, knew Latin and Greek. A man who understood etymology, that is to say, the meaning of words.

However, this particular script was a miniature exercise in gothic regularity and so harmonious that one could barely detect where the writer had paused to dip his pen into the inkwell. It was the writing of an early Chironi who, without clearly revealing why, had been careful and mannered; the Chironi family had needed a past as well as a future. Maddalena could not say why this handwriting disturbed her to the point of tears. But this is what writing ought to do, make us face the point of no return – the abyss within ourselves.

Maddalena was at home but not alone, because her mother Nevina had formed the habit of coming in every day to help with the baby, thereby giving Maddalena time to be alone and reflect. She had not read a word of the manuscript yet, but she did understand why Marianna had left it to her. It was more than an inheritance. It was a position, a coordinate in a world short of positions and bearings. A call to resistance. An incitement to change, something to remind her that she was herself only twenty years old and had a husband, a lover who was dead, and a son.

The first lines of the long manuscript, which seemed quite ancient, looked as if they had been added some time later on a separate page. Maddalena recognised the quotation from Epicurus on why there was no point in fearing death, and Cristian's handwriting. She stroked those lines with her fingertips, enjoying the feeling that they contained a fragment of the person who had guided the pen, even something of what had been needed to exert such exact pressure. Cristian had had good handwriting, with a tendency to emphatic stress, and that was obvious.

Now, all she could think of, was that Cristian too had read those pages. She could imagine him bending over the little desk in his room in the Chironi house at San Pietro, which he had only been able to reach through Marianna's garden. She could see him studying the genealogy that his grandfather Luigi Ippolito, who had died a war hero, had pieced together so carefully to make it clear that one need not live without a past if one is capable of imagining one.

Whatever the truth of the matter, it had all started with a Spanish ancestor, a certain De Quiròn, who had been sent from Castile to Sardinia as a punishment, like any old policeman or carabiniere. With time this De Quiròn had become so fond of Sardinia that he could not and did not want to return to Spain. So he had pressed on recklessly towards the centre of the island, where indomitable mountain folk, the bloodthirsty *pelliti* (or hairy Sard savages) lived. He had been following in the footsteps of the Bishop of Galtellí who was searching for a healthy climate for his diocese, so as to escape the infected air and relentless pestilence of the coast. This had brought him to Nur, a settlement on a delightful plateau fringed by woods and watered by clear streams. A miniature Garden of Eden where the bishop and his followers immediately settled. And here De Quiròn, who had already changed his surname to the more locally acceptable Kirone, met the woman who was to be his life companion. He let his beard grow and gave up his ruff, and probably the rest of his previous life with it. He took to wearing coarse woollen cloth like the locals, and fathered a son whom he dedicated to the archangel Michael . . .

Maddalena was so absorbed in reading this manuscript that she did not notice her mother at her shoulder. "Will Domenico not be back for dinner?" Nevina asked.

"He must have been detained at one of the building sites," Maddalena answered just a little too hastily.

"But hasn't he told you anything?" insisted the mother, who had not failed to notice her daughter's reticence.

Maddalena finally raised her head from the papers on the table. "He's sure to let me know if possible," she snapped.

"But can something have happened to him?" her mother persisted.

Rather than continue this conversation, Maddalena crossed the room and turned on the radio. "Turn It On Again" burst from the speaker as if nothing could be more normal than for such a sound to fill the house. Nevina pulled a face. Her daughter gathered the manuscript together and replaced the pages carefully in their correct order in the folder, which she then put back in its place on the shelf.

Domenico did not appear for dinner. Nor did he come home that night. Next morning, towards six, Maddalena finally heard the hall door open. She wanted to get out of bed to confront her husband, but instead went on lying on her side, watching luminous stripes of dawn appear through the blinds.

Domenico came cautiously into the bedroom. He did not undress but checked whether his wife was asleep.

"Who do you think I am?" she asked the emptiness in front of her, a question that ripped into the stillness of the room.

Domenico screwed up his eyes. "I've been drinking. I don't like you seeing me in that state, so I went to sleep at Babbo's."

"You've been drinking," she said, as though repetition might make this more acceptable. "You've been drinking," she said again without looking at him, because addressing him directly would have implied that she was ready to understand him in some way, when in fact she wasn't.

"Yes," he agreed. And that was all.

They remained silent for several minutes. Both had within them words that would have filled the silence. But the words rebounded meaninglessly inside their heads without finding any way to rise to the surface.

Domenico started undressing. "I've got a work appointment at nine," he said.

"Good for you." Then seeing he said nothing more, she added more clearly: "You'll be in a great condition for work, then."

"I know, I know," Domenico interrupted. As if admitting that he deserved some sort of criticism if she wished to make it, he went on, "Listen. This is not an easy time for me."

"Whereas for me of course, it's all roses and flowers."

". . . That's not what I meant . . ."

"Oh no?"

"I just wanted to say I'm not quite sure what's happening to me."

Maddalena turned. He was standing at his side of the bed in vest and pants. She noticed a livid stripe from his thigh to his buttocks. "What's happened to you?" she asked.

"Nothing," he said quickly, taking clean underwear from the chest of drawers and freshly pressed trousers from the wardrobe, before heading for the bathroom.

Left on her own in the bedroom, Maddalena thought how quickly and unexpectedly things can happen. She was sure something must develop in connection with this crisis of Domenico's. He, terrifyingly, had given everyone to believe that his recent experience with his father was as understandable as fresh water. But that was not so.

When he came out of the bathroom he was fully dressed. Maddalena was on her feet and had opened the bedroom window wide to let in fresh air. Now she could see him in full daylight, pale and suffering.

"I'll be alright now," he said, attempting the smile he knew could melt rocks. But Maddalena's expression showed there was little to melt. "Some coffee and I'll be fine," he assured her.

He had shaved, and every time he did this it reminded Maddalena of long drawn-out waiting and cheated expectations. Suddenly she wanted to cry, but controlled herself. She would rather have died of suffocation than let a single sob escape her. So without saying anything, she went into the kitchen to make coffee.

After Mimmíu's death, Domenico had begun to cut himself off from others. It was not so much that he had changed, just that he had become more cautious.

More and more often, he went back to sleep in the house he had shared with his father. To Maddalena, this seemed entirely logical; hers was not a marriage that depended on togetherness. She had to get things in perspective. Now that everything was clear, she had no problem in accepting that she had not married the man she loved, and so never expected her husband to behave as though he believed himself to be loved. But she did unquestionably feel great tenderness for him. Perhaps even more than for her son. And she knew that Domenico would never abandon her, or ever demand anything he would not get. Paradoxically, now that he had found the courage to establish a certain independence, she felt more confident. She stopped asking him why he spent so much time away from home, and about his frequent pain and drinking. In fact, about everything. So, as was her way, she solved the issue by telling him if he wanted to sleep in his father's house he should feel free to do so, but that he must never embarrass her in public. This was what Maddalena liked to define as "keeping things as they are", but, more than anything else, it was her way of saving herself from being caught unprepared. Cristian's sudden death had upset her vision of the future and such a thing, she promised herself, must never happen again. She was prepared even to be a fake wife to love the man who happened to be in her life, now that the fiction of their close union was all that remained. She was a woman who would not accept anything she could not foresee.

Her mother Nevina adored her grandchild, and spent a lot of time in the house, tormenting Maddalena with what she imagined to be her unobtrusive silence.

"What is it you're always reading?" Nevina asked one day, seeing her daughter constantly at the desk.

"My inheritance," came the answer, with the hint of a smile to show her mother how true her little joke was.

After that Nevina stopped asking questions and Maddalena had no need to look for more answers. The manuscript's narrative had developed a sustained pace, a sort of tense urgency . . . She realised that Luigi Ippolito Chironi, who had written it, had felt a need to give precise meaning to emptiness; it was a rejection of aphasia, a story to fill the lack of a story. The land he described as being a benediction and simultaneously a malediction was something she could understand. Cristian had been able to understand it too. Domenico, at best, could intuit it. Which was no sort of privilege.

None at all, the poor suffering creature.

Missing his father, and enjoying the freedom that his father's death had brought, he came to experience a sort of euphoria. Especially

211

when he found himself alone in his father's house, and was able to rummage through the furniture and in every remotest corner, turning out the pockets of the jackets, trousers and overcoats hanging in the wardrobe, and checking through drawers that had previously been closed to him. It was exciting to have such power, but also subtly embarrassing to have uncontrolled access to what had once been so private to his father.

The empty house fascinated him, reminding him that everything was accessible now, that there was no envelope he could not open, no document he could not examine, no failure he could not expose. The first nights he stayed there he could hardly sleep, living on the surface, like someone scratching paintwork with a nail to reach a deeper layer without damaging the object that had been painted. But very soon the urge to reveal himself made him cast all caution aside. He was grabbed by a fierce hunger, by a need to expose any possible lie, but also simply to rescue ostensibly defunct objects from their obscure tombs in wardrobes, cabinets, bedside tables and wall-units . . . Mimmíu had never thrown anything away, even preserving linen that had belonged to his long-dead and quickly forgotten wife Ada. He had stored hundreds of photographs, both black-and-white and coloured, in albums and tins. Snaps of himself as a child, of Vincenzo Chironi, of Cecilia, and even of Marianna when young. There were coloured photos of Mimmíu with Domenico when small, being raised by a single father and already dressed like a little adult; Domenico studied his own expression in these photographs. He looked at the child's chin, pinched as if in an effort not to cry. He was overcome by a sort of adult melancholy, almost as if there was nothing he could deny to the child staring so relentlessly at him from these photos.

One drawer contained reels of film. These he could remember, of course. Occasionally, after getting out the large humming projector which he kept packed away in a cupboard near the bathroom, Mimmíu would enjoy showing them and explaining. By the time he was a teenager Domenico had sworn to his father that sooner or later he would destroy these films. His father had smiled, somehow embarrassed, but to keep them safe had always put them carefully away. Now here they were. The box containing the first reel was marked *Cala Liberotto, July 1967*.

Now frames in over-exposed colours sprang to life on the blank wall of the living room, showing a beach strewn with deposits of seagrass. Thin as a rake, Cristian peered out from behind a big sand dune, his bathing suit hanging down, barely held up by a cloth belt. He was waving at Mimmíu who was shooting the film. Mimmíu's hand had not been steady, but the subject of the film had the expressionist obstinacy of the work of cinema's early pioneers. A close-up of Cristian revealed his strange beauty, his lineage. Then Domenico appeared, like an aboriginal afraid of his own image when faced with a camera. Plumper and overdressed, wearing a ridiculous little hat, he seemed as inhibited as his companion was free. Domenico studied himself, full of tender pain, thinking of the nine-year-old boy he had been, and remembering every single moment of discomfort and incomprehension he had felt every day so long ago. He slipped out of view when Cristian, aged seven, ran into the sea to wet his feet, while he himself concentrated on backing away from the water. Then the projector switched itself off.

After a while it came on again, though Domenico could remember exactly what had happened on the rest of the short film:

Cristian, noticing his fear, had gone back to persuade him to join him at the water's edge. Domenico had refused, and the more he resisted, the more Cristian had pressed him, pulling him by the arm. Mimmíu with the camera, clearly amused, had not missed a moment of this little battle. Then Domenico, all resistance at an end, had given way to uncontrollable tears. There the film ended.

Though it was so late at night, a tremendous heat still lingered. The kind that makes old folk shake their heads in disbelief.

AUGUST 1980 GOT OFF TO A TERRIBLE START WITH THE disaster at Bologna. For the love of God, one wanted to ask, to what foul depths could humanity descend?

"The poor creatures," Nevina murmured between her tears. "The poor, poor people . . ."

From the other room the voice of Luigi Ippolito Giuseppe sounded like the lament of an abandoned animal. He was ten months old now and beginning to pronounce a few syllables, but sleep was still a problem for him. When Maddalena appeared in his room to reassure him that he was not alone in the world, he quietened down.

Even on the television screen, the devastation seemed to be mostly dust. We all know so little about each other, Maddalena found herself thinking.

Nevina found her daughter still drying her eyes. "What can we do?" she asked herself.

Her mother shook her head. "Those beasts!" she murmured.

There was a strange atmosphere in the room, as of things coming to an end, of farewells and parting statements.

"I've switched the T.V. off," Nevina announced. "I really can't take any more . . . Do you think the child is too hot?" She was trying to swallow the bitterness in her throat. "Perhaps there are too many blankets on him; maybe that's why he isn't sleeping."

"No, no, he's fine," Maddalena answered. "The only reason he isn't sleeping is he can't sleep. That's all there is to it, it's just something I've got used to now."

"Do you remember what the paediatrician said?"

"That he must be taken into daycare?" Maddalena was beginning to sound aggressive.

"I'm sure he said that more for your sake than for the baby's," her mother went on.

"I'm fine. And so long as I can I shall keep him with me, I'm not handing him over to strangers!"

"Alright, alright," Nevina said to ease the tension. Then nothing more.

"Now what's the matter?" Maddalena asked after a pause, her nerves on edge.

"Nothing. Nothing. It's all fine. But I mean, is everything alright here at home?" Maddalena, unable to tell a lie, just nodded. "But why do I never see your husband at home?"

"It's all so new to him, you know what he's like, the slightest thing can upset him."

"Just be careful, though. Upsetting rumours have been reaching me ..."

"What kind of rumours?"

"They say he drinks rather too much and too often. They've seen it," she stated, as if she had been preparing for this moment for days. Maddalena shrugged, though she knew these rumours were not without foundation. "But does he come home afterwards?" Nevina went on, to make the most of the tiny advantage she had gained over her daughter.

Maddalena shrugged again. "Of course he does. What sort of questions are these?" She was struggling.

"Perfectly reasonable ones. I'll get your father to speak to him, if you like."

"No, just you keep out of this!" Now Maddalena was losing control of her voice. Luigi Ippolito Giuseppe jumped. "Keep out of it, both of you." Maddalena had reverted to the strained tone she had been using earlier.

Nevina screwed up her eyes as if that were the only way she could cope with the woman before her, who despite a certain resemblance, no longer seemed like her daughter. "If you speak to me like that again, I swear that I'll slap you, I don't care how old you are now. And that's that," she added firmly.

The box for the second reel of film was marked 1971, *Performance*. The opening shots showed preparations prior to going on stage. The schoolteacher, Signorina Pinna, was giving the actors their final instructions. Basic make-up, cardboard crowns, cloaks made from cheap material, wooden sceptres painted gold. And the strange fever that overcomes those who have to get up in front of their parents and perform the result of a whole year's work. All this was obvious in this performance in a school hall disguised to look like a theatre. And there was Cristian, who though in a lower school grade, had been recruited because Pinna had "taken a fancy" to him.

This is how it had happened: Domenico, in eighth grade, had been recruited with other eighth-grade students for this performance at the end of the school year. One day when they were rehearsing in the school hall, Cristian had brought in the lunchtime snack which Domenico had accidentally left at home. This interrupted a rehearsal of Shakespeare's *Henry IV*, at the moment when the Prince of Wales is protesting that he wants nothing to do with the throne, because his father the king much prefers Percy, who unlike the Prince, seems to have been born to be king. Domenico remembered the speech delivered by Costantino Cossu, who had been cast as King Henry IV because he was not only big and heavy but although only twelve years old was already sprouting a beard. Domenico perfectly recalled the king's exact words: *"O that it could be proved that some night-tripping fairy had exchanged in cradle-clothes our children where they lay, and called mine Percy, his Plantagenet! Then would I have his Harry, and he mine."* The images on the film were distorted, the only sound the hum of the projector. The shots were poor and all taken at the same distance, two or three metres from the stage: fragments of scenes with children, pathetically dressed in leotards and cardboard armour, aping grandiose tales of blood-thirsty heroes from a bygone era. He could not hear the words, but still had a strangely precise memory of them. Because this was their own scene, where Percy and the unreliable Crown Prince Henry meet. In the midst of a forest of plants that could never have existed in nature, painted by boys on strips of wallpaper during art lessons.

In the scene they had to pretend to have met during battle; becoming irreconcilable enemies though they had been fighting on the same side.

Domenico: *My name is Harry Percy.*

Cristian: *Why, then I see a very valiant rebel of the name. I am the Prince of Wales; and think not, Percy, to share with me in glory anymore: two stars keep not their motion in one sphere . . .*

Domenico: *Nor shall it, Harry; for the hour has come to end the one of us: and would to God thy name in arms were now as great as mine.*

He could remember it all. And also that, a few seconds after pronouncing those fine words, he had had to die at Cristian's hand. A sword made from cardboard and *papier mâché* had penetrated between his arm and side thanks to a theatrical trick which had deeply impressed everyone at the time.

Domenico rewound the film and returned it to its box with exaggerated care, almost as if afraid that Mimmíu might come in and realise he had been watching it. Then he put the box back in its place next to the film of Cala Liberotto.

Now in the silence he suddenly felt alone. He looked around himself. His father would never have tolerated a mess like this. As he scanned the whole scene, his eye fell on a folder he had not noticed before. It had ended up under a pile of newspapers. Domenico had discovered that Mimmíu kept some pornographic magazines. But this was an anonymous folder made of stiff cardboard, the kind with a flap that fastened with elastic. There was certainly nothing special about it except that Mimmíu had written CRISTIAN on the front in neat block capitals of a kind familiar to Domenico. There could have been any number of reasons for Domenico not to open it, but he ignored them all.

Inside he found a little pile of cuttings in perfect chronological order, newspaper reports of Cristian's death. There were also a few handwritten notes mainly with large numbers in ascending order: 10 000, 200 000, 450 000. Then a series of receipts for telegrammed money-orders credited to someone called Schintu Federica.

*

That evening Domenico went home to his wife. He understood from the expression on Maddalena's face that she wasn't expecting him. This in itself, in some inexplicable way, made him anxious. But he pretended to have noticed nothing. Nevina was still there, getting ready to go home. She gave him a glance more worried than angry, and asked him if he had eaten. Domenico looked at Maddalena without answering his mother-in-law, but the older woman had clearly not expected an answer. She headed for the front door, putting on her overcoat. "See you tomorrow," she said to her daughter as she went out.

Husband and wife stood facing each other. "There's a piece of meatloaf on the sideboard." Maddalena waved vaguely towards the kitchen.

"Made by your mother?"

Maddalena nodded. Domenico found the meatloaf on a plate under a clean dishcloth, carried it to the table and looked around as if to remind himself where the cutlery would be. He took a fork from one drawer and a napkin from another, then sat down.

"Are you staying?" Maddalena asked, coming up behind him.

"Yes, if that's not a problem," Domenico answered with his mouth full.

"No, no problem." She found herself unintentionally resentful.

"That's good," Domenico said, to fill the increasingly awkward silence.

"And tomorrow?" Maddalena asked. From her tone, it sounded as if she felt no need to add anything else.

Domenico wiped his mouth. Maddalena opened a kitchen cupboard to get a glass and took an open bottle of wine from the draining-board by the sink. She poured half a glass and held it out to him. "Take this, or maybe people will say I choked you with the meatloaf."

Domenico laughed and swallowed, then knocked back the wine. "Your mother would be happy," he said.

"We have an appointment to take the child to the specialist tomorrow morning. Will you come with me?"

"Tomorrow morning?"

"Oh never mind, forget it," Maddalena snapped, irritated by her husband's hesitation.

"No, no," he intervened. "I'll come, tomorrow morning's fine. In the afternoon I've got some people I have to see, but the morning is fine. What time?"

"Ten," Maddalena said. "You'll be sleeping here tonight then?"

"Yes, yes," he said.

"In any case, the bed in the other room is made up too."

Domenico poured himself more wine.

Nevina felt as dark as midnight. She took a more circuitous route than strictly necessary to get home. She had absorbed a little of the evening's freshness, but it was not enough to overcome the terrifying sense of imminent danger she felt every time she entered her daughter's house. She needed to calm herself before reaching home so as not to seem too worried.

She had only been home for a minute when her husband Peppino came to find her. "I've just called Maddalena," he said. "She told me you left half an hour ago, I was just about to come and look for you."

"I needed time to meet my lover, didn't I?" She entirely failed to sound as witty as she had intended.

"What's going on?"

Nevina took off her shoes and overcoat before answering. Then picked up an old receipt that had fallen out of her pocket. Peppino waited patiently. "I've no more idea than you have what's going on. But every time I go into that house I have a bad feeling." She looked around. "Are you alone?" she asked.

"Our son has gone dancing."

"It's the same every evening. But this business of Maddalena doesn't seem right to me. Domenico's never there, and when he does appear, you should see the expression on his face."

"And what does she say?" Peppino guided his wife towards the sofa so she could sit down.

But Nevina remained standing. "She says nothing. And even seems happy to accept the situation. And if you ask what they've decided about the child, they don't even seem to know that. Ten months old and he's not even been baptised. I ask you."

Peppino shook his head and shrugged. "These days such things don't seem to matter as much as they used to . . . If it suits them, I suppose it's alright." Then, instead of pushing Nevina towards the sofa, he pulled her towards him. "You must learn to keep calm," he whispered. "Relax. Come here." He hugged her tightly. "How long since we last danced together, the two of us?" Nevina did not answer, but gradually began to relax.

"*As the music echoes, that found us together, I shall again tread the path that brings me to you . . .*" He began to whisper in her ear as he took the first few steps of the dance. She followed obediently, pretending to agree. "*. . . Wherever you are, just listen, and you'll find me at your side. Just a little of me, in this concert I give to you!*" he sang tonelessly, miming a high note as he led his wife into a pirouette.

Nevina shed a few tears, weeping not only for the present, but for the past as well.

The visit to the paediatrician revealed nothing special. All was fine. The child was healthy, if a fraction overweight. Nothing to worry about. Domenico and Maddalena were obviously a perfect couple. Everyone at the surgery admired the young father for having felt it important to accompany his wife for this regular check-up on their child.

Soon August would be gone and with it the festival of the Redeemer. In that very period when the summer was likely to break, either suddenly turning autumnal or even more ferociously hot. In that particular year, 1980, the stones of the main street were radiating a heat so intense that one could imagine them erupting like a volcano. And they had not yet had time to solidify again under their feet.

Yet when Maddalena leaned on Domenico's arm as he pushed the pram, she felt as if she was walking on a carpet of flowers. So much so, that even the most distracted passers-by turned to gaze at them.

Back home, they ate a quiet lunch. Luigi Ippolito Giuseppe slept like an angel. After lunch they enjoyed a long kiss, a kiss with no particular meaning or promise, like when they were both teenagers.

"I'm always afraid I'll say something wrong." Domenico spoke carefully.

Maddalena thought this clear-sightedness must be a miracle, or at least a way out of the tunnel. It was true she had asked him firmly, "Why do you never say anything to me anymore?" But she had not expected him to answer with equal clarity. "And I do understand what you must be going through," she said.

Domenico shook his head violently. "I always have the same dream," he tried to explain.

She assumed he must mean the moment when he thought he could still save his father's life. "We'll sort it out," she reassured him, putting her hands on his shoulders.

He suppressed a groan, since both his wounded life and his wounded flesh were just under the thin cloth of his shirt.

Maddalena began unbuttoning his shirt, but Domenico grasped her wrists: "No, please don't."

Maddalena pulled back her hands abruptly, as though her husband's touch had scalded her.

"I told you, I have to see some people about work," he explained, buttoning his shirt again.

Once outside the house he began to breathe normally. It turned out that Federica Schintu lived in a modest block of flats in the suburbs, among uncultivated fields and land still midway between nature and civilisation. An area still searching for meaning, no longer green but not yet built up either. A paradoxical district that should have promised rebirth and progress but instead seemed the product of some recent conflict, with its development interrupted at destruction stage so that any further human development seemed uncertain. Such places were now described as "satellite" or, more presumptuously, "residential" estates. But in fact they were accumulations of building materials in the middle of nowhere. Portions of mangy territory like threadbare velvet, waiting for some attempt at town planning to give them purpose. Yet it was in such places, so it was said, that in the midst of a now sterile countryside apparently afflicted by alopecia, all prosperity had its origin. So initial enthusiasm for a rosy future had given way to a sort of environmental resignation, a daily acceptance of everything that was unfinished, including thoughts. Even the street-lamps were standing there without light lining, like the ribs of whales, unsurfaced carriageways that turned into quagmires whenever it rained. Small blocks of flats floated amid the bleakness of supposed communal areas that were gradually developing into an undergrowth of dumped furniture, mattresses and discarded white goods. This was where Federica Schintu lived.

It seemed clear to Domenico that "living there" must mean having a very cynical view of the world. But his realisation of this helped him to understand, for the first time, how far he had been pushed to react. His own interior too was becoming more of a desert. All the same structures of abdication were inside him. And they, too, had the same horrible front doors of anodised aluminium and frosted glass with perpetually defective locks that were swept by draughts at the first breath of wind. Their squalid lifts were lined with fake wood (formica pretending to be beech), and they had horribly cylindrical push-button panels with a yellow button for the alarm and the other buttons all red. Where cigarette-smoke adhered like a layer of icing-sugar, and combined with both human and non-human odours of food and armpits, soot and shit.

The outer door yielded before Domenico had a chance to discover whether it was open or closed. He found himself in a small entrance hall that stank like a combination of school dining-hall and gymnasium changing-room. The intercom proclaimed "Schintu 3rd floor", indicating top floor. He was tempted to take the lift, but decided to walk. After every two flights of stairs there was a small landing where the doors of two flats stared across at each other, while the lift door in the middle wall resembled the entrance to a telephone kiosk. Again it was the changing smell that told him he was moving from one floor to another, as it varied from cabbage to deodorant, mildew, and old clothes.

The door marked Schintu was on the right at the top of the stairs, near the end of the grey banisters and a handrail covered in blue plastic.

He rang and waited.

Footsteps approached from behind the closed door.

"Who's there?" came a tentative female voice.

Domenico cleared his throat. "We don't know each other, I'm the son of Mimmíu Guiso."

"Ah," the woman said, looking through the spy-hole. "Who are you looking for?"

"Schintu Federica." Domenico put the surname first, as though to add an official touch to this strange conversation.

"That's me," the woman said, her eye against the tiny glass lens in the door. The man's face outside on the landing, seen through the little hole, resembled the snout of a strange fish.

"We need to speak," Domenico said. Imagining the woman must be looking at him, he took a step backwards and opened his arms to show he was not dangerous.

He heard the sound of the lock, but did not step forward until the woman became visible, still defensively holding the door. She was small, thin and nervous, wearing a pair of orange leggings and a green blouse two sizes too large for her. Her toenails were painted dark red. In appearance she was not plain so much as unkempt; her make-up indeterminate, her hair distorted by an aggressive perm.

"Who gave you my name, signore?" the woman asked, speaking formally, even if it was obvious that Domenico could well be even younger than herself.

"My father." He seemed to anticipate the question. Then he reached into his jacket pocket. The woman gave a start when he pulled out a small bundle of papers held together by a rubber band. With his other hand he showed her a hundred-thousand-lire banknote.

She stood back to let him in.

The interior of the apartment seemed curiously over-tidy. It made Domenico think of how some quartzes can look rough on the outside but have a violet core as smooth as marble. The taste shown in the choice of flooring, wallpaper and furniture was not of the best, but everything looked clean and respectable. All was new but at the same time unremarkable, like a lodging-house planned for old people or students.

Walking a step ahead of him, the woman led him into a sitting room packed with too much furniture: small tables, glass display cases, chairs, dressers and a chest of drawers which carried a television set that was switched on without the sound. Inside the glass cases and on the flat surfaces was an indescribable collection of knick-knacks, lamps and framed photographs.

Federica Schintu pointed to a chair for Domenico, but he remained standing. "My father used to send you a money-order once a month," he said briefly, then fell silent.

The woman watched him uncertainly. "Really? . . ." she began, then interrupted herself as if suddenly realising that her answer might lead her astray.

Domenico waited, but she seemed to have no intention of adding anything more. So he pulled a small green receipt from the bundle he was holding and read, "Five hundred thousand lire to Schintu Federica. Every month. For a year."

"Yes," she said, unable to deny the evidence. "That's my name written there, but the money wasn't for me . . . I drew it then passed it on, that's all."

At that answer Domenico gave a jolt, as if beginning to understand for the first time what this was about. His heart beat faster in his chest. "So the money wasn't for you," he repeated slipping into the more familiar "tu", trying to sound more decisive and less condescending.

Federica's leg began trembling, as though she were at her wit's end. "No, it was for someone who wanted me to look after it for them . . ." she said in a sudden rush.

"And what was there in that for you?" Domenico asked, waving his hundred-thousand-lire banknote.

"Well," she said. "What there was in it for me was the bother of queuing up at the post office and the bank."

Domenico held out the banknote in such a way as to indicate he was not prepared to let go of it without a proper answer. "Let's do it this way," he said with extreme calm despite the fury boiling up inside him. "I'll say a name, and if that name is the correct one, you keep this hundred thousand. Right?"

Federica Schintu nodded.

"Raimondo Bardi," said Domenico.

After a moment's hesitation, the woman took the banknote.

*

He did not go home to Maddalena. And she had not expected him to, because she had understood everything he had not told her. As soon as Domenico had left the house, Maddalena had telephoned Nevina on the pretext of telling her what the paediatrician had said, and let her mother know that this evening it would be better if she stayed at home. Nevina said that was fine, since she had some ironing to do and a mass of other things, implying that these were things she had had to put aside for the last few days for her daughter's sake.

Maddalena rang off and smiled into the surrounding silence. Sitting down on the sofa, she relaxed and closed her eyes. Such moments of surrender had sometimes produced masterpieces. She had read somewhere that "the unfortunate Mr Karenin", for example, had owed his birth to a late summer afternoon, when Tolstoy had been lying on the sofa at his dacha trying to make up for a sleepless night. The only person Maddalena liked in *Anna Karenina* was Anna's husband, who had tried to keep their marriage going in spite of everything. And anyone who imagined he did this out of a sense of duty was wrong. He was an honest man, foolish, melancholy and in love. Maddalena was the kind of woman who loathed Anna Karenina herself from the first moment. So stupidly perfect, so meaninglessly unsatisfied . . .

Luigi Ippolito Giuseppe started whimpering in his room. Maddalena got up and went to him, and passing from sleep to wakefulness she was forced to leave the racecourse where Anna, ignoring her husband's presence, laments Vronsky's fate in public.

Reaching her son's room, Maddalena leaned over the child's cot so he would understand that she was there with him. When the baby stretched out his arms, she picked him up and hugged him to her breast. They stayed like that for a long time. Reality now seemed no more than a poor appendix to her imagination. Expanses covered with snow did not exist, nor did sledges hauled by tame horses. There were no such things as opening nights at theatres or receptions. Nothing. Domenico did not exist; only Maddalena herself and her child.

The unfortunate Domenico Guiso saw from his watch that it was now two o'clock at night. It had not been difficult for him to understand what had taken place between his father and Raimondo Bardi. He knew Raimondo well. After his arrest in the port at Livorno, Raimondo had claimed to know nothing about what had happened, but had been sentenced to five years in prison nonetheless. The fact that Mimmíu had been paying him every month through Federica Schintu as a cover said everything: it explained how much Mimmíu had actually known about Cristian's death. And everything else.

Domenico felt his nerves getting the better of him. When he was alone he would give way to extreme reactions such as sweeping dirty plates and glasses off the table with his arm and letting them smash to pieces all round him on the floor. He was just as capable of turning the apartment into a pit where he could wander naked and unwashed like a savage. He thought he now knew what to do.

It took him a few days to get the permit he needed. As for the travel, that was no problem; he told Maddalena it was for work. But faced with the orderly who asked to see his papers, he did feel a little unsure of himself.

The beginning of September that year was soft and welcoming. Domenico drove calmly to Cagliari, his car window a little open so as to experience the exhilarating fragrance of the countryside. If he had been able to bottle that perfume he could have made a fortune, he thought. Once he was out of the built-up area, the countryside ran towards him, filling the windscreen before dividing into two streams that ran along either side of the car. The cloudless sky was compact like blue plaster. On either side of highway 131, self-seeded privet ran past him like the wake of a ship, as did groves of citrus, plantations of artichokes, silvery rocks emerging from a desiccated fleece of undergrowth, whole tiers of wild fennel, clumps of asparagus, and clay chewed up by excavators. All this flashed by Domenico's car doors. He pressed down the accelerator, more as a challenge to the viscous countryside than because he wanted to arrive sooner. He was in no hurry; he still had three hours before they would let him into Buoncammino prison.

When he reached Monserrato he stopped at a bar, ordered a coffee, and asked for the toilet. The barman gestured with his chin at a door where the letters W.C. had been marked in green felt pen on the back of a shoe-box. Then he knocked back his coffee which had been cooling on the counter, and made his way back to the car.

He had been very nervous all the previous day. So much so that in the afternoon he had needed help. It had taken a fair number of blows with the belt to restore his equilibrium. At one point, despite the fact that he had offered to pay her more, the woman had refused to go on. So his left shoulder was rather sore, and driving a car did not help. The pain reminded him how much he was to blame for letting himself be so distracted.

A month after the event, the car radio relayed the ongoing obsession with the horrible carnage at Bologna. They said it had been an ending, or was it a beginning, not that it made much difference. And that the bomb had marked a sudden awakening from an overly prolonged sleep. And that from now on, nothing would ever be the same again. From bright colours to lead-grey.

Then the reality beyond the windscreen suddenly became drab. Cagliari announced itself with sheds and clusters of tower blocks like the periphery of a real city. There it was, the *finis terrae*, the final piece of the known world before emptiness. He was already becoming aware of a strange swarming, as of too many human beings crammed into a confined space. As though they had all run there only to find themselves crushed together a mere step from the precipice. Ever since he had been a child, Cagliari had seemed far away, and now he understood why. He realised that this sense of finding oneself on the edge, directly facing the open sea, placed Cagliari further away than any possible distance. More distant than the most distant city possible, whether real or imaginary. In fact, Domenico had been in Cagliari three times before, so this was his fourth visit. And now on the radio, there was Renato Zero singing to him that no *tristezza*, no sadness, can ever really have existed. Quite so. The truth was, the car was still heading for Buoncammino, while Domenico himself was moving backwards.

Take for example an afternoon three years before. Late June and the first days of July: an utterly crazy heat, enough to make you faint in the street. The hottest summer for two hundred years, so they said. He and Cristian lived in their underpants. Whole afternoons needed filling after school, almost as if time itself had unexpectedly slowed down. No matter how hard he tried, Domenico could not remember any other time when the clock had moved so slowly. In fact, what he remembered most of those sultry afternoons spent in his underpants, was the theatrical slowness of the hands of the clock as it struggled to follow minute with minute and second with second.

There had been a confusion of bodies and sweat during those slumbering afternoons. Cristian seemed bent on revealing his vulnerability, perfectly fluid in the stunned listlessness of those closed rooms. Especially when, amid that darkness of curtains and shutters, you were forced to close your eyelids tight and keep your breathing to a minimum so as not to disturb the treacly air.

And Cristian had sung softly during that afternoon turned to artificial night:

When you eat an apple you and the apple are part of God
When you think of God you are part of every part, and nothing lies beyond it
When you live you are the centre of a wheel while the spokes are rays of life

Listening to Cristian's rough but tuneful voice, Domenico had experienced a sweet discomfort, a bodily response almost beyond his control.

He could understand how delicious that malaise had been by the brute force it had needed to lock his jaws shut. And the heavy reverberating pneumatic sound every time he swallowed in that silence. Cristian had been immobile, his song blending into the

233

creamy heat with no obvious connection with it, murmuring now rather than singing, as if he had used up every available breath:

When you think you are creative, the illusion is to call it an illusion
When you ask, you must give, and when you give you achieve love
When you cry out, there's no reality, but you have decided you are
God and creative
When you call all this real, you have found everything inside itself

Then, his song finished, the silence seemed even more powerful, like a spasm of expectation. When he felt Cristian's hand lightly touch his shoulder, a handful of eternal moments went by during which he could not move, as though afraid to surrender to his heart beating in his breast as violently as a cat in a sack.

He parked the car. Buoncammino seemed less a prison than a fortress. As he faced the official who checked his papers, Domenico had a moment of uncertainty. As though his journey had satisfied every other need. He gave the official his identity card and passed through the automatic gate that led to a fine courtyard and the principal building.

The interview room lay beyond a long side corridor, where Domenico began to realise how closely literature could reflect life. He walked in the footsteps of the warder ahead of him, exactly echoing the sound of the footsteps of Edmond Dantès in the hideous prison of the Chateau d'If. Shoes striking metal create an atrocious chime, he thought, realising he must be exceptionally agitated to summon up his beloved Dumas on such an occasion. The fact was, he was not one of those people with a quote for every moment but, he told himself, this was the right occasion to dig deep inside himself for *The Count of Montecristo.*

The area set aside for visitors was a long narrow room over the entrance, bisected by a wall about a metre and a half high, extended up to the ceiling by a heavy grille like a cage for apes. Several screens divided this wall into small numbered niches. Guided by the warder, Domenico entered number five. Numbers seven and ten were already occupied by people he could not see, but he was aware of a subdued whispering from them.

Raimondo Bardi presently appeared from a small side door, accompanied by an extremely young warder, who removed his handcuffs and showed him where Domenico was waiting. A year in prison had changed Raimondo, who now seemed more muscular, even slightly taller. His shaven head made his face look older without ageing him. His singlet emphasised his remarkably hairy shoulders.

"What a coincidence!" Raimondo exclaimed before sitting down in front of his visitor. The cage framed his face and Domenico noticed a large blood-clot at the corner of his mouth. "I dreamed about you last night," Raimondo said. "You were here in the prison car park sitting in your car, waiting for me to come out . . ."

"Are you trying to make a fool of me?" Domenico interrupted. Raimondo stopped, the rest of his dream stuck on his lips. "Are you trying to be clever?" Domenico insisted, trying not to raise his voice, though at the same time making it clear that he was in a determined mood.

Raimondo shook his head almost as if wondering what Domenico was talking about.

"Federica Schintu," Domenico said.

Raimondo attempted a laugh but failed. "Oh, that," he commented, leaning towards the grille. "That's nothing."

"Nothing?" Domenico said angrily. "You beg money from my father and you call it 'nothing'?"

"By the way, I did hear what happened. My deepest sympathy . . ." Raimondo said with odd formality.

Domenico gave him a long look, like a teacher disappointed in a promising pupil. "You should not have done that," he said sharply.

"I never asked him for anything. But your babbo wasn't stupid, Domé . . . The money was his idea and I wasn't going to turn it down."

"But what were you giving him to believe?"

"What difference can that make? Live and let live . . . Nothing has changed between us and nothing will change. I'll be here four more years, and when I come out I want everything just as we agreed."

"Yes, but you haven't answered my question."

"What question?"

"What were you giving my father to believe?" Domenico tried to use the same words as before.

"Nothing, because he worked it out for himself . . . when he saw at the last minute that you were not setting off with us for Carrara. It was he who took me on, right?"

"Yes, of course."

"And when he realised you were not setting off with us, he added two and two together. He realised you must have been connected in some way with Cristian's disappearance. Fathers sometimes pretend not to understand things, but they do understand them.

He came to see me here, sitting just where you are sitting now, and said 'we arranged something for Cristian'. And when he said 'we' he meant you and me . . ."

"I know, that was his style," Domenico conceded. "So?"

"So nothing, just that he was ready to pay me more than I was getting from you," Raimondo concluded, wiping the haematoma at the corner of his mouth with a grimace.

"And you?"

"I told him if he wanted to help me financially he was welcome to, but it was not related to anything 'to do with Cristian Chironi'. I swear to that."

"So what did he do?"

"He looked at me, pulled out a cheque-book, and wrote down a sum of money. He told me he would pay that sum every month to anyone I liked to name so long as I didn't get you into trouble. And when I said 'What do you mean, trouble? There is no trouble', he tore out the cheque and showed it to me . . ."

An embarrassing silence followed.

Domenico pursed his lips as if to hold back tears. "And then what did he do?" he asked again.

Raimondo looked at him with a certain benevolence but also with some curiosity, as if unable to grasp that inside the same man two such contrasting beings could exist side by side. One moment gentle and docile, the next cruel and vindictive. "And he said that in any case, even if there did turn out to be trouble, I was covered. That's what he said. Then he looked at me with that particular look of his, you know it well, don't you?" He waited for Domenico to agree. "I told you, fathers pretend not to understand, but they do."

Domenico's face revealed a glimmer of hope, which Raimondo

registered before the other could fake it. And he took fright.

"Cristian?" Domenico asked. And said nothing more.

"What?" Raimondo said.

"What was it like?" Domenico demanded, but without managing to conceal a hint of satisfaction.

"No," Raimondo cut in. "This, no. Warder! The interview is over."

Cristian was waiting for him in the front passenger seat of the car parked not far from the entrance to the prison. Domenico opened the door and got in. Although he noticed Cristian when still a few metres away, he gave no sign that he had seen him. He got in, started the engine, and turned on the radio which croaked at him, as though full of frogs drunk on caustic soda. Cristian was naked and wet as though he had just come out of water. There was a big gash in his left shoulder, and he was trembling. Domenico put the car heater on. A light buzzing of bees joined the frogs on the radio. He drove off without saying a word and without looking towards the passenger seat, making out that he was totally absorbed on the road that would take him out of Cagliari and onto the 131 for Oristano.

The same suburbs that he had passed through only an hour or so earlier from the opposite direction, now seemed totally different. Almost as though, as he left the city, this previously undesirable expanse had at a stroke become more agreeable. He told himself this must be because of the direction in which he was travelling, with the sea now no longer approaching him but behind him. And with such a wide distance still to be crossed. Now the sheets stretched across the balconies of the last blocks of flats waved him *ciao ciao*, as the so-called industrial zone opened before him in its desperate randomness. Domenico accelerated a little, his eyes firmly on the road ahead. Even the colours were changing, passing from empty to full, from over-exposed to chiaroscuro, from arid to leafy, from horizontal to vertical.

Cristian turned towards him. The radio was belching out a tangled skein of fragmentary phrases and illogical splutterings, interspersed with occasional scraps of music from a confusion of channels. There could be no doubt that Cristian and Domenico were together in some inscrutable limbo, some shadow zone.

The route from south to north very soon revealed itself as much more intricate than that from north to south had been, with this side of the highway constantly interrupted by road works. Three or four kilometres after the city a sign indicated a detour via the old inter-city route, some ten minutes of road that seemed only just reclaimed from thorny bushes. Nature has a sneaky habit of taking back anything that man has abandoned.

Domenico's road, therefore, found itself crossing a section of neglected land which had just been taken back into use. The road ran over an unfinished flyover and through a short excavated area before re-emerging onto the 131. Suddenly the radio became clearly audible: "Cristian wishes to dedicate to Domenico this piece by Claudio Rocchi called "There is no such thing as reality". He knows why," announced a voice with a strong provincial accent. Dom-enico turned the radio off.

"Why don't you tell me what it is you want to know," Cristian asked sharply. He did not turn to ask the question, as though it were more important for him too to keep his eyes fixed on the windscreen.

One would not have realised Domenico had taken in Cristian's words but for further light pressure on the accelerator, almost like a conditioned reflex. "How was it?" he asked suddenly.

"How was what?" Cristian said.

"Now we are both asking questions and never giving answers," Domenico added.

"It would help if you could explain yourself better. What exactly is it you want to know?"

"How it happened, just that. You do understand, don't you?"

Cristian turned towards Domenico but looked beyond him. Outside the car, houses, trees and sky were running past them.

Finally he answered: "It was like drowning. Like waiting on the platform to meet a train that's late. Someone, the woman I loved, or a friend, or a dear relative, had promised to come to me, but never arrived. I had come in good time to meet them because, as you know, I hate keeping people waiting almost as much as I hate waiting myself. I'd taken a lot of trouble getting ready, because I was taught that being properly prepared and looking respectable is essential when meeting people. I'd bought wild flowers for the woman I loved, had a smile and handshake ready for my friend, and had already prepared a clean bedroom for my dear relative. I held my breath when I saw the train puffing round the final curve in the track. I waited for it to stop, then looked apprehensively over the shoulders of the passengers crowding the platform.

"It was as if this was how I imagined life in general to be, waiting with anxiety and worrying that I would let people down. The fact was, nobody came. Suddenly the platform was empty again, and I was left there with my wild flowers, my smiles, my uneasy calm, and the thought of the pointlessly prepared bed with clean sheets. The final imponderable moment before it happened and before everything vanished, took me back to that platform as though I was obstinately still struggling to meet Life rather than Death."

Cristian fell silent.

Domenico swallowed. He was passing from light into darkness, entering a bitter, unreal, shadowy, silvery world, suffused with blood from the drowning sun. "What did you do to your shoulder?" Domenico asked, feeling he must speak to fill the silence.

Cristian turned to glance at his wound. "I don't know," he said. "It doesn't hurt, anyway."

"It's like a broken wing," Domenico said.

He felt Cristian smile. "Have you taken me for your guardian angel, then?"

"Oh, the things you put into my mind!" Cheerfulness struggled with melancholy in Domenico's voice.

"*Angel of God who art my Guardian* . . . remember?"

"Of course, Aunt Marianna's obsession: *light us, guard us* . . . How did it go?"

"*Support me and govern me* . . ." Domenico prompted.

"Yes, yes." Cristian was getting excited.

It seemed as if the old times were back, lit by the very streetlights now ripping through the heavy darkness of the Abbasanta road. "*Because I was entrusted to you by Celestial Pity* . . ." Domenico continued.

"*Amen*," Cristian concluded, but with such agony in his voice that Domenico could not help turning to look at him. He had drawn up both legs onto the seat, and was hugging his knees with both arms.

"Yes," Domenico agreed. "We must have an *Amen*, what sort of prayer would it be otherwise?"

Cristian moved his head as though his neck were giving him pain.

"You know why I did it, don't you?" Domenico asked point-blank.

Cristian gave a very slight nod. "The hour has come to end the one of us," he declaimed, but in a whisper, as if wishing to confuse Domenico. "In any case, what happened, happened."

"Are you trying to say you forgive me?" Domenico asked hopefully.

But at that moment the car entered the Sedilo tunnel. There was no answer to his question.

PART II

In the Meantime

BY THE TIME OF LUIGI IPPOLITO GIUSEPPE'S THIRD birthday, the business of keeping up appearances had already been tacitly settled. Maddalena and Domenico had decided without discussing it that they would keep the family functioning in public, while in private each would continue not to interfere with the other.

Certain financial matters had become so pressing that Domenico had been forced to sell some land by the sea at a loss. This was land Mimmíu had bought only five years previously in the hope of getting planning permission that had been slow in coming through, though certainly not for environmental reasons as was claimed at the time. Teams of builders had put pressure on local politicians not to grant building permission until the builders considered the moment was right. Domenico found himself excluded from two important projects, one connected with the building of a tourist harbour in the Ottiolu area, the other for a tourist village at San Teodoro. If Mimmíu had been alive he would have been able to take control of both projects and the relevant teams of builders, but Domenico did not have the same degree of influence. It was clear that, apart from what had come to him directly from his father, he couldn't touch the inheritance. Clearly not all of it had come to him as his father's heir. In any case, he would never have disposed of the major part of the property, the Chironi bequest, unless sure of being able to turn it to profit. He would have been willing to take a risk, of course, but in that case he would have had to be ready to refund his son for any potential losses. So the simplest thing was to sell the estates in question, which he had decided were in any case unprofitable investments. But he realised only months later, how much more profitable it would have been to have held on to them. Someone else must be enriching himself by standing on Domenico's shoulders, as he often put it. But this faceless "someone else" remained the ghost of a ghost.

When he understood that the contract for the fixtures for the new multi-purpose centre in via Roma would go to a firm on the mainland that had proposed similar services at barely half the price he had anticipated, Domenico was forced to borrow from a trustworthy banker to meet his firm's cash flow requirements. The loan arrived two months late, guaranteed by a holding company in Milan that had agreed to take on in full the debts of the firm of Guiso & Figlio. The notary, Signor Sini, explained to Domenico that this was virtually a miracle, as though a sacred hand had pulled him from the water at the last minute to rescue him from drowning.

"But who are these people?" Domenico had asked nervously.

Sini seemed struck with wonder. "What do you mean, who are they? Edilombarda, of course. A financial organisation with solid capital and earnings."

Domenico pressed on: "Yes. But what interest can they possibly have in me?"

"Don't waste too much thought on that," Sini said, in a more moderate tone. "Everyone's looking for business in Sardinia these days, and Edilombarda probably see 'assistance' of this kind as a way of getting themselves a foothold on the island, so to speak . . . It may even be that they were expressly looking for a struggling business, do you understand?"

"Maybe they just want to get their hands on the whole lot," Domenico said heavily.

"Well, if that's how you see it, all you can do is turn down the credit they are offering, I do know the people in Milan asked for all possible information, even from this office. So they are well aware that the Guiso firm will, in effect, be solvent as soon as the Chironi inheritance is released."

"But what should I do?" Domenico exclaimed, drumming his fingers hysterically.

"Accept. Stop giving away family jewels. Is it true you want to sell your father's house?"

"Yes."

"There could also be some interest in the old Chironi family building. That could be worth quite a considerable sum."

"Ah." Domenico hesitated. "But who would be interested in it?"

"I don't know. Though one international foreign firm active in the hotel business has shown an interest. It would be a good deal, and considering what they are offering, there'd be a good percentage in it for you as well. It would give you some breathing space . . ."

"I'd have to think about it."

"Think quickly, because they could easily change their minds and look elsewhere. They've also had their eyes on the Hotel Sacchi at Monte Orthobène . . . that's just between you and me, of course."

A few days after this interview with Domenico, Sini happened to comment over a business lunch that the firm of Guiso & Figlio was like a football team that was always playing in the penalty area without ever scoring the vital goal, and to anyone who asked him what he thought of their general prospects, he said they were coming to a period when anything was possible. That after years of disaster they were all now on the cusp of something interesting, a period full of opportunities. In any case, if Italy had managed to become world champions at football after such a dismal prelude, it was obvious that all sorts of things were now becoming possible. Free and easy investments were changing the face of the country, and by country, Sini meant the whole of Italy, north and south, islands included. In his view it was precisely this world of finance that would finally transform the country into a first-world nation. He planned to stand for mayor in the local elections, but years of dealings as a lawyer had taught him how important it was never to reveal his intentions or, still more, give away his preferences beforehand. Take football, for example. It had never meant much to Sini, but since Italy had just been so lucky in the recent World Cup, you couldn't avoid mentioning football. As Sini saw it, this sudden interest of speculators in Núoro particularly illustrated the shamelessness of modern times, in which people were searching for money everywhere and nowhere was out of bounds. Naturally, people said, ethics appropriate to such a period of transition would be required, a form of restoration for every minor transgression. It was necessary to become new men, more fluid and elastic than before. Because after such a relentless struggle, after such madness, rebirth was essential. And the resistance Sini had detected on Domenico's face convinced him that the man had not adjusted to these new times, so that it would be necessary to work through his wife, who seemed so much more approachable.

"That's how it is," Sini finished.

Maddalena looked at him and asked the question she had been wanting to ask from the moment she arrived: "Why did you want to see me alone?"

Sini nodded enthusiastically. Exactly the right question, he told himself. "Because I believe you can help me to resolve some what we could call indecisiveness on the part of your husband." He knew that with Maddalena it was best to get straight to the point. "I believe you are au fait with the situation concerning the inheritance?"

She looked down. "There are some problems."

"There are some problems," Sini repeated. "And what is the source of these problems?"

"Delayed concessions? Repayment on credit? Unsuitable investments?" Maddalena speculated.

"All that and at the same time none of it. If I had to summarise the whole thing in a single word I would say, 'inflexibility'. Do I make myself clear?"

He stopped to see what effect the word was having on Maddalena.

"Meaning?"

"Meaning that your husband has not understood the connection between the estate as it is now and the mandate of the will. You see, as I have explained before, it's a matter of Chinese boxes . . . The Chironi inheritance, which is more or less constant, will go to your son who will be free to dispose of it on reaching his majority. In the meantime, the guardian, that is to say your husband, is at liberty to increase the estate, but not to subject it to . . . unnecessary risks. I am deliberately putting this in the simplest possible terms so you understand the situation. So who will there be, as the appointed referee, to define what I have just described as 'unnecessary risks'?"

"Yourself," Maddalena answered at once.

"Exactly." Sini smiled. "For this reason, to make sure that things go forward in the best possible way, if one may put it like that, we need a community of interests. Which brings us back to the word 'inflexibility'. I do have to say that such fixed ideas in a man as young as your husband do surprise me." Sini waited for a reaction from Maddalena, but none came. "There are times when an instinctive response is necessary, or at least a realistic approach. And, let's be frank, your husband is obstinate in not understanding that in order to build he must have the right friends. This, my dear lady, is no longer the world of your late lamented father-in-law."

Maddalena said nothing, only the merest twitch of her chin betraying how nervous she felt. "So what needs to be done?"

"First and foremost, get him to see reason." Sini referred to Domenico without naming him.

"He's worried about ending up surrounded by the wrong people. You must understand that?"

"No," Sini said abruptly. "What he must understand is that he is trapped in a corner, and will get no assistance from this office unless he acts at the very least to ensure the stability of the Chironi inheritance rather than breaking into it. When the estate is in the hands of its legitimate heir, that is to say your son, he can do what he likes, but until then my office has to remain responsible . . ."

"I understand," Maddalena interrupted. "But may I speak frankly?"

Clearly this idea did not appeal to Sini. The only frankness that ever interested him was his own. But if speaking frankly would make this woman happier, so be it. He nodded.

"I simply believe that my husband, Domenico, has been shut out of the building business, and that you, *signor notaio*, know perfectly well who is to blame for that." Sini seemed about to react, but Maddalena did not give him time. "Let me finish. We may look as if we're chained up, but we have no access to these holiday villages and never will have until we accept this providential help that seems to mean so much to you . . ."

"You are being harsh," Sini said, pretending resentment. "I assure you that Edilombarda is an extremely reliable firm that turned to me as a direct referent, in fact you would do better to thank me for having, in the first place, suggested yours as a business worth investing in."

"We do thank you, sir. But I would also like to make it clear that I am not my husband. He still thinks people are capable of acting without ulterior motives . . . However, I do understand what is involved, and I have also understood how far it applies to me. We'll let you know." Maddalena stood up.

Sini, his mind on the imminent mayoral election, understood that there was absolutely no point in attempting a reply.

*

Mimmíu had grown extremely light, lacking all substance, apart from a yielding exterior that was difficult to grasp. Like one of those paper lanterns that float up into the air when heat is applied to them.

For Domenico, still as always struggling to save his father, this lightness came like a dismissal. He did not know whether to be happy or sorry, because their recurring contact had begun to feel as much a condemnation as a reassuring certainty. He was beginning to moan about this in his sleep, as if finally admitting that the effort of holding on to something that was always escaping him had become too much.

Opening his eyes, Domenico remembered that he was now in the house in via Deffenu, and that he had spent the whole of the previous evening arguing with Maddalena, who had been trying to convince him that if he wanted to continue to work, he must come round to Sini's idea of a "bailout". Domenico resisted because he did not entirely understand what this meant: did it mean that if he did his work he would be saved, but that he could not do this work unless he was ready to put himself in the hands of a holding company that wanted to use his difficulties in order to play the market? Was that how it was?

Maddalena confirmed that this was the case. And explained to her husband that the question only seemed strange to him because he had not taken into account the percentage that would have to be paid to Sini upon ratification of the agreement. Domenico, this time, understood everything. Sini was guaranteeing to the consortium of developers, that in order to honour the agreement the Guiso company would have to sell the land that Mimmíu had bought. And not at market price, either. So thanks to local connections, Sini had closed off concessions to lower the price and to compel Domenico to let the land go. At the same time, the notary had taken a percentage from Edilombarda to compensate for the debt that Guiso & Figlio had contracted through the previous operation. "Chinese boxes," as Maddalena said.

For his third appointment with notary Sini, Domenico prepared himself with the meticulous care of a goldsmith, because he felt he needed to engrave his words, thoughts, actions and omissions on his mind, as the dear departed Father Virdis would have put it.

Maddalena had taken care over her make-up and also with her husband's appearance, and no sooner were they outside the front door of their home, than she took his arm as if they were still a couple who could not bear to be separated.

It was an indifferent sort of afternoon, neither hot nor cold, of the sort that settles on objects and people like almost imperceptible cosmetic powder, visible only against the light. An ordinary powder, with the smell of sugar-coated almonds and almost pink in colour. It was imbued with a melancholy expectation of solitude rather than the reality of solitude itself. For Domenico the suspense seemed unbearable torture, but Maddalena held his arm to prevent him escaping, and to make it clear to the whole world what a close couple they were. In her own special way of looking at things, literature counted at least as much as reality. And often more, because if anyone had dared to doubt the solidity of their marriage, they would now need to get these doubts out of their head, since Maddalena Pes Guiso and Domenico Guiso were on display to all and sundry, walking to Sini's office, elegant and beautiful, arm in arm. Just as it should be. And nothing else – reality included – mattered a damn.

However, as a capitulation it was indeed a capitulation, in the sense that once the interview was officially over, and once he had sat with Maddalena in the notary's office for a good twenty minutes, all that remained for Domenico was to sign the documents in the appropriate places marked with crosses, the stuff of idiots. Not only that, but he did this even though he knew he was laying his head on the block. Even so he signed, under the vigilant stares of Sini and Maddalena, in the hope that the executioner would miss his stroke. Once this 'formality' was over, the would-be mayor hastily withdrew the precious documents from Domenico's sight, for fear that he might change his mind – not that the ink he had used to initial and sign the documents even needed blotting. Then he smiled and handed the documents he had just so rudely snatched from the signatory to his silent secretary. Then, having registered the proceedings, he turned back to the effectively decapitated man before him, to assure him that the results of his wise decision would very soon become clear.

In fact, the effects became clear only a few days later when the local council of Porto San Paolo that controlled the Cala Girgolu district, unexpectedly gave unrestricted permission for the construction of holiday homes, immediately substantially increasing the value of the land that Mimmíu had had such bitter difficulty acquiring from its previous owners. Good news, perhaps, but not for Domenico. Rather it was the ultimate proof of his absolute ignorance and lack of vision in handing that land to Raimondo Bardi – by means of a private document – to recompense him for having deceived Cristian Chironi and forced him to travel in a Transit van loaded with firearms. And this explained how Cristian's death, which had far exceeded Domenico's intentions, came to cost him the loss of such a valuable property. Mimmíu, in turning directly to Raimondo, had realised that his son Domenico had been the main instigator of what had happened, perhaps even the anonymous informer who had led the police to discover the weapons. And it was clear that when Mimmíu had offered to pay Raimondo a sort of annuity via Federica for as long as he was in prison, he had done so to prevent Raimondo ever denouncing Domenico. So there was the twisted sneer that sealed the young Guiso's utter defeat. Because now that he had given way on all fronts, now that he had let himself be saved by strangers who would not have given him any leeway, now that he could have evened it all out thanks to something as profitable as the construction of a holiday village at Cala Girgolu he, in fact, no longer owned the land it was to be built on.

Domenico realised only too clearly that his defeat would be total when, waiting with his wife for the notary to receive them, he had noticed two employees, unimpressive junior figures at the office without authority or qualifications, point at him and laugh, like all cowards on this earth who are arrogant towards the weak and lick the arses of the powerful. One of these two, who had a job in the office only because he was a distant relative of the notary, thinking himself out of sight had made a gesture to the other, raising his two index fingers to chest level to indicate a space of about ten or fifteen centimetres – the maximum length of the leash they allowed for that mongrel Domenico Guiso.

Domenico had been able to understand this without being able to hear clearly what the two were saying, because by now he had understood that the level of resentment people felt towards him was proportionate to the bile his father had once forced them to swallow.

A few days before this, an engineer who had worked on all Mimmíu's sites, had come face to face with Domenico in the street and allowed himself to voice certain disagreeable things relating to presumed acts of dishonesty that he had witnessed and suffered while working for Guiso & Figlio. Domenico had looked about himself, wondering whether a punch on the face might be the best option, but noticing that three or four others had also gathered, as if in anticipation of a fight, he let the matter rest, restricting himself to a scowl at the former works director who, despite the scruples of his conscience, had turned a blind eye to every single one of those acts of dishonesty of which he now claimed knowledge. There were limits to slander, Domenico thought. But such a thought seemed light-years away from the world he was actually living in.

There had been another obvious signal, too. This had been an impulse, immediately after the unpleasant encounter with the engineer, to return to the Chironi house at San Pietro. A strange Pavlovian instinct had made him realise how violent his future surrender would be and that he must prepare for it. When he slipped the key into the lock of the smaller door within the larger main gate to the courtyard – two doors that lived one inside the other like father and son, or twins of different sizes – he became aware that something was preventing him from getting in. It took him considerable force to push hard enough to squeeze through into the courtyard. It was only then that he understood that what had obstructed his entry had been a vine that had grown to an inordinate size and attached itself to the woodwork of the gateway. Passion-flower, wistaria, ivy, jasmine, false jasmine, and this vine in particular, had inflated like boa constrictors over the lemon trees, hibiscuses, medlars and all the other shrubs and small trees that, like Laocoon with his sons struggling against sea-serpents, had been trying to force their way to the light. They were like wrecked ships about to sink under a steely green blanket of climbing plants. The powerful fat plants had prospered in sap-filled indifference, while whole bushes of hydrangeas had withered away till they resembled the horns of male deer. And dried-out hydrangeas had pressed down the bushes, reducing them to mere heads of curly hair. The *schlumbergera truncata* or mother-in-law's tongues, left free to grow with its natural tendency to spread, had now reached out to lick the bottom of the cement laundry bowl where, in the appropriate compartment, a dry amber-coloured fragment of Marseilles soap still survived like a cyst. And the dragon-trees, which when kept indoors had seemed so exotic and unnatural, had now expanded from the corner of the courtyard where Marianna had planted them to imitate Caribbean palms; the sort that thrust themselves forth, sinuous and keen, on travel posters of white beaches edging crystalline water.

This forest, which had once been Marianna's garden, moved him to tears. It was as if, somehow, it had failed in its duty to guard and preserve what had once been a garden haven. These plants had not protected the garden they were growing in nor shown the slightest inclination to do so. They had swelled in wild neglect, an Amazonian confusion, a chaos without reason. Unrestrained, they had struggled strenuously against each other. Domenico had to fight his way through this exuberant luxuriance to reach the French window into the kitchen, and the window itself was also obstructed by plants armed with suckers like the tentacles of an octopus or a whip with claws. He had to tear aside vibrating branches, arterial spirals and cyst-like ganglions of berries and pods, before he could reach what turned out to be utter nothingness, an interior that smelled of the grave, a house now parched by death and silence.

When he entered the empty echoing room that had once been the vast Chironi kitchen, a sudden silence exaggerated the noisy, sibilant intensity of the growth outside. Domenico had absorbed the resonant fever of the verdant flood swamping the courtyard. He understood the bitterness with which the forces of nature had crept back in retaliation after being held down for so long. And he was able to judge the full depth of his own surrender, and perceive the nothingness bound to follow it, since he was actually living inside it, exactly like when, after an explosion, nothing remains except a compact vibrant silence.

Someone had emptied the kitchen and cleaned the fireplace. The walls still carried the marks of the furniture that had once stood against them and the units that had been fixed to them, like the footsteps of bodies no longer alive. Further on, beyond the corridor, the bedrooms were closed as far as the stairs leading to the upper floor. The small landing at the top of the first flight was a metre and a half long and the same wide. There, in a corner, a blacksmith's hammer still lay, its wooden handle so dry that it resembled rope or a great dried-up intestine. And on that handle, long ago domesticated by the grip of a hand as strong as it had been tender, vibrated a shaft of light from the corridor above, where the shutter of a window had perhaps been left open. This luminous presence, in fact more an absence, was enough to inhibit him from climbing the stairs. Once, what seemed a thousand years ago, during the fierce inconsistency of childhood, Cristian had crouched there, arm outstretched to catch Domenico by surprise as he crossed the landing on his way from the lower to the upper floor.

He had read somewhere that atoms migrate in the greasy complexity of existence, changing into something else. And now, as he listened to the hostile silence in that buried house, that *sepulta domus*, he measured the extent of the terrible cost of his defeat.

Domenico had done terrible things; he had killed the real love of his life. He had carried the weight of the universe and had died because that universe, that love, had died; much more completely than the body of Mimmíu, which, even in his guilt, he had not been able to save. Now the walls of the house were drenched in the melancholy backwash of that agonising afternoon. As if infinitesimal fragments of all those who had once lived there were peering out in search of a place for themselves, in a pneumatic emptiness that was allowing them no rest.

He took refuge in the bedroom where, his voice suffocated by heat and his skin glistening with sweat, Cristian had once sung for him. All that was left now were two nets like unique relics of archaeological sediment. Apart from these, nothing had survived except in his imagination: the purpose of the room, as an immobile setting for the act of sleep and the fever of sexual desire. And the act of falling in love, in the instant when one knows it only as an arrow, the downward stroke of the tritest metaphor, or like a knife; things that only really hurt at the moment they penetrate or when one tries to pull them out; but so long as they remain lodged, the pain they cause seems bearable, even acceptable. And, sometimes, allowing them to remain stuck in your body is the only way you can survive.

Domenico, in that room, could see his life clearly despite everything. He did not know who had decided to empty the Chironi house, or what had happened to the furniture that had been in it. He knew nothing. And since no thought can exist, whether disturbing or comforting, that does not pull another thought in its wake, he remained certain in that emptiness that he himself, as a person, had no value at all, either as a son or a father. Now, as he tried to pull the arrow out of himself, he understood that this action was causing him an unbearable agony that had nothing to do with his body, but was a dormant emotion reawakening within him at that moment.

The emptiness allowed him clarity, shifting theory to practice: he had killed his love, had buckled under his father's dead weight, and had ignored his son. He was a failure.

Cagliari, Buoncammino, July 1984

A JAIL THAT OPENS TO ALLOW A PRISONER WHO HAS
served his term to leave is like an unconscious mother expelling
yet another child from her body. This is not the way it is usually
viewed. Prisoners have no nervous loved ones waiting in front of
the main entrance to welcome them. At Buoncammino they leave
from a side door, very much offstage, and very often no-one is
waiting for them at all. At least, so it was for Raimondo Bardi.

When the prison closed behind him he was almost shocked
by the immensity of the expanse that lay before him, stretching
from the summit of hills to the sea, with nothing to interrupt his
view. It occurred to him that the purpose of detention is to direct
the prisoner's gaze precisely where his jailers wish to direct it.
He pointed his nose into the salty unfiltered air from the port
below, and was overtaken by a subtle euphoria, not the blatant
euphoria he had expected. He had discovered that a good dose
of cynicism helps and that poetry not only kills reality but destroys
one's instinct for survival. Within his cage, he had developed
entirely new views of the world. Elementary facts, bodily func-
tions, carnal thoughts. It was a place where he had been forced
to choose between life inside and life outside, in a physical no less
than in a metaphysical sense. And he had learned that anyone who

261

can survive inside, can reasonably hope to survive outside too. So after three steps outside the prison door, he decided to forget he had ever been in there at all.

Raimondo had spent the last three and a half years in what was called "the politicians' lap", and had learned that, like himself, most of those connected with politics knew nothing. They had ended up in politics because some action of theirs, either spontaneous or forced, had become a part of that world. If you asked them what they had done they would have replied that, just for a change, it was they themselves who had been cheated.

Once past the outer wall, he discovered the sky was huge, something he had never consciously noticed before. And tilting his head towards that uniform blue, he risked a moment of weakness that he stifled by heading for the bar-trattoria on the far side of the road. He needed a coffee, a real one.

The man who ran the bar, a small man with an unbelievably cirrhotic complexion, studied him as an entomologist might examine a familiar species. Without even waiting for an order, he turned his back to activate the puffing coffee machine. When a small quantity of dense dark liquid began emerging from the beak of the filter with its projecting handle, he placed a spoon and saucer directly in front of Raimondo who was waiting for his fragrant cup, but he did not fill it to the brim. He told Raimondo he had made him a specially good cup of coffee. Raimondo thanked him without bothering to check whether the coffee was as good as the man claimed.

But in fact it really was good.

Raimondo left the bar and looked at his watch. Federica was late. As usual, she must have miscalculated how long it would take her to reach Cagliari. He wandered about for a bit, and checked the knapsack in which all his property was stowed, both what had served him in his cell, and what was going to be useful from now on. He had grown wise, learning much during his years inside. For instance, that keeping your gaze fixed on a single point can save your life in prison, just as it can outside. But, distracted for the moment by all the sky pressing down on him and so much fresh air wrapping him like a cocoon, Raimondo Bardi's eyes had grown inattentive. If he had not let himself be distracted, he would have noticed that life was teeming below him, with cars struggling up the hill and housewives festooning tiny balconies with huge quantities of linen . . . and large cargo vessels in the port unloading containers onto the quayside.

Not to put too fine a point on it, his senses, so closely confined during his years in prison, did nothing to help him understand that this would be the final day of his life.

THERE HAD BEEN THE BEGINNINGS OF A FIRE AT NÚORO that July morning, on the hill at Ugolío. Which made the cynics say: look, that's the area beyond the new hospital, ear-marked for yet another residential estate. Naturally there was nothing straight-forward to support such a theory, but in that part of the world, fires always indicated more than mere carelessness; in fact they often defined precisely which neglected natural areas would even-tually end up built with exceptionally solid cement.

Anyway, in the Guiso household they were discussing the fact that, two years after building permission had been given, nothing had yet been done about the land at Cala Girgolu. This was a treasure in serious need of development and Domenico was shaking his head over it.

Meanwhile, on the Carlo Felice road to Cagliari, Federica Schintu was driving as best she could, which was not very well. She slowed down on curves or when going uphill, and hurried past junctions, which worried her, and in tunnels, which terrified her. In any case, she was late. The heat was fierce, but driving with the window open gave her a terrible headache and on top of that, as if sultry weather were not bad enough, there was the tension caused by noise, her fear of running out of petrol, and the constant checking of the clock, not to mention smoking an occasional cigarette.

Ten in the morning. Another fifty kilometres to Cagliari, and she was already half an hour late.

She had dragged herself out of bed at dawn, gone into the kitchen to make coffee and switched on the T.V., which she always kept tuned to Videomusic. The solemn close of Queen's "Radio Ga Ga" filled the room, followed by Lionel Ritchie and "All Night Long". Federica loved that song; wiggling her hips as she waited for the coffee to rise. Then as she drank she looked through the window at the countryside, which still seemed half asleep.

It was an orange dawn. If she had known his work, Federica could have put Turner's nose out of joint to the extent that everything out there was verging on an extreme monochrome, with the sun giving the same dusty tone to both sky and land. Now the T.V. was pouring out Bronski Beat's "Smalltown Boy" while on the screen rails carried the train bearing the small-town boy in question towards the big city. Federica scooped out the sugar that had collected at the bottom of her little cup before putting it in the sink and running water into it. The video reached its climax as the train finally brought the small-town boy into the arms of the great tolerant city where he would build a new life for himself . . .

She turned the T.V. off; it was already seven and she could not afford to waste more time on the enchantment of the screen. She dressed hurriedly but with care, easy enough because she had planned everything the evening before – peach-coloured socks and jeans jacket with the sleeves rolled back, and a Madonna-style lace vest, with necklaces and the earrings with the crosses. Then she rushed out, only to come straight back because she had forgotten her cigarettes, which she found on the edge of the bath with her lighter. Since she was there, she squeezed another drop of pee out of herself into the toilet. Then, closing the hall door behind her, she crossed the landing, deciding to ignore the lift and walk down the stairs. At the third stair she suffered a brief attack of vertigo and a spasm in her chin, then stopped abruptly, bending forward as if to anticipate the impact of a wave she knew she could not avoid. The attack only lasted the fraction of a second, but long enough to indicate that this would not be just another ordinary day, though not long enough to make clear that it would be the last day of her life.

Federica had started out at half-past seven, leaving the city behind her without even having to cross it. After the unmetalled track that, sooner or later, would give way to an asphalted road, she passed between farms to reach the Macomer–Abbasanta road and, once past Oristano, the road to Cagliari. She was inhibited not only by the lorries that flashed past her in the fast lane, but by the tiresome fact that she needed to keep stopping to pee. This was mainly because she was feeling so nervous. But, to be honest, the strange turn suffered on the stairs at home had not been entirely without its hints too, but of course it is typical of such hints that they are never seen as hints at all until it is too late.

The previous afternoon, she had spent an interminable half-hour on the phone talking to her sister Pina, who had wanted to know why she was going to Cagliari, and Federica had not quite known what to say. The very fact that her sister had asked such a question had deprived it of much of its meaning. But for an instant, she had experienced profound panic, like clear evidence of depth in water measured by an exceptionally precise lead-line. Then, when Pina weighed in with her usual grumble that for herself, having a husband and children was no sort of benefit but rather clear proof that hell undoubtedly exists, Federica had willingly let herself be distracted by what was obviously a loud and clear warning sign.

In her car she had what could scarcely be described as a radio so much as a source of indistinct voices with music superimposed. As they headed down this funnel that would only end when they reached the furthest limit of the land, a confusion of programmes pressed on one another like too many people jostling for space in a small area. In this way scraps of reality emerged from the machine which she tried to make sense of by small flicks of the tuning button. And every so often she did for a moment grab some fragment of complete sense; a snatch of song perhaps: "and for a moment you regain the urge to live at a different speed" . . . or a snippet of local news: "blue tongue" . . . "assumptions at Ottana" . . . or a sliver of dialect poetry: "duminica ando a missa e mind'intendo duas dae soru de sa janna . . ."

If she had had the time to think of it, even with all that remixing the ghosts in the ether, and the brief re-enactment that occured each time she tried to fix on one particular broadcast or another, she would still have been wandering about as if without body or weight. Seen from above by a gull or a goshawk, Federica Schintu's cherry-red hatchback would have been nothing more than a simulation, a single blood cell in the faint arterial flux of that comatose land.

A CONVICT'S LAST DAY IN JAIL IS SEEN BY THE PRISON community as a practical demonstration of the meaningless nature of such confinement. Watching your cell-mate collecting his things and packing his bags with the air of someone who feels a need to excuse himself for having survived to the end of his sentence, is like being present at the graduation of a son. That is to say, realising what effect the passing of time has had on one's body. What had once been a new-born baby prattling meaninglessly, eventually began talking and then, still at first unsteady on his legs, made his way through kindergarten, elementary school, middle school, senior school . . . and there! Eventually earned a doctor's degree. And how much time did that take? Nearly a whole lifetime. Rather sad.

That's how Mario felt when Raimondo Bardi handed him a pair of headphones for the radio and walkman which were both still in reasonable working order; you just had to adjust the contact for the right ear by pressing the base of its tiny speaker. Mario, from Sassari, had used his fists to put a supporter of the Torres club into a deep coma; he was a shard from Raimondo's shattered time in jail. A mere memory to be quickly forgotten the moment he exited the door reserved for freed prisoners. But at that particular moment, with his foot still on the doorstep, Raimondo imagined he might even miss Mario, if only briefly. Raimondo had served his sentence like a man, but now he could expect a period of relative affluence. He was going home richer than he had been when he started in prison. He had a little money set aside and some land to claim. He checked his possessions to make sure he still had the certificate signed by Guiso Domenico that guaranteed him a six-hectare site at Cala Girgolu. He had already packed his more important possessions into a single backpack before supper. All the other things he had accumulated in nearly five years – utensils, gadgets, clothes, magazines, a few books – he had left in his cell for Mario or for whoever Mario might decide to give them to.

The morning of liberation, as he liked to call it, seemed in no hurry to dawn. Yet, thanks be to God, it eventually did. At nine in the morning, after breakfast, the prison governor summoned him to recite a speech he had heard others mention in the corridors or courtyard. Something like: "In half an hour, or at most an hour, you'll be leaving us. Make sure you don't come back." That was all.

After another half an hour or an hour at most, he was outside talking to the cirrhotic barman just a few metres beyond the Buoncammino prison wall.

And Federica was late.

They scarcely knew each other, but he had asked for her telephone number the moment they met, something he had never done with anyone before, proof that their meeting had made some impression on him. In fact, even in prison, he had often thought of Federica.

Now he was on his way home. Away from Cagliari, and the building that served as a refuge for local brutes. But Raimondo could still remember the first time he had seen Federica, tidying hotel rooms and cleaning toilets, despite her outstanding marks at school and commendation in her studies.

As soon as he recognised her car, Raimondo jumped out of the green plastic chair outside the bar and rolled up his sleeves. Federica went straight to him. She told him that for someone who had spent so long in jail he seemed remarkably fit, and that having his hair so short suited him and made him look more of a man.

"You're looking well," she said.

"You flatter me," Raimondo said, and without even giving her time to stretch her legs, took her place in the driving seat of the car: "Let's go."

She looked at him. "I thought I'd have a coffee first . . ."

He was impatient. "Later, on the road."

She cast a glance at the prison wall towering above them and shook her shoulders decisively. Then she walked round to the passenger side and joined Raimondo in the car. They looked at each other just long enough to judge how long it had been since they had last kissed. Then he started the engine. She stroked his back while he engaged first gear. He did not react. Very little seemed to have survived of their former intimacy.

Until they were clear of Cagliari they let looks and gestures do the talking. The radio, fussing like a deep-fryer, kept them company without either making any effort to control it. The invisible voices that filled the silence relaxed the tension that had kept Federica on edge during the journey out, and she fell into a deep sleep. Raimondo, his eyes fixed on the windscreen, kept the accelerator pressed down, gripped by the ripeness, like sourdough, that dominated the scrub, the picturesque perfection of the fields of sunflowers, and the sad obstinacy of the fallow lands. He kept the car at a fastidiously steady distance from the side of the road just as he had been used to calculating distances in prison. From the corner of his right eye he controlled the road's edge and watched the centre line as if it had been a changing guard.

"Light me a cigarette," he said suddenly.

Federica started. "What?"

"Cigarette," he repeated. "Light me a cigarette."

"Oh, of course." Bewildered, she searched the pocket of her jeans jacket for cigarettes and lighter. "One of mine?"

"But no filter." He still kept his eyes on the road.

She broke the filter off the cigarette, then put it into her own mouth, tasting tobacco with the point of her tongue, before transferring it to Raimondo's lips. She spat repeatedly as if to get the last scraps out of her mouth.

"I've woken you," he admitted.

She indicated that was nothing . . . that she hadn't been asleep; but her eyelids were growing heavy again. Meanwhile smoke from Raimondo's lungs was invading her space. Keeping his hands on the wheel, he let ash fall on himself. When he reached the end of the cigarette he checked to make sure he was still in the middle of the carriageway. From the side rear-view mirror a world normally concealed from his sight revealed the arrogant consistency of a reality that could not be ignored, no matter what. In that world of opposites, reflected in the mirror, the fronts of cars darting in the opposite direction appeared in reverse, and the road that had seemed as if strangled through the windscreen, now stretched out as if inflated by the heat. A white car indicated, overtook them and sped on. But another car, a green one, seemed to be carefully maintaining a certain distance behind them.

The man driving the green car, which he had hired in the port at Cagliari, stuck his chin out at the car ahead for the benefit of his three passengers. These were four shady-looking types, though the sun whose direct glare was strong enough to force a squint, and the sky so blue as to flatten out every detail of facial expression, would have ensured even the kindliest of men a sinister appearance. The pitiless contrast of extreme light and darkness emphasised prominent cheekbones and strikingly arched eyebrows, so that the four would have perfectly suited a film about a group of hired cut-throats pursuing an unusually important victim.

Not that much conversation was going on in the green car. When its occupants did speak, it was in generalisations like how incredibly hot it was, that they must keep their distance, and that they still had plenty of time.

The driver, who had a shaven neck, sweated as he struggled to activate the fan on the dashboard, but all he succeeded in producing was yet another blast of the extremely hot air that had the surrounding countryside in its grip. The man beside him was checking a small map, while the two in the back seat stared at the rear of the car in front, almost as if their stare in itself could prevent them losing concentration. They were so tall that their heads touched the roof of the car, and so heavily built that on the rare occasions when the car bounced, their shoulders bumped together.

When the moment they had been waiting for arrived, everything happened at once. The green car accelerated at the turning for

Macomer (marked with a red line and an arrow on their map). Then they closed in on the car they were shadowing, while the driver turned and stared into the other car and saw, as he expected, that its occupants were a man and a woman. And that the man was the person they were after.

When he noticed the green car accelerate, Raimondo, unsurprised, told himself that these people, whoever they were, had at last decided to show themselves. For a brief moment the two cars ran side by side. For no apparent reason the radio now gave up its frog-like croaking and switched to a honey-sweet song: "Remember that piano, so delightful, unusual / That classic sensation, sentimental confusion" . . . Federica had time to think: "Even if this song has nothing to do with it, it reminds me of the summer we went camping at Gonone", and she was about to ask Raimondo if the same thing had come to his mind, when a sudden braking hurled her towards the windscreen. As the singer on the radio confidentially asserted *I like Chopin*, Federica opened her eyes and saw Raimondo throw open the driver's door, swing out his feet, and shout, "Run for it! Run!"

She grabbed the handle of the passenger's door and was about to open it when an enormous man stopped her. A man from the green car. She had no idea why they had got out of it, but clearly they were unfriendly. They had stopped at a place forgotten by both God and man, a sort of upland plain, well out of sight of anyone driving on the 131. A place where it would have been pointless to cry out, though in fact Federica did yell at the ferocious emptiness of the infinite sky that so well matched the rocks and bushes now surrounding them.

She could not see Raimondo, but when the bastard on her side realised she was planning to escape from the other side, he flung open her door and grabbed her ankle. She tried to kick him away, but was overcome by a sharp pain in the ankle held in the man's vice-like grip. Sultry, almost unbreathable air filled her mouth and her heart pounded loudly in her chest.

"Who are you?" she asked, noticing that not far away three other men, like devils on the Day of Judgement, had seized Raimondo. But her attempt to introduce herself to this stranger with malicious intentions elicited no response. Without relaxing his grip he pushed her back into the seat from which she had just tried to escape, not caring if he was pressing her against the gear lever or the handbrake.

More stunned now than frightened, Federica had often wondered what dying would be like. As a child, she had sometimes forced herself to stop breathing for a few seconds. Now, possibly faced with the actual immanence of death, she understood how ridiculous such experiments had been. The good thing was that after the initial injury to her ankle – the fiercest pain she could ever remember – she was now feeling almost nothing, except that her lungs seemed to have become infinitely small, and her sight, never brilliant, was reduced to a mere miscellany of objects, noises and colours. She knew she must be dying because the tattooed forearm of this unknown man was pressing against her neck, and soon there would be no air left in her lungs.

Still able to hear, she was aware of Raimondo shouting, further away in the hands of the three other devils. It had not needed much for the song on the radio to fade away, its chorus reaching towards the ether for a new audience: "Rainy days never say goodbye / To

274

desire when we are together / Rainy days growing in your eyes / Tell me where's my way" . . . then an ugly piano solo brought everything to an end.

When he had finished with Federica, the man with tattooed arms retrieved Raimondo's backpack from the car and joined his three companions. To judge from the state of their victim's corpse, they had made the most of the encouragement they had been given to enjoy themselves. The language they were speaking was as unfamiliar as their appearance. The one who seemed to be their leader, the one who had strangled the woman, emptied the backpack by turning it inside out like a sock. Among the things that fell out of it was the sheet of paper that Domenico had signed to make Raimondo Bardi a future landowner; a man who had started life with nothing, been clever for an hour or two, and briefly become a man of substance. But now his brief future had been extinguished amid a hail of kicks and stones near Macomer in an area local people called Fort Apache, and his sheet of paper had been taken by the Four Horsemen of the Apocalypse, who now got back into their green car, rejoined the main road, and returned to Cagliari. There a cargo ship flying the Soviet flag had just enough time to take them on board before starting its return journey to the Baltic.

NEVINA WAITED FOR MADDALENA TO FINISH PREPARING Luigi Ippolito's meal. This consisted of a vegetable soup that her daughter had overcooked, and now she was using a fork to mash into a puree any fragments of carrot and celery that had survived in one piece. When she began mixing in processed cheese, Nevina went up to her and said, "You're doing it wrong," trying not to sound too critical.

The younger woman went on with what she was doing, then pushed past her mother saying "Let me through" to reach the child, who was waiting in his high chair; she straightened his bib and began to feed him.

"That child's four years old and you treat him as if he were half that age . . . he can't eat without help, finds it difficult to talk and can't even be bothered to walk," Nevina said.

"That's enough," Maddalena said, continuing to feed Luigi Ippolito and paying no attention to her mother. "That's enough," she repeated with greater force, despite the fact that Nevina had said nothing more. "Why do you always go on and on about everything?"

"Because I'm worried, surely even you can see that." Luigi Ippolito gave his grandmother a suspicious look. Nevina stared back. "He can't do anything for himself. It's not good at all," she added, still with her eye on the child.

Maddalena, obstinate and silent, continued to feed him until the bowl was empty. Then she wiped her son's hands on the bib and straightened a rebellious lock of his hair, before taking him under the armpits and lifting him out of the high chair. Luigi Ippolito stayed as passive as a puppet. He was light and slender, and looked younger than his age. Depositing him on the floor, Maddalena asked, "Would you like to watch the cartoon?"

The child nodded and climbed onto the sofa in front of the television. Meanwhile his mother inserted a VHS cassette into the old-fashioned video player. The title "101 Dalmatians" came up on the screen that only a moment before had seemed lifeless. When the film started, Maddalena rejoined her mother in the kitchen.

"Please don't talk to me like that in front of the child," she said desperately. "You think he doesn't know what you're saying, but he hears everything and he understands it too."

Nevina took little notice, though it was clear that her daughter was seriously exasperated. "Look, I'm not saying he's backward or anything like that," the grandmother answered. "I just mean you aren't helping his development."

"Why?"

The bare simplicity of this question took Nevina aback. "Isn't it quite clear why?" She waited for more from Maddalena, but nothing came. So Nevina continued: "Because if you fuss over him so much now, everything will be more difficult later on . . . What, do you think you'll still be able to do everything for him when he starts going to school?"

"That's still two years away," Maddalena replied.

"Two years will pass more quickly than you think," her mother snapped. "The boy's like a defenceless nestling."

"Defencelesss? But I'm here!" Maddalena was beginning to get even more annoyed.

"And you think you are enough?"

Her daughter searched for an unanswerable reply, but was forced to accept that one never thinks of the right thing to say until it is too late. Instead, with no obvious connection, she said, "When I was pregnant I was always dreaming."

Nevina looked at her. "And now you don't dream at all?"

"Not at all," Maddalena confirmed.

"Since you mention it . . . I dreamed of my mother last night," Nevina said.

"Grandmother Iolanda. Did she give you any useful lottery numbers for us to play?"

It was as if Maddalena had forgotten her previous remarks.

"Of course not," Nevina protested. "No numbers . . . it's not that I remember much anyway."

"Don't give me that. When I was pregnant I had the most incredible dreams that seemed real."

"I read somewhere it's impossible not to have dreams."

"And so it is," Maddalena said, with a touch of her earlier disputatiousness, but stopped herself in time before reverting to the annoyance that had made her attack her mother over little Luigi Ippolito.

Even so, they seemed on the point of resuming hostilities when something drew them back into the living room. The child had got hold of the remote control and the screen was no longer showing the cartoon but was giving the rough account of a sensational local news item: "There are no theories yet about the Macomer murders. The victims have been identified as Raimondo Bardi from Núoro, a convicted criminal, and Federica Schintu from Pattada, also resident in the Barbagia capital. Enquiries centre on the letters FR retrieved at the site of the crime. The possibility of a failed robbery has been excluded . . ."

The news item ended with the usual sequence of gruesome images apparently chosen for their blandness. Maddalena snatched the remote control from the child and struggled to restore the cartoon. But once she had found it, whether because of the news item or because no-one any longer seems to notice how terrible children's stories often are, the cartoon seemed less innocuous.

The two women remained standing behind the sofa on which Luigi Ippolito was sitting, until normality had been restored. Then they looked at each other. Nevina thought of many things she could have said about the lifestyle her daughter insisted she had deliberately chosen, but in fact said nothing because she judged silence more powerful than any of their recent skirmishes.

"I'm going to take the curtains down . . ." Maddalena said suddenly. "Do you put them in the washing machine, or is it better to wash them by hand?"

"In the washing machine, of course. It's not too rough with curtains," Nevina said.

"Okay. Then can you help me with the stepladder?"

Domenico crouched, but this could not stop him feeling the leather tongue scalding his skin from hip to buttocks. It had been a tremendous blow. He had forced himself not to cry out, and in so doing had released a sort of terrible howl from his diaphragm, causing him to gesture to the woman to give him a few seconds to recover.

This he did by nodding his chin, the sign they had agreed on before the session to make clear the limit beyond which she should not go. Over time this limit had generally been allowed to increase. Now Domenico usually pretended to be tied up and, often, gagged as well. At his sign, she had stopped. The pain, atrocious but intimate and by now utterly familiar, restored him to peace with the world.

That afternoon in particular he had asked her to redouble her strokes with the belt, adding the verbal abuse they both liked: "You cowardly worm, you impotent queer, you poofter, you fucking murderer!" Time and mutual familiarity had refined the woman's skill. She sensed how important it was to him that things should go beyond a game and approximate in some way to reality.

Occasionally she worried that her client's degree of resistance seemed to have developed to such a point that she feared she might unknowingly cross a line. But if she hesitated and paused for a moment too long, he begged her to strike again even harder. He no longer wept as he had the first few times. He became terrible, immobile, inexpressive until the blow hit him, when he dissolved into a kind of acute relief.

Afterwards, as if it had all been nothing, he would dress, recover his normal voice and the self-possession he had temporarily abandoned, and pull banknotes from his wallet. On this particular afternoon he added what she called "a generous tip".

"I see we're feeling good today," the woman said, knowing Domenico's generosity always related to his mood.

He nodded. "I've found something I thought I'd lost for ever," he explained. And putting the banknotes on the little table for her as usual, he went out.

Cala Girgolu, September 1988

AS HE HUGGED MADDALENA FOR THE PHOTOGRAPH, Domenico's smile was like the dark depths of a pond.

They had organised something simple and informal to inaugurate the villa at Cala Girgolu. This was to be their holiday home, in appearance halfway between "colonial" and a rather tired approximation to the folk style of the Costa Smeralda. Just what you would expect in the provinces, perhaps, but the house was generally sober and well-proportioned. Standing on a rocky outcrop with the small island of Tavolara directly opposite, it included a shady pinewood and was about two hundred, or at most three hundred, metres from the sea. From the covered terrace it was possible to admire the perfection with which turquoise and white, green and orange, yellow and blue, filled the canvas.

Domenico asked the professional photographer engaged for the occasion to take another picture from that position. After all, this was his house, and he wanted a view that would at least look official. He felt strangely at ease, though he was the only formally dressed person present. It was September, but the heat was still beating down like August. Maddalena was blossoming in middle age, one of those women who become increasingly attractive with the passing of time, ever more refined and in control of their looks and gestures. Luigi Ippolito, now nearly nine years old, was still withdrawn, and as his grandmother Nevina had predicted, it had needed infinite patience to get him used to school. Now he was circulating among the two dozen invited guests, showing no particular interest in any of them. He had grown tall and slender, with the particular look some only children have, halfway between wise man and serial killer. To put it another way, he was more inclined to solitude than reflection. It had required all Nevina's influence to persuade him to go to catechism in a sort of private section of the class, where he did not have too much to do with anyone else. This was not because the family wanted to isolate him, so much as that he clearly did not get on with strangers. Even now, on this day of celebration and inauguration, he circled the event, walking its fringes like a wolf observing a flock of sheep before selecting which one to attack.

"Come and have your photograph taken," Domenico urged.

Luigi Ippolito started by refusing, but when his mother insisted too he lowered his head and went over to join his parents in front of the photographer, whose professional patter included comments like, "Well done, just one more, yes that was perfect, real top quality . . ."

At last it was finished, and Luigi Ippolito was able to escape, while Domenico went over to Mayor (formerly notary) Sini and his builder colleagues, and Maddalena retreated to the kitchen to check that the refreshments were ready.

The following June's elections were anticipated as a mere formality that had long been settled. It was said that anyone who expected another strong performance from the Communists had another think coming, because the Berlinguer effect could not last for ever, and seen from an international perspective that whole model was falling to pieces. Had they not heard about Hungary? A "white whale" was navigating with swollen sails, they commented, while the cleverest socialists had discovered how to settle their bums on two seats at the same time.

At this point the ladies intervened to say that was enough politics, while a small group of musicians specially brought in from Sassari struck up some dance music that drove the remaining young people to the beach. A few of the guests took a closer look at the site in general and the house in particular with a view to the possibility of getting something for themselves in the village, which apart from a few public buildings, street-lamps and English-style lawns, could now be considered virtually complete. Only three or four villas a little higher up and slightly further from the sea, still needed to be sold.

Here was something Domenico thought he had lost for ever but had recently rediscovered. Here, before his eyes, was the first real project he had carried through without his father. He reflected on this without being conscious of its significance. An obstinate chant was coming from the sea, but you could only hear it at all if you shut out reality. Moving towards this dirge-like song, Domenico took a few steps towards the rocky ridge above the site on which his country house had been built. The sea lay open in front of him.

Lost in his own thoughts, he did not notice Maddalena roll up her sleeves and come towards him. It really seemed as if the sea had deprived him of any ability to communicate, so that although he became aware that his wife was trying to attract his attention,

283

he nonetheless seemed unable to respond to her in any way. She had to go right up to him.

"The child!" was all she said.

For Domenico it was like when the hypnotist reaches "three", and the victim over whom until a moment ago he had total control, suddenly wakes up amid general laughter.

"What's happening?" he asked, in the conversational tone natural to people in the first moment of waking up.

"The child!" Maddalena repeated. "He's disappeared!" she added in a loud voice that seemed to convey a new and absolute gravity.

"What do you mean, he's disappeared?" Domenico said, still not moving.

She sounded impatient. "I've been searching for him everywhere."

"He'll have gone to the beach with the kids." Domenico moved closer to his wife.

Maddalena shook her head. No, that was the first place she had looked, obviously.

They headed for the villa.

Luigi Ippolito was not in the house, and the children on the beach had not seen him.

An immediate search was organised. The carabinieri maresciallo tried to sound encouraging, but murmured that of course anything was possible: the child could have gone somewhere on his own initiative, or someone might have forced him to go.

"You mean been kidnapped?" Domenico asked.

Maddalena widened her eyes as if suddenly realising how

simple the answer to what had seemed an infinitely complex question can be.

"Unfortunately that possiblity can't be excluded," the maresciallo admitted. By now it was four hours since the child had last been seen.

HOW HE REACHED THE PLACE WHERE HE FOUND HIMSELF, Luigi Ippolito would never know. But he could imagine that the way he felt must in some way relate to the fact that he had never felt pity for as long as he could remember. He believed that everything that he was, and everything he would ever become, must derive from that absolute fact. Luigi Ippolito Giuseppe had always and absolutely despised compassion. Compassion for his parents, but for himself too. Beyond that there was little to say: he cultivated doubt and thrashed about – without letting it be seen – in the mud of his own obsessions. For example, his obsession with kindness, and with the idea that ultimately this could benefit the person who exercised it more than the person who was the object of it. Wasn't kindness perhaps nothing more than a form of pride? If it had been normal, why would they have invented the Saints? Who anyway were merely professionals or champions, people so proud in the exercise of their altruism as to be able to annul themselves, and thus raise themselves through altars to the height of the heavens. They said any such person would become a Saint.

He looked around. The place where he was was unfamiliar to him. A tangle of bush and broom. He had been crouching under a shrub growing from a granite base and still giving off heat, since with the coming of darkness the air had grown only a little cooler. He knew people were looking for him, but that was of no interest: if he was to become a Saint he must learn not to feel compassion, accepting the fact that his mother was distressed and his father annoyed; in fact he understood everything perfectly.

He walked for a couple of hours before stopping when he found the shelter. He would not have been able to say why he had chosen it; he only knew that when he started walking the voices from the villa gradually faded. He began to feel euphoric, and the better he felt, the further he wanted to walk . . .

But now he was tired. He could hear that someone was calling to him from far away, but he was too tired to answer . . .

The setting sun and the increasingly feverish activity all around Maddalena put her into a strange state of trance. She sat down in a corner among the majolica tiles in the well-fitted kitchen of her house by the sea, and from there watched people fussing about, but though she was aware of their general appearance, she had no sense of whether they were officials in uniform or not.

When one man in uniform did come up to ask her something, she merely stared at him. The man accepted this and moved away.

"She's in shock," he said. "Signora, can you hear me?"

Maddalena could hear him, but understood in some way not to hear him. The man shook her a little, as if to restore something that had come adrift inside her. An elegant and highly perfumed lady came up to her.

"Maddalena, darling . . ." she murmured in the tone of one mother emoting in sympathy with the pain of another. "Everything will come right, you'll see," she said, "but we have to go now." She lightly touched Maddalena's head with a sunburnt hand heavy with rings, her wrist jangling with bracelets.

Domenico, outside with the others, was "searching every inch" of his territory. He was not so much worried as irritated; this melodramatic culmination to what had otherwise been a perfect day annoyed him intensely. It reminded him too much of the curse he so often laboured under, which made him sweat over things that came easily to other people. As now for example: what harm could there be in his celebrating his seaside house? Why could the day not end as happily as it had begun? All these were questions with answers that were only too familiar to him, but which nonetheless continued to hammer away in his head. He was particularly annoyed with his son because, it was increasingly clear, the only reason that creature had come into the world was to destroy his father's peace of mind.

"Cursed creature, why inflict this on me?" he muttered to himself, "you are utterly without compassion."

The suspense was driving Nevina mad; she was used to hiding her feelings, but this was becoming increasingly difficult as she wandered round the house, cleaning hysterically. Nonno Peppino had immediately joined the group searching for the child but they had discouraged Nevina from coming with them.

Meanwhile night fell.

THE SECRET WAS TO GRASP THINGS AT THE VERY MOMENT they happened. The darkness, which had so suddenly become total, fell on Luigi Ippolito's narrow shoulders. He could hear voices and see lights, but even though he knew he was walking forward into glaring light out in the open air, no-one seemed to see him. He almost believed he must have become invisible.

Turning towards the house, he crossed a line of men who remained unaware of him, with the one who was his father looking angry. If only for this reason, the boy did not dare draw attention to himself, but kept out of their way among the bushes. As he came nearer to the house, he could see his mother in the distance looking out from the terrace into nothingness, but when he tried to attract her attention, it was again without success.

He felt no pity. Something that could make him a Saint. School had brought him an agony of glances and words. He hated it when anyone looked at him or spoke to him. He had understood the precise harmony of absence and had cultivated it, until life grabbed him and catapulted him into a world full of others of his own age with whom he had nothing in common, but to whom everyone expected him to relate. This is hell, he told himself. The words of the catechism were nothing. Mere theatre. To him, hell seemed the impossibility of being isolated.

At home, each day was longer than the one before, with his mother asking him why he never spoke, and his father staring resentfully at him because he was so clearly not the son he had hoped for.

Though he did have occasional moments of illumination, as once when Maddalena in exasperation asked him, "Why are you like this?"

Then he heard himself answer, "Because I am a child."

This answer apparently hit the mark, since his mother immediately relaxed into a sort of loving, even if rather exaggerated, reaction, and agreed that yes, indeed he was a child, he was her child.

He would be able to tell her that he had decided to be a Saint. Perhaps his mother might be the only person in the entire universe who could understand perfectly that this might be a legitimate aspiration for him, and that like all aspirations, it would require an act of faith on his part. Plus the consciousness he possessed of precise suffering. Luigi Ippolito understood this consciousness was the biggest obstacle he had to overcome. And he knew it would require an act of force, like a wrench that though at first it might cause unspeakable agony, in time would prevent other and even more painful agonies. Yes, that was the point: he must never feel pity, not even when face to face with God.

Anyway, what pity had God ever felt for him in abandoning him to the delirium within himself? When He had transfixed him through and through before he was even born with the unbelievably sharp blade of constant unrest? When, in striking him, He had proclaimed, "You will never find peace," assuring him he would remain for ever sleepless and alone. And what pity had God granted him even now, at this present moment, while creating a sky to drive him mad and everywhere stunning him with the scent of thorny broom? It never spared him, it never let up, that grip round his stomach. What pity had he ever felt when suddenly – though he realised it had in fact happened gradually – he had found himself in the midst of a whirlwind like those described in the hagiographies, when the divine manifests itself?

Try to imagine a shapeless soul wandering about on a sunny September afternoon, with no weapon with which to confront the beautiful light except its own weakness. This was a sky in a million, because if the world had been turned on its head, it would have been an infinite universe of nothingness. He could see a bushy tree, like an old man with arms outspread, straight from the usual rhetoric of nature and nature's power. And, scarcely needing the fact to be mentioned at all, invisible but deafeningly loud cicadas. And then there was the sea, a real mirror for reflection. An extremely sensitive surface, intensified by the fire of excess in which rays of the sun insinuated themselves into empty spaces between the clouds. God was presenting Himself to Luigi Ippolito in the most commonplace iconography imaginable. And he himself, this also as in the tritest of hagiographies, felt himself at a loss. He was nearly nine years old now, and already knew there was no escape for him.

This was not happiness. The time would come when he would defy anyone not to believe that such revelations brought peace, though in fact what they brought was war. And violence. At the heart of his ecstasy, when he believed he had joined the company of those who have a precocious understanding of their vocation, doubt still flourished. Because, as the parish canon pointed out,

291

although repudiated by God, Lucifer had still not been able to bring himself to keep away from God.

Luigi Ippolito felt a pain in his chest, a minor yet agonising pain. The sort of pain that finds no way to express itself fully but wanders in the antechambers of our personality, like a troublesome intruder whose presence we refuse to accept.

He could have described this with equal accuracy as a benediction or a malediction, because though inconstant it was precise, just as shadows become precisely either short or long depending on the time of day.

It was September now, and there was the countryside, and the sky, and that majestic tree . . . what disgrace. And that strange feeling of being unwell . . .

The searchers, carabinieri and local people were called off towards three at night; by which time the lost child had mysteriously returned home alone. No-one could discover exactly what had happened because the object of their concern, a young boy, refused to speak to them.

Several weeks more passed before matters came to a head.

It would be his ninth birthday in four days' time, and school had started well. Luigi Ippolito seemed calmer and more at ease than before. He was playing football on the little sports ground near the house and everything seemed perfect. He felt well; the pain had left him, apparently no more than an illusion.

He dribbled the ball past two opponents and faced the goal, feebly defended by the weakest and fattest of the opposing players. Luigi Ippolito was about to kick the ball into the top angle of the goal, exactly where he knew the goalkeeper could never reach it. He was shrouded by the pneumatic void that enwraps every hero before his great deed.

He waited, though he had little time to adjust the ball before kicking it into the corner where he had so precisely planned to put it, in the way that any champion would. He knew that to be a champion you must play within your limitations, and rid yourself of everything superfluous.

Giving a little jump, he advanced on the ball with the grace of a young dancer. The boy in the goal looked as if begging for pity, but what pity can a hero feel if an important part of his destiny is never to feel pity? So no pity. Luigi Ippolito's instep was about to give the ball a delicate touch to impart the unstoppable curve he had planned.

As he jumped, he fell backwards to the ground, almost as if swept aside by a gigantic hand to prevent him kicking the ball, or an axe strong enough to slice a concrete wall in two had smashed into his chest.

Opening his eyes, he found himself lying on the ground with others bending over him, including the fat goalkeeper. Above their heads the sky was indescribable, and above the sky was a kind of certainty.

He sat up and said it was nothing, he had just missed a breath and his eyes had clouded over, but he was fine and they mustn't worry.

He headed home alone, a distance of a mere two hundred metres. Leaving the little sports ground he took a few steps, then stopped and waited.

He looked up and everything was resolved. The pain had gone, and so had his distress. All that remained was the certainty. He started walking again, unexpectedly euphoric.

Coming into the house, he sat down at table as usual. It must have been a really special day, because even his father Domenico was sitting at table with them. So it seemed a good moment to speak.

"I'm going to be a priest," he said firmly.

That stopped Domenico in his tracks. "*A paragulas maccas uricras surdas*" ("Stupid words deserve deaf ears"), he exclaimed in Sard to cover his surprise, half-smiling with incredulity. "A priest? We've never had any priests in this house!" He stared at the boy, torn between disbelief and pity.

Luigi Ippolito smiled back. He was learning how to deal with such reactions.

So when Domenico bared his breast before saying another word, the boy gave him a guarded gaze as if he were himself the Almighty Creator; instead of backing off, Luigi Ippolito waited for his father to speak. He was the only son, his father reminded him, was he determined to bury a promising future in such a sterile present?

"You are pitiless," Domenico told him.

But the child held his head high, not even searching for complicity in his mother's face. Nor did he back down before his father's anger. He realised he would never be able to prevent this sort of revelation to which he could give no name, but which had a precise physical consistency somewhere between his stomach and his chest. Languorous and painful, yet nonetheless pleasurable and tremendous.

*

When he had fallen to the ground that day, it must have come to him that there can be no such things as a minor pain. Because – and this was clear – God demands exactly the same strength from us whether we are fighting a louse or an elephant; two such creatures may have different dimensions, but their power of resistance is the same.

So when Luigi Ippolito had hit the ground and smelled the bitterly acid peat of the football field, he had come to realise that there is no such thing as slight damage – there is just damage.

IN THE YEARS THAT FOLLOWED, LUIGI IPPOLITO SOMETIMES wished he could go back on what he had said that day at table. But he had never anticipated any sort of compromise. At the seminary there was no time for second thoughts, at least not for anyone who had committed himself to the extent that he had. Someone without pity, someone who had never intended to go back, someone who had armed himself against the Evil of the world.

Armour-plated, yet at the same time a human being of flesh and blood in all the pride of puberty, he was ready to accept pain in exchange for renunciation, as though forced to fast while tormented by biting hunger. That was his body, tormented by appetites he must not satisfy. Tempted by his eyes and by his dreams, snared by physiology. He understood there was nothing he could do about it because he had had no voice in the construction of the machine, so that he could not beg for no moderation or respite from this genetic fury. Having a body in a state of transformation while himself unable to take any part in that transformation, almost unable even to touch that body, was already in itself a proof of sanctity, because without despising God Himself, he was in no position to criticise the circumstances in which God had placed him in the world. But it was impossible to love his flesh with a love greater than the love felt by the God who had created it and loved it. God had not foreseen any compromise in that sense, so Luigi Ippolito Giuseppe Guiso himself could not foresee any such abdication either.

As he felt himself growing physically, he needed to exercise this antagonism bravely. Against his own body, certainly. But also against the evidence of a universe unquestionably secularised though it proclaimed itself to be partisan. He felt as angry as a mastiff puppy on a lead, a dog too canny ever to be profoundly faithful. He had been sure of this ever since that afternoon when he had crashed to the ground at the very moment when deceived by the illusion that he was fully in control of his life.

He had cultivated a mad passion for stories of blind spirituality, stories of martyrs embracing their executioner, smiling at instruments of torture, and begging for suffering. He had convinced himself that this was the only way to live. To have a sense that though the body was soft, destructible and mortal, it was at the same time impalpable, compact, irreducible, incapable of pity or adjustment, and ready to fight. Ultimately restless.

He had never prayed for himself, but had knelt before the image of a heart, more swollen than the real thing, red and throbbing like a fruit reaching the acme of ripeness in the last moment before it breaks from the branch, falls and lands on the hard surface of reality. Like some dark figs on the branches of city trees, that split open to expose their flesh to birds, insects and grubs, before being recalled by gravity to smash to a pulp against cement or asphalt. That was what he imagined it would be like to be martyred, to be like ripe flesh incongruously striking hard earth.

He had learned to adore certain crowns of thorns that

resembled infancy more closely than he was able to understand. Like brambles, where the best and largest blackberries are out of reach, unless you offer your hands and arms to be scratched. That was exactly how he imagined dedication to be, having blind faith in a reward that would compensate for pain. He had indeed prayed for the agonies of others: of his father, of his vulnerable and tentative grandmother Nevina, and of his mother, who did not understand to what extent giving birth to a Saint might be a privilege or a curse. He had prayed for everyone apart from himself.

And although he was now on the painful path to priesthood, he was still attracted to vestments and the rough fibre of hair shirts, in the way of simple-minded people, and of those who are incapable of imagining a complex universe but nonetheless have some grasp of the general idea of complexity. He understood and at the same time did not understand. That was the fact of the matter and had been from the start, ever since he had first become aware of his ability to provide answers that he had never consciously worked out for himself.

Luigi Ippolito's vocation was a feverish vocation, a feverish and ferocious sickness.

THE IMAGES OF THE CROWD KNOCKING DOWN THE BERLIN
Wall spoke for themselves. It was clear now that the world was
entering unknown territory. And those concrete barriers so pathetically caving in conveyed the idea of whole swathes of what could
be defined as History crumbling under the weight of an unforeseen
change of heart.

For a long time now Maddalena had wanted nothing to do
with History. Her life had been stranded on a sandbank, precise
and predictable and leading nowhere. Everything on television
interested her like a documentary about life on an unknown
planet. She had played her cards and, as far as she could see,
had lost, tied to the wrong husband and, still worse, to the
wrong son.

Since he had begun to attend the seminary, Luigi Ippolito
Giuseppe had grown ever more distant from her, which made
her feel more alone than anything else in the world. More than her
absent husband, who dabbled unproductively in business, always
one step from the edge of the cliff, deluding himself that it was
enough to make others rich to become rich oneself.

There could be no question that Domenico's business affairs
were going badly, even extremely badly. He was able to maintain

a degree of wealth, but had also gained the reputation of being a braggart. Even so, he must have had a guardian saint in paradise, because every time he seemed on the brink of bankruptcy, some mysterious associate on the mainland that he often referred to – but whose actual existence no-one could prove – rescued him from his problems.

If they had asked Maddalena Pes what kind of a man she had married, she would have said a good man, though she was not sure she knew him very well. And in fact, though they had now been married ten years, there had never been any real intimacy between Maddalena and Domenico.

Nevertheless, as the television ushered in the new age, with crowds knocking down the wall that had divided East from West Berlin, she felt emotionally involved for the first time.

Luigi Ippolito Giuseppe was doing so well in his studies that he had been approached by an observer from the Young Persons' Pastoral Vocational Organisation, and decided to accept an invitation to move to a junior seminary in Rome.

These were difficult days. A young priest called Padre Filippo Tomei arrived at the Guiso home to discuss the matter with Domenico and Maddalena.

"There can be no question that Luigi Ippolito has a vocation," Padre Filippo said.

Domenico looked at him without opening his mouth.

Maddalena seemed to want to think over the priest's words despite the simple clarity of what he had said. "But he's still a child," she eventually managed to say.

Padre Filippo grimaced. "Of course," he began. "But that does not prove he may not have a genuine vocation . . . many children are not taken seriously when they show an interest of this kind, but I have had long experience in the Young Persons' Pastoral Organisation, and I can assure you that I have many colleagues who first felt their vocation when they were children and whose vocations went on to prove valid and stable."

"What is there to stop him entering the seminary in Núoro?" Domenico asked, disinclined to embark on a devotional discussion.

"Nothing, nothing at all," the priest said quickly. "It's just that the house in Rome could offer him more . . . – " he searched for the word – "opportunity. And with a vocation like Luigi Ippolito's, nothing would be better than to give it every possible chance to develop."

"But he would be so far away," Maddalena sobbed.

"He would be studying with the best teachers, and enjoying sport and the company of other equally talented boys."

"Talented," Domenico repeated. "What sort of talent?"

"The talent of those who have answered Christ's call. Look, I've spoken to him many times over the last month. The boy has particularly attracted the attention of Don Pirodda . . ."

"Yes, yes," Maddalena intervened rather nervously. "So he has told us . . ."

"And he has also told us that you would look after his education and care," Domenico added firmly.

"Exactly," the priest confirmed.

"But have you, Father, really succeeded in talking to us? Why do you tell us so little?"

Father Filippo took time to find the right words. "Luigi Ippolito and I have prayed many rosaries together, and that has brought us closer. The boy is absolutely constant in his vocation, there can be no doubt about that."

Luigi Ippolito's meeting with Father Tomei had taken place about a month earlier in the seminary chapel. Don Pirodda had pointed out Luigi Ippolito praying by himself in a secluded pew. Padre Tomei had gone over to him. "So here we are," he had said, as if he had arrived early for an appointment and wanted that noted.

Luigi Ippolito had looked at him diffidently, but since this was a priest he nodded and returned to his prayers.

"You know," Padre Tomei had continued, "I'm certain you and I haven't met simply by chance. I'm sitting beside you now, and I'm sure that can't be an accident, what do you think?" Luigi Ippolito did not turn to look at the priest, or answer him.

Padre Tomei gave the hint of a smile. "Perhaps it's Providence. Perhaps Our Lord and the Virgin Mary have arranged for you to be exactly where you are at this moment, and have deliberately placed me by your side. What do you say to that?"

"I say it's possible we may be calling providence what other people may describe as an accident."

Padre Tomei could not help laughing, and decided to tease Luigi Ippolito . . . "What 'other people' do you mean?"

"People like you and me," the boy answered calmly.

"Yes. I agree it could be put like that," the priest conceded. "But people like you and me know that it's not the same thing, don't we?"

"They should do."

"Then we agree our meeting has been no accident," the priest went on. "And that not every thought that Our Lord inspires in us is necessarily a random one." Seeing that the young man made no response to this, Tomei continued. "I'm here to suggest a plan to you, to give a concrete response to your questions . . . "

"But not to answer them," the boy added.

Padre Tomei looked as if he had not understood what the boy was saying.

"'A concrete response', but not answers," Luigi Ippolito repeated, as if to imply that they again had a choice of meanings.

"No, not answers, I have no answers," the priest had to admit. "Let's just say the rosary together, shall we?"

The boy agreed that would be fine.

From then on the relationship between the two had grown ever closer, reaching a form of closeness that was utterly chaste and respectful. Day after day, Luigi Ippolito felt he could talk with this man in a way he had never been able to talk with anyone else before. It was a strange feeling, searching for words to describe his own thoughts, and finding someone else willing to listen to his words.

One afternoon, when it was raining outside – it is important to remember that it was raining outside because this was an extraordinary moment that would remain firmly fixed in Luigi Ippolito's memory – it was November 11, the feast of St Martin of Tours, and the Entrance Antiphon involved I Samuel 2:35: "And I will raise me up a faithful priest, that shall do according to that which is in mine heart and in my mind".

Father Tomei had sent for him while he was changing his clothes after serving at Mass. Luigi Ippolito knew what the priest was about to say, but nonetheless felt confused. He did not want to doubt, but could not help doubting. So he presented himself at the appointed time with an anxious expression on his face.

"First I want to thank you," his spiritual father began, "because in all the years during which I have worked in this field, and in which the Lord has granted me the opportunity of getting to know souls like yours . . ."

Luigi Ippolito blushed violently. He had the impression that this man knew things about him he did not know himself. His experience certainly must have given him the ability to recognise the incontrovertible signs of vocation, when even the person receiving the vocation does not clearly understand it.

"Now I have a question for you: do you want to say yes or no to Our Lord?" Padre Tomei continued.

Luigi Ippolito felt like an athlete about to make a jump: should he think carefully or answer instinctively?

"If the Lord wants me, let Him take me," he said softly, but firmly.

Father Tomei embraced him: "I don't know if it's permissible for anyone to be at the same time so happy and so close to God."

ON THE MORNING OF JANUARY 4, 1994, JUST BEFORE THE end of the school holidays, Luigi Ippolito Giuseppe Guiso of the parish of Nostra Signora delle Grazie in Núoro left home to enter the Junior Seminary Sangue di Cristo in Rome.

It was an extremely cold morning. Maddalena was looking at the straight shoulders of this son who was about to leave her for ever. She had not noticed him growing so tall, and just as one suddenly becomes aware that one's hair has grown longer, she realised her little boy was now a youth, and that his cheeks were shaded by a light chestnut down that resembled her own.

The previous evening he had insisted on packing his bags himself, and had firmly refused all offers of help from both his mother and his endlessly tearful grandmother Nevina. He understood the reason for this crying. He told himself it was right to shed tears for a love that would inevitably grow more distant, although he was glad to be going where he had decided to go and where he knew he would be happy. He had started playing football again. He had prayed to meet The Lord in an appropriate fashion. And he had been studying . . .

His luggage, consisting of a suitcase and a single large bag, was waiting in the hall. Maddalena, Nevina and Luigi Ippolito dined together in silence. Domenico had gone out that afternoon, and had not returned by eight in the evening. The whole day had seen a coming and going of friends and relatives, and several seminary companions had come to say goodbye.

The days before, on the other hand, had seen a real ordeal. The arguments between Domenico and Maddalena had reached new levels, the mood in the house increasingly acrimonious. Domenico complained that whoever these people from the Youth Pastoral Organisation might be, they were clearly not interested in his son because he was special, but only because his family was well off. This idea infuriated Maddalena who, like most mothers, did think of her child as special. She was sure Domenico was mistaken: Luigi Ippolito stood out because of his exceptional seriousness and conviction. But her husband shook his head with the sceptical, cynical and resentful expression so characteristic of him, dismissing the whole subject as a matter not worth discussing. Maddalena began to wonder whether she herself had been partly responsible for Domenico becoming like this. But she did not press her case; knowing well that arguing would be a waste of time, because once Domenico was convinced of anything there was never any way of making him change his mind.

All the same, her anxiety was not without foundation. Now that the old systems had crumbled before a new world full of hollow statements, Domenico understood that the former time of established rules (which admittedly had never existed for him anyway) had definitely passed away, and they were now clearly entering the golden age of the devious.

Two years earlier, mayor Sini had been arrested for embezzlement during the Mani Pulite or "Clean Hands" investigation, which had extended even to this remote corner of the world. But now, more brazen than ever, Sini was once more standing for election, this time for a new party no-one had ever heard of that favoured wearing ties and double-breasted suits. Meanwhile Luigi Ippolito was leaving for Rome, which meant he would soon be beyond the control of those still in Núoro.

This was what Domenico was blaming Maddalena for but she did not understand, because she herself had profited during those years without ever asking herself how this advantage had come about. She conceded that Domenico was right, though it would have been enough for him to acknowledge his wife in public without ever feeling any sense of duty towards her. So that was where their arguments ended, since neither of them had any interest in taking things beyond a point of no return.

But on that particular January 4, the feast of Saint Ermete, all Maddalena had to do was go near the windows for her teeth to begin chattering. She had left the heating on all night because she knew Luigi Ippolito always woke up feeling cold.

She had risen in a hurry the moment she heard him moving about in his room. Even though it was so early she found him sitting on his bed fully dressed. She stood in the door gazing at him, trying to memorise every smallest detail of his appearance. No-one would ever have described him as a happy child because he was a fighter, one who could never accept anything as settled. One might have thought him contentious, but he was not really that. It was just that he had a particular way of looking at the world that did not make his relations with other people easier. Her son had always walked alone, Maddalena told herself.

Even now, despite having heard her approach and seeing her standing there at his door, he gave no sign of acknowledging her presence. This hurt her and reminded her of how difficult it had been to get him to take her milk when, newborn, he refused her breast from the start, and how she had always felt she was invading his privacy every time she tried to exercise any authority over him as a mother.

Domenico had come home very late and rather drunk, and had not even got out of bed that morning. Luigi Ippolito glanced into his room five minutes before leaving, as if dutifully waving goodbye to a stranger.

His father peeked out from under the bedclothes, opened sleepy eyes and breathed, "God be with you."

Luigi Ippolito said yes, that was exactly what he wished for, but added nothing more.

Maddalena waited outside the room with his scarf, gloves, woollen cap and warm coat. She had repeatedly checked that the boy had packed all the new linen she had bought for him, and made him coffee with mocha, the smell of which invaded the hall, now scene of a long-drawn-out but feverish farewell between mother and son.

"I'll write," Luigi Ippolito promised.

She, fearing this promise might have to bridge an infinite distance, said, "But phone me too."

He agreed to do that and buttoned up his heavy coat, allowing his mother to adjust the scarf round his neck.

The roar of a car engine broke the frigid silence of the dawn.

"They're here," Luigi Ippolito said. "Don't come out or you'll catch cold."

She hugged him very tight, knowing it was her last chance of real contact.

He let himself be hugged, but with a certain embarrassment at her eagerness. "They're waiting for me," he cut in and pulled away. Then picking up his suitcase and bag, he went out.

Maddalena mimed a step towards him, but those shoulders so suddenly transformed into the shoulders of a man surprised her again. So she stayed exactly where her son had wanted her to stay, aware the closing door was taking him away from her for ever.

When she heard the car start, she went back to the kitchen, poured herself more coffee with a lot of sugar, and gazed at the crystal world beyond the window as she drank it . The wonder with which even pain could be expressed was a mystery she could never come to terms with. Luigi Ippolito has abandoned me, she thought. And the winter outside was a triumph of lace and rock-crystal, the garden a display of blown glass and diamonds. Precious yet inaccessible. Terrible yet incredibly fragile. How could this be possible?

She held back her tears even though no-one could see her, and indeed, Domenico was not there. But that was simply how it was and how it would continue to be. She could see the pitiless balance of her life. She had decided to put her faith in security, and had got it wrong. And she told herself, not by way of consolation, that she would have got it wrong anyway. So she decided that, after all, this was the moment to begin crying.

She looked once more at the pale light beyond the window, noticing the glass transparency veer towards violet and, at certain angles, even towards the full colours of the rainbow. This world had the static quality of a staged photograph, unless that was no more than her mind struggling to make sense of her life. She was surprised when tears ran down her cheeks, as though she were a statue, to whom the ability to cry had been granted in some utterly miraculous way.

Wiping her eyes with the back of her hand, she went into Luigi Ippolito's room. His bed was still impregnated with his smell. There were a few garments on the chair: a pair of jeans, a printed sweater, and a torn vest. And a couple of pairs of shapeless shoes.

She picked the jeans up to put them away and noticed something in the pocket. A folded sheet of paper. A letter.

Mamma,

I have seen clearly how this gift has developed in me, and I have come to understand that if nothing satisfied me before, it was only because I had not been aware of my goal.

I shall be fine now because this is what I want. I found myself at a crossroads and made an instinctive decision. Then I suddenly felt completely at ease in a way I never had before. I do not know how far you have understood my choice, but I assure you I have done this for myself, and not as an attack on you or Babbo. I know he has taken it particularly badly, but I hope that with the help of Our Lord in time he will come to understand.

I always knew the Lord would call me . . .

L. I. G.

PART III
Later

January 1999

THE NOSE OF THE AIRCRAFT RIPPED INTO THE COMPACT
quilt of clouds with a loud short shock. A metallic-sounding
electronic bell introduced another announcement. The carefully
modulated voice of a stewardess begged to inform passengers
that preparations for landing had begun and they would arrive in
no more than a quarter of an hour. This was, of course, not the
personal opinion of the speaker, since she spoke with the authority
of the commander, Captain Nostromo, a name that to any literary
or superstitious passengers might suggest splashing down on
water rather than wheels on a runway. Speaking, like the Archangel
Gabriel, with the voice of God, the stewardess requested everyone
to fasten their seat belt, to raise their seat to its upright position,
and to close their table.

Meanwhile, like a massive polar bear lifting its head above the
ice, the plane allowed a glimpse of *terra firma* lapped by sea. This
was a merely chromatic event: dark red, brown, and bottle green
against a watery and gelatinous greenish blue that shaded into
Prussian blue.

The earth had a variety entirely of its own, a sort of genetic
incapacity to be uniform, while the sea stubbornly drew together
its own various elements, calm or rippled, though appearing

313

homologous and solemn in its feverish consistency. In contrast, the land expressed motion in its immobility, and variety in its solidity. Which goes a long way to explaining why qualities often seem to be what they are not, when seen from an unexpected angle.

This is how birds and reptiles are always able to grasp reality, each with its own specific relativity. So that a clump of grass seen close up will seem enormous, while from far enough away it will be merely the infinitesimal fraction of a chromatic mixture, rendering both views equally relative and partial. Eagles do not have better eyesight than snakes: they just see differently.

The metallic bell that had introduced the announcer also woke the passenger in window seat E in row 6 of the McDonnell Douglas MD-82, as it descended in its Meridiana Airways livery towards the Costa Smeralda airport at Olbia. This was the last leg of a journey that had taken him from Riga in Latvia via Rome Fiumicino to this point, and if the announcement could be trusted, in fifteen minutes he would be in Sardinia.

A passing stewardess reminded him to raise the back of his seat to an upright position. The man smiled as he did so. He was about forty years old, his hair a very light brown, almost fair. He was dressed in very new Italian clothes, though his modest if rather shabby golden beard merely made his jaw look unclean. But this apparent carelessness, so far from detracting from his appearance, made him seem all the more elegant. He was one of those men whose appearance has something otherworldly about it, as if they are visitants from another world. Yet his expression also conveyed that he was at home anywhere he chose to belong.

Was he coming to Sardinia on holiday? the stewardess asked him in careful English, despite the fact that it was January and she knew the holiday season on the island extended at most from June to September.

"Business," the man muttered, mispronouncing the English consonants.

The stewardess raised artificial eyebrows. "You speak English so well," she began untruthfully.

"Oh no," he mocked her.

The plane hit a gust of wind and regular passengers told each other that this must be a premature surge of the *maestrale*. As if the island were a grumpy old woman who had little time for foreigners even though she was forced to accept them.

The plane touched down with a bump, and the Archangel Gabriel reported that they had landed on time, that the outside temperature was 7 degrees Celsius, and that Captain Nostromo thanked everyone for having chosen to fly with them (meaning the firm that had chartered the flight).

The stewardess watched the man she had just spoken to make his way out down the flimsy retractable steps.

The wind hissed and filled the man's lungs with an indescribable aroma, making him feel dizzy and worrying him, because it seemed not so much the embrace of a stranger, as the reaffirmation of some ancient affection, like the familiar litter-tray of a cat impatient to bury its faeces. The combination of wind, vegetation and saltiness seemed natural . . . suggesting to the visitor an adversary squeezing his opponent's waist to stop him breathing, like a picture he had once seen, of a statue of wrestlers by Michelangelo in which one man was standing and trying to twist his body out of the grip of another who was holding his legs; when even though one man was contorted, the other seemed in no way ready to admit defeat. This was the physical effect this place had on the arriving passenger: a dream of shrubs and evergreen leaves as thick as hide and correspondingly fragrant, but also the breathing of a lethargic earth, as solid as a fired pot and just as fragile. Like tormented crêpe, the earth was exhaling a smoky breath of January chill, as if confronting the night of time in a distant past when granite had not yet solidified from having been a mass of incandescence. Like when the tongue of his white dog Tatra licked his lips and neck, as if to make sure of being recognised. And like everything he could imagine beneath the frothy blanket of snow covering the hill an hour's walk from the farm where he lived. He remembered that feeling perfectly; it was like home to him.

"Excuse me, may I push past?" The speaker was a man standing behind him at the entrance to the airport building.

"Of course, please excuse me," he answered, letting the other through.

When they met again shortly afterwards in the luggage retrieval area, he gave the other a slight nod. At the exit, since he had not come from the European Union, he had to go through Customs. He presented his passport.

"Krievs Oskar," the duty official read.

The man responded with a minimal movement of his head.

"Riga, September 4, 1960," the official continued.

"Yes."

Outside, beyond the sliding door marked "arrivals", someone was holding up a sheet of paper with his name written on it. Oscar Krievs came to a halt in front of him: he was the taller of the two by a good twenty centimetres. The other realised this must be the passenger he was waiting for. Making an awkward gesture with his hand as if in greeting, the smaller man led the taller out to the car that was to take him to his destination.

They were not more than ten minutes into their journey when the little man behind the wheel started asking questions as if to ensure that everything was as it should be for this clearly important passenger. Was it too cold in the car? Would he like to stop for something to eat? Oskar answered no to each question. The driver said no more.

In the white season he had fallen in love with the emptiness, but now a major invasion was pressing in on him from beyond the shaded windows of the car which, having left the coast, was beginning to penetrate the living flesh of the island, like a huge whale accepting that a minute but ferocious parasite was determined to walk over its body.

Oskar closed his eyes, trying to recapture the icy silence of his *ciems*, or home, with its red roof, and the snow-covered field that led his eye to the loop of the river, in the sharp air of autumn mornings pressing on his chest like a lament punctuated by the squeak of his dog's paws on fresh snow.

The gloom of the present January afternoon reminded him of his own well-remembered black season. When he had not yet learned that worlds existed in which nothing can suffice to screen the sky. Soft, flattish places, where his gaze could take in immense stretches of grain without being interrupted by the menace of sterile rocks. In his black season Oskar had learned to distrust the earth and the men who lived on it, soon exposing every cautious theory of survival. He had lived in constant anticipation of being ambushed, as is always the danger in a land full of gorges and ravines. Then, born again in his white season, he had learned to accept the burden of amplitude, to the point of having to admit he must adjust a long view of expanding time to his new self and the attitude to waiting that this involved.

You could not dismiss Oskar as a man happy to sit on the fence, or one who loved long periods of waiting for the white hare to decide to emerge from its underground burrow. But after returning three or four times with his game-bag empty when everyone else had managed to hunt successfully, he had been forced to learn. To learn everything. For example, that if he wanted to bring home a bag full of game, he must be prepared to be patient enough to wait for the right moment. And now another right moment had finally arrived.

"Please stop here," he unexpectedly ordered the driver, speaking without any foreign accent or unfamiliar rhythm, so that the man behind the wheel was afraid for a moment that the passenger behind him must have mysteriously changed into someone else. But, ignoring the fact that the road was deserted, he made the appropriate signal, braked and pulled over.

They were in a sort of no-man's-land just after the fork to Lula, a place where the disordered structure of false level areas and walls of rock still suggested a time for illusions, permitting one to imagine new opportunities. If one turned one's back on the west with its prominent mountain slopes, one could see the east open on a sort of descent to the sea teeming with plots of land that had been torn from the granite.

Oskar got out of the car and crossed the road to the barrier between the lanes. In that limpid, swooning afternoon, nothing gave any real sign of life: not a single car, nor leaves moving in the wind, nor birds flying through the air. Only the imposing aroma of the primordial mixture that, an infinity of ages earlier, had gone to make up that land, as though it had been built on a foundation of mortar.

This was how the black season could penetrate his nostrils and reach through his nostrils to his stomach, and through his stomach to his groin. Oskar closed his eyes and and had a precise déjà-vu, something he had pushed aside but which now returned, over-bearing and unavoidable. Shedding a few tears, he swallowed odours and regrets.

Meanwhile the driver had taken advantage of the break to smoke a cigarette, leaning on the warm bonnet of his car. When he saw Oskar coming back he threw away his cigarette and hurried to open the car door.

"We're nearly there now," he said, suddenly feeling a need to reassure this strange but surprisingly emotional passenger.

"I know, I know," Oskar answered, getting back into the car.

They entered Núoro from the slope where the new hospital had been built. It was not yet four in the afternoon but already begin-ning to get dark. The last few kilometres had been uphill, as if there was really no way of avoiding the clump of houses between the hills. A nest of greedy people, like land pitilessly palmed off on younger sons in the kingdoms of ancient times, inaccessible and sterile. They went over the crossroads, known as the "station cross-ing" despite the fact that Núoro had never had a proper railway station, only a terminus with two narrow-gauge tracks. Then they climbed towards via Trieste, a high, winding arterial road not far from, in fact very near to, the via Deffenu slope, and went on without Oskar even looking out of the window on that side. From piazza Italia they rose to the top of via Ballero, next to the entrance to the cemetery, which was certainly a monument with all the trimmings, almost as if the only way to be accepted in that city was to have oneself buried there. The cemetery had converted this provincial capital into a metropolis. But Oskar's fixed stare ignored that too. Then they entered via della Solitudine, leaving on the right the church of the same name, which had once been countryside, and tackled the hairpin curve before Monte Orthobène. For another six kilometres they shook their hips like a belly-dancer through Solotti and Fonte Milianu until, at the summit, they came to the Hotel Ristorante Fratelli Sacchi.

It had been getting colder, though not cold enough to persuade Oskar to add an overcoat over his impeccable clothes. When he got out of the car he looked about: the low white building had been built in a style somewhere between local and Mediterranean, on the edge of a mountain ridge directly facing the plateau and the city. The whole could be reached through a small open space like a terrace, that had been made by filling in a deep hollow. The hotel was linked to its restaurant by a covered veranda intended eventually to be enclosed behind large windows.

A man, solidly built but so timid as to seem diffident, came forward to meet him and introduced himself as the manager of the hotel, adding that everything had been made ready exactly as Oskar had wished.

"I hope you will excuse the room," he explained. "For several years now the hotel has been closed . . . but we have redecorated a fine big room specially for you." Then he looked at Oskar without being able to wipe doubt from his face: what could such a powerful man want in a place like this?

Meanwhile the chauffeur had found a boy from behind the bar to help him carry Oskar's suitcase from the boot of the car to his well-heated room.

Oskar thanked him, and held out a fifty-thousand lire note to the man, who took it a little hesitantly.

Judging by the decor as a whole, they had not restricted themselves to restoring just the one room, but also the whole of the otherwise disused hall and corridor that contained the room. By now it was 11 p.m., or 23:00. Oskar looked at this number as though it had some meaning for him.

In his black season, it would have reminded him of his mother. Was that possible? That a number could remind one of a person? By its form, perhaps, or by its sound. Twenty-three was his mother. He remembered that because he had been with her when she lay dying, and had gazed at the luminous figures on the electronic clock on the bedside table in her hospital room, and this clock had recorded the exact hour of her death. Twenty-three.

He went into his room. It was indeed large, decorated in a simple, mildly rustic manner. Three large windows in the eastern wall looked out over the valley, as far as Baddemanna. The heavy loom-woven curtains had been deliberately left open so that coming into the room the guest could enjoy a stunning view of oaks and ilex trees clothed in frost. This forced him to change the convention he had been subject to for nearly twenty years, which was to describe the first season of his life as "black". Now, and he was absolutely certain of it, that season had been of the same glazed green as these humble trees, little more than dry thorns,

(

would have been, with none of the silver wonder of the birches where he would take Tatra to run. He noticed that, exactly as the manager had said, everything had been prepared as efficiently as possible in his room, and that as the central heating had been turned on in advance, it was comfortably warm.

The hotel, and consequently this room, had been his property for four years now. He ran water into the bath while undressing, but before getting into the bath, he rang hotel reception which also served the restaurant, to ask if everything was ready for the dinner he had ordered for an hour hence. The man answered yes, it was all sorted, he need have no worries.

"WHO'S THIS YOU'RE GOING TO DINNER WITH?" MADDALENA asked, joining Domenico in the bathroom.

He spat out toothpaste. "What do you mean, who is it? The boss." He forced a laugh. "The chairman of the Edilombarda finance company, the people who took on our debt. A Russian." He added in a low voice: "The person who has us on a lead."

"What?"

"Nothing, nothing . . ." Domenico checked to make sure he was properly shaved.

Maddalena shook her head. "A Russian," she repeated.

"The new frontier . . ." Domenico said. "Russians and Chinese. Should I wear a tie?"

"Will it be a formal meal?" she asked. Domenico did not know what to say, so she advised, "Keep a tie in your pocket, then if need be you can put it on at the last minute. But what does this man want?"

"Krievs, that's his name, Oskar Krievs. What should he want? Perhaps he wants to have a look round to see what he's bought. Now that they've opened the international borders . . . I know he's going to meet his Italian colleagues." Domenico felt it important to seem unruffled with his wife even though a wordless disquiet was growing inside him.

Maddalena went ahead into the entrance hall to make sure he took his best coat and the cashmere scarf that made him look like a young man who knew what he was doing. Domenico took a moment longer to find his gloves.

"I don't think this will take very long," he said quietly, giving his wife a kiss between cheek and temple. "See you soon."

Watching him go, Maddalena had a strong feeling she should be protecting him in some way. "Wait a moment," she said.

Domenico stopped on the threshold.

"Aren't you going to take your hat?"

"No," he said. "It messes up my hair." Then he gave her a smile and closed the door.

He knew the restaurant well, but the warmth inside made him unbutton his coat. Two tables were occupied by couples, and a table for six was filled by what looked like a family celebrating some sort of anniversary or promotion. Then, wedged into the furthest corner between the fireplace and the last shutter of the panoramic window, he noticed the back of a sitting man.

Just before he reached the table where Oskar Krievs was waiting for him, the restaurant manager came up to indicate the direction in which he was already heading.

"Sit down," Oscar Krievs said without turning to look at him.

"Yes." Domenico stopped in his tracks as if continuing a conversation in his head, then advanced to the empty seat before him. Then he took off his gloves, coat and scarf and placed them on an empty third chair, before coming forward with his hand outstretched.

Oskar, thin and impeccably dressed with his untidy beard of curly fair hair, turned to greet him.

"Please sit down," Oskar said, looking him intently in the face. Then it suddenly became clear that Domenico was not about to sit down. "So it's you," Domenico said, using the familiar form "tu" and feeling a sort of laugh rising inside him. "So you're not dead after all," he added casually, as if to say, "long time no see".

"Of course I'm not dead," the other man confirmed. "Not in the least."

And so they remained, one standing and the other seated, without adding to what they had just said.

"Have you got a cigarette?" Domenico eventually asked. "And what should I call you?"

"Oh, so you smoke now, do you? Call me what you like," the other said, beckoning the manager.

The man came running to find out what his employer wanted, then rummaged in his jacket pocket for a packet of cigarettes, which he opened and offered to Domenico, who took one, and stuck it between his lips. The manager then produced a plastic lighter decorated with images of footballers.

Domenico, who had not smoked for a long time, sucked in his first breath. "Cristian," he decided. And remained standing.

"Alright, Cristian, then," the other man agreed, showing none of the emotion he might have been expected to feel on hearing his real name for the first time in nearly twenty years. "Shall we order something to eat?"

Domenico shook his head. "Not yet. Let's get a little fresh air first, what do you say?"

*

325

They walked to the car park where Domenico had left his car, and stood contemplating the city lit up below them, which now looked like a muddle finally beginning to fall into shape, while only a few hours earlier, in daylight, the effect had been entirely different.

"I have often asked myself what a Martian arriving here in a space-ship would think of us and of this place," Cristian said, contemplating the bustle of lights.

"He'd say we're mad. All of us. And that this is a place for madmen, you should know that." He dropped his cigarette butt on the ground and extinguished it with his foot.

"Yes, without a doubt."

They went on standing in silence.

"Well, what shall we do, then?" Domenico asked, as if his question had been a direct consequence of their agreement about the madness of Núoro.

"What would you like to do?" Cristian asked calmly.

"I can't think of anything in particular."

It was as if, during the last twenty years, they had already said everything and there was now nothing else left to say. It was a struggle to fill the silence, and here in the dark it was getting colder.

Domenico shivered. "I didn't bring my coat. But I don't think that would help much."

"I quite agree." Cristian started rummaging in the pockets of his jacket. He too was beginning to feel the cold. Finally he found what he had been looking for: a crumpled piece of paper marked with a few brown stains. He handed this to Domenico, who took it, understanding instantly what it must be. He unfolded it, as if determined to drink the bitter draught to the end. It was the document in which he had undertaken to cede his land at Cala Girgolu to

Raimondo Bardi. Seeing his own writing again after such a long time worried him. "Yes, that's how it was," he confirmed, deciding the stains on the paper must be blood. He remembered that this document had cost Raimondo Bardi and Federica Schintu their lives. "Don't forget, I brought up your son," he began, but immediately stopped; what he was saying sounded too much like a speech, when all he had wanted to do was to make a striking revelation.

Cristian continued gazing into the emptiness before him, with its epileptic vibration of lights that represented the city by means of contrast like some medical image seen through fluid. He seemed to have no interest at all in what Domenico had just said about his son. "When they fished me up out of the sea it was a struggle for me to understand that you could have wanted me dead," he said, as if simply stating a fact of no great interest.

Domenico put the paper Cristian had given him into his pocket and opened his arms. "Do you remember the play? 'The hour has come to end the one of us.'"

Many people who lived in the Ciusa Avenue area, piazzetta Aspromonte and Sant'Onofrio, later said they heard a rumble, looked up and saw a flash against the total black of the mountain wall.

Domenico Guiso, a young Núoro businessman, had decided to end his life – like his father before him, after all. Which confirmed a feeling, in this town now become a city, that this was a story that was being endlessly retold. The incinerated remains of the suicide were examined with care, and all those who had had anything to do with him on that fatal evening were interviewed.

Oscar Krievs answered all the questions he was asked, explaining that he had come to Sardinia to sort out some outstanding debts owed by the firm of Guiso and Figlio, despite repeated extensions over several years allowed by the firm's financial backers (among whom he himself was the principal shareholder). Speaking broken Italian, he declared that during their brief conversation he had no reason to believe that Signor Guiso had any intention to end his life. He said he had heard the roaring engine of the car just after he returned to the restaurant. On this point in particular, he was less than truthful. In fact, he had still been in the car park when Domenico, putting the paper into his pocket and pronouncing his last words, had got into his car, started the engine and accelerated towards the edge of the escarpment. The car had then followed a curve through the air before crashing twenty metres further down the hill. A few seconds later, it had burst into flames.

A strictly private funeral was held two days later, to give time, so it was said, for the dead man's only son who was studying to be a priest, to return home from the mainland.

But at Domenico's funeral there was no trace of his son, Luigi Ippolito Giuseppe. Nor did the former notary and mayor Sini, now a member of parliament, put in an appearance.

Maddalena followed the coffin with her relatives and one or two workmen. The poor tormented soul of the dead man had been allowed the benefit of the doubt. The powers that be had concluded that his appalling act had not been deliberate, so much as a failure to come to any decision at all. So he was allowed a quick Mass in the presence of a few curious onlookers, and even a place in the vault where the Chironi and Guiso families rested together.

Cristian had followed the little procession at a distance. Maddalena, dressed in black, seemed a woman from another age, the sort poets once celebrated in sonnets. Her mother Nevina was old now, and Cristian kept his distance, so he could see without being seen.

Yet Maddalena did see him.

To begin with she thought he must be a strange vision generated by the stress of the moment. But then she convinced herself that it all made sense. In any case it was her habit to take facts at face value, without trying to analyse them.

As for Luigi Ippolito, he simply had not wanted to come home for the funeral. She could accept that, and restricted herself to telling anyone who asked after him that the boy was upset, but that he could not be expected to travel such a long way at such short notice. It was not as if he were being held back by just any old employer, she said, implying that the business that had detained her jewel of a son must be considerably more important than the mere death of a father. Even a death of that kind. This was why, people told each other, the parish priest had been able to give the suicide a religious burial. Among themselves, people told each other, priests can sort things out.

Nevertheless, just as they were leaving the church to take the body to the cemetery, Maddalena saw Cristian. For little more than a second, but she did see him. And she had a shock, which others interpreted as a consequence of the dreadful blow the sudden loss of her husband must have caused her.

"Come and sleep with us," Nevina begged her, once the attendants had fastened the bronze clasps to seal the huge slab of marble that closed the vault, "at least for tonight."

"No. I must go to my own home," Maddalena said with a mixture of anxiety and expectation that the old lady found hard to interpret.

*

So they left the widow at the gate of her house in via Deffenu, where she stood waiting until the car moved on. Then Cristian emerged from behind the house next door.

Maddalena stood still and looked at him as if about to accuse him of some oversight. Though it was nothing that could in any way diminish her love for him. Cristian pursed his lips, as always when searching for words.

"So it really was you," she said.

"Yes. It was me."

"I knew you weren't dead."

Cristian took a step towards her. "You're even more beautiful than I remember," he murmured.

Maddalena backed away, as if to keep him at the same distance. "You've changed, though you're still the same. What happened to you?"

"Will you let me come in?" It was his turn to ask questions.

"It's your home." Maddalena opened the gate.

Cristian followed two steps behind her down the familiar path. "Nothing has changed at all," he commented.

"Wait till you see inside," she warned him, as though to prepare him for who knows what changes.

After they had entered, Cristian looked about himself. In the white season he had often dreamed of finding himself in that exact place. But not from nostalgia.

"What did they do to you?" Maddalena asked, with infinite emotion.

For a moment Cristian was afraid he would not be able to find words to answer her. Then he said, "I returned from the dead."

But Maddalena would not let him say more; their love had

always been expressed in painful emotion. She grabbed his face and kissed his cheeks, his eyes, his nose, his lips, his ears, his neck, in an obstinate fury, as though determined to taste every millimetre of his face. While Domenico must have been paying his fee to the ferryman in the underworld, Maddalena and Cristian touched each other with their eyes closed, as if needing to learn to know each other anew in every possible way. No excuse seemed possible for what she was doing now, nor did she need any. He searched under her clothes to find her skin and rediscover exactly what he had been torn away from before. But nothing could ever again be quite the same as it had been before. Despite the fact that they were once again in the place where they had first made love.

He has changed, Maddalena thought, playing at pushing away the one thing she wanted. His skin had become denser and dryer, his whole body had developed into a machine built for survival. He still had the same broad chest but not the same colour; he was now milky white, pale in the way skins seldom uncovered are pale, especially those accustomed to cold climates. There could be no doubt that his second life had taken the upper hand with him.

She did not ask him how he had survived or been saved, and for the moment he did not seem much interested in telling her.

They made love with precise passion, and it was just as they had always imagined such a moment would be.

She has grown more beautiful, Cristian thought, undressing her. He had always loved complete nakedness, and basic sex without elaborate passion. In this he was primitive: the woman had to suffice in herself. And Maddalena not only answered his need but, he was afraid, he would never be able to have enough of her. She had filled out without becoming fat, her body mature and sweet like the fruit at the top of a tree where most exposed to the life-giving kiss of the sun. And he was where he had always wanted to be, even if in being there he risked severely hurting himself.

Further than that it was impossible to think.

Later they said everything. How he had been saved from the water by a sailor from a Soviet cargo ship. The sailor's name had been Juris, and he had pulled Cristian from the water with a whaler's harpoon: couldn't she see the scar on his left shoulder? Soaking wet, more dead than alive, he had been hauled on board their ship. And taken away. That was how his white season had started, he said, because in the place where he had gone there was so much snow. On the farm where they had taken him in, they had called him *Zivs*, which is Latvian for fish. They laughed. It had taken him several months to recover his health. Then he worked on the farm like an ordinary lad, sharing the family's salt meat and gherkins in vinegar. His work was to shovel dung and keep the cowshed clean. Not light work, but he did learn the local language, which he spoke with an accent that made everyone laugh, Latvia was not independent then but part of the Soviet Union. When she asked him to say something in Latvian, he murmured "*Es esmu šeit*, which means, I am here." She smiled as though all along she had known that perfectly well. Then later he had been able to do business with the local authorities. Russian bumpkins, half asleep, so that a natural entrepreneur like Cristian had in due course been able to get all he wanted. An official identity, for example, and a passport with a new first name and surname: "Oscar Krievs". Then a few small jobs, and in due course control of the local customs. A sector in which the previous incumbent had grown rich by his own limited standards, and which Oskar Krievs had been able to develop into a goldmine . . . The rest had simply been unlimited access to everything, which had grown even greater after Latvian independence. This was how he had recovered what he had previously owned.

Maddalena looked down. Her years had not been so easy. And he, Cristian or Oskar or whatever his name now was, had become a father, was he aware of that? He hugged her and said yes, Domenico had told him that before he killed himself. But Cristian did not seem much interested in the subject, as if his son not being physically present made the boy irrelevant. Maddalena, still naked, rose to her feet, ran into the next room and came back with a photograph album; she wanted to show Cristian his son.

Could he see the great resemblance? Yes, Cristian said, he could see that. But his eyes were closing, he was so tired.

That night, when the white dog came twisting right and left to meet her, she did not even wake. She watched it from the furthest corner of the blank sheet of paper to which the surrounding space had been reduced. Everything else had vanished: farm, hayloft, nothing was left. All that remained was a blinding whiteness. And beyond that, nothingness: just the brown of the dog's eyes and the red of its dangling tongue. She was afraid for a moment that the dog might push her over in its eagerness. But she stood firm. Standing on its hind legs, it rose to her own height, as if trying to look into her eyes. Then moving its snout it seemed to ask to be stroked. Maddalena did not wake.

"*Paklausīgs suns*," the man whispered, appearing behind her.

Maddalena indicated that she knew that, she realised how

affectionate the animal was, without even turning to see who had spoken. She sensed the man was smiling. Even when she felt him brush her neck lightly with his hand, she did not wake.

Now, all round her, the light was doing no more than whitening a pulsing sky, almost like a quivering backdrop of neon lights. If she looked carefully she could make out, beyond the whiteness, a spinney of silver birches and, beyond that, the shape of a village in the far distance. To the extent that Maddalena wondered what extraordinary power it could be that enabled her to distinguish so clearly the onion domes at the top of a couple of identical bell-towers and the spires of a castle.

The man was just as she had always dreamed him to be, with his well-fitting jacket and the cuffs of his high-necked jumper turned back over his jacket sleeves. And his skin and eyes, thin untrimmed beard and untidy hair, were almost the colour of honey.

"*Esmu šeit,*" he reassured her.

Maddalena gave a slight smile to show she had no need of reassurance. The dog gave her a last look before running off and disappearing into the whiteness.

"What's your name?" Maddalena asked the man. Her voice was like that of a child.

"*Mani sauc zivs,*" he answered.

"Fish?" she asked, to be sure she had understood correctly.

"*Jā, zivs,*" the man confirmed.

In her sleep Maddalena had that look her father had always described as her "old lady's face", but which was merely her particular way of looking puzzled. "Fish," she repeated. "But there's no sea here."

"*Nemāku peldēt,*" the man said, trying not to laugh. He was standing in front of her now, just as the dog had been a little earlier.

They laughed together as if they had always known each other and were used to this level of closeness. "Fish is a very good name for someone who can't swim," she said.

The man said nothing, just looked at her. But it seemed that, suddenly, he wanted to kiss her.

She waited for his kiss, because it was clear that she wanted the same thing too.

When Maddalena Pes woke, she discovered she was alone. "Cristian?" she called.

A few seconds later he answered from the sitting room: "Here I am."

She slipped from the bed and, taking the blanket with her, joined him. He was shaved and fully dressed, which made her feel exceptionally naked and distant from him. Suddenly she felt ashamed of having given herself to him so easily.

"I was waiting for you to wake up," he said in a remarkably neutral voice. "I didn't want to go without speaking to you and I didn't want to wake you." This explanation had to stand for some form of kindness that seemed light-years away from his intentions.

Maddalena looked at this man as if she suddenly realised that despite the fact that he was there, he had never actually come back at all. And she knew there was no prospect whatever of any joint life with him.

"You will lack for nothing," he assured her.

She pulled the blanket closely round herself. "So you're going?" she asked, but not as if it were something she had only just realised.

"Yes," he answered. He was a man used to giving a name to everything and giving everything its name.

"And what about us?" She clearly understood the chasm into which such a question must throw her, blurted out without control, allowed to burst from her like that . . .

"There is no 'us'," he continued with the same cold precision. Then he stood up, seeing that Maddalena, for no apparent reason, had run to the kitchen with her blanket round her shoulders like a Native-American wife.

Cristian Chironi made his way to the front door where his suitcase was witing for him. Once out of the house he would call his driver and head for the airport at Olbia.

"I'm off, then. Goodbye," he announced, speaking into the emptiness behind him.

At that moment something sharp seemed to penetrate his ribs and stop his breath. He was so astonished that at first he felt no pain. Bending backwards as if surprised by the sharp impact on his lower back, he tried to free himself from the knife. Then, realising that extracting the knife would merely hasten his end, he swung round.

The last thing he saw was Maddalena, completely naked and with her hair loose, her gaze fixed and her posture proud, like the Nemesis about whom so much has been spoken and written for thousands of years.

PART V
Finally

WORSHIPPING ASHES
Gozzano, February 2000

LUIGI IPPOLITO THREW OPEN HIS WARDROBE DOOR TO reveal a full-length mirror, and faced the other self that appeared before him. He had no difficulty in recognising that self. He was certain who he was, which gave him the confidence of a foot soldier in ancient Greece hurling himself against an enemy phalanx . . . Calmly loosening the top three buttons of his cassock, he practised repeating his new name: Luigi Ippolito Chironi.

He searched his childhood memories for clues to what he had so easily been able to understand of himself when he read the documents his mother had left for him. He had grasped immediately that this was something more than a simple manuscript. In fact, each generation had left at the very least some sign or comment on the folder that contained it. Messages in a bottle floating on a sea of circumstances.

His father Cristian had impatiently jotted down little notes, as if scribbling impulsively under pressure for fear of forgetting what he wanted to say. What particularly struck Luigi Ippolito was a long quotation from Epicurus presented in the form of a deliberate announcement: "Death, the most terrible of ills, cannot exist for us. For when we are alive there can be no death, and once death has come for us we are gone." A quick calculation told him that this must have been written by Cristian at the age of eighteen, at the time his mother Cecilia died. There was also a page torn from a book on art history with a reproduction of Caravaggio's "St Matthew and the Angel", which has been preserved in the Contarelli Chapel. Luigi Ippolito had himself seen the original in the church of San Luigi dei Francesi in Rome, and could confirm that this reproduction bore no relation to it. He asked himself how it would have been if his father Cristian had had a chance to see the original masterpiece with his own eyes. It might at the least have helped him to understand something that he, Luigi Ippolito now face to face with himself, knew for certain: that reality is always more difficult to understand than anything imagined. Which is why we find it so terrifying.

At the end of the first group of manuscripts, written by the great-grandfather whose name Luigi Ippolito had inherited, Cristian had attached a letter to the folder with a piece of sticky tape. This was a will, or at least a tentative farewell to life, written by the old man who had been his own earliest known ancestor:

I, the undersigned, Chironi Michele Angelo,

hereby declare I do not wish my relatives when I die to dress me in black – no mourning. Mourning my Beloved Ones will do nothing for me mourning is in the heart. Another point I don't want masses said if I am not present. I don't want to be put in a tomb like my Grandson my Son and all the others . . .

Each person had tried in his own way to give meaning to something that did not necessarily have any meaning. There were two photos: one of his great-grandfather Luigi Ippolito in First World War uniform, standing in front of a small Romanesque church; while the young man in the other was his grandfather Vincenzo Chironi wearing a dark double-breasted suit and white shirt without a tie, smiling into the camera and leaning on a motor-cycle.

There were also, on other pieces of paper, lists that were whole genealogies updated from time to time in Marianna Chironi's beautiful handwriting:

Michele Angelo and Mercede begat Pietro and Paolo, then Giovanni Maria and Franceschina, Luigi Ippolito, Gavino, and Marianna. Marianna and Biagio begat Mercede known as Dina. Luigi Ippolito and Erminia begat Vincenzo. Vincenzo and Cecilia begat Cristian.

Cristian and Maddalena begat Luigi Ippolito . . .

Here it was, already written down and recorded for ever, without any mystery. Black on white, things that without realising it, he himself had known from the beginning. This accounted for the feeling of inadequacy that had characterised every choice he had made. And which he had attributed to chance and disquiet. Yet he had never assumed that he must be an orphan.

He was unexpectedly overcome by a sudden affection for Domenico Guiso, who in spite of everything had struggled to be a father. A supposed father like Giuseppe or Joseph. And Giuseppe had also been the name of his own maternal grandfather – dead many years ago – who added the other name, that of destiny. Domenico would have liked to have been a father but he had never had the strength to stop being a son long enough to become one. That tormented soul, how well he understood it now; Domenico had tried in every possible way to ignore something he had certainly known: that he was in fact bringing up Cristian's son. Just like himself who, in the same way, had tried to ignore what he had always known: that Domenico was not his real father.

But he had very affectionate memories of Domenico, there could be no doubt of that.

And now here he was staring at himself in the mirror, slim in his cassock, but proud and arrogant too when faced by the Chironi he had discovered himself to be; at least he was now in a position to say a prayer to help rescue poor Domenico from purgatory.

A little earlier he had stretched out on his newly made bed fully dressed with the buttons on his tunic bright and his shoes polished till they shone. He had tried whispering his full name into the silence: Chironi Luigi Ippolito. No longer Guiso. In fact, with the Chironi lying on the bed, the Guiso he had previously been had stood there contemplating that other self lying there composed, dead, and ready to weep. The One was lying there, precisely himself, while the Other stared down at him, unquiet and petrified but nonetheless turbulent, straight and dry as an insult hurled into one's face right there between the bed and the window. The concentration of the One was obvious while the concentration of the Other was a form of control. At first sight one might have thought them identical in all respects, Luigi Ippolito the One and Luigi Ippolito the Other, except that the one stretched out on the bed had the imperturbable expression of the serenely dead, while the other, standing there observing himself, was frowning with the stiffness of the confused.

Thus while the One lay immersed in the indescribable peace

of total surrender, the Other was struggling against an inevitable feebleness. Nonetheless, the Other came almost close enough to steal the One's breath, like a loving father who needs to reassure himself that his newborn child is still breathing. But it was certainly not from love that Luigi Ippolito submitted to Luigi Ippolito. No: the Other submitted to the One to read his life. And even to insult him, because this was not the right moment to die, still less to impersonate death, nor was it a time to surrender.

The One continued to listen without moving, obstinately and farcically pretending to be dead. He refused to move despite the fact he would have preferred to return to life.

Surrendering to this clear obstinacy in himself, the Other sat down on the edge of the straw-seated chair by the bedside table like a young widow who has not yet understood the shame she has suffered. He continued to watch the One who was scarcely breathing.

"What is it like to explore this land of silence?" he asked him. "What is this cursed journey like?"

Then the light seemed to leave the room suddenly, so that the dense eyebrows overshadowing the closed eyelids of the One revealed his pallor in full. The Other then, just like the fading light, lowered his voice and subdued his thoughts to declare himself definitely ready to play the game of compassion. Could the One remember the solitude of exhausted fields in summer heat? And waiting by the animal trap? And life spitting from his lungs after racing? And battles in the olive grove, accompanied by the fierce chirping of cicadas and the churlish hiss of the *maestrale* wind . . .

"You were determined to stare into the light because you

wanted shadows, but I wanted to be fully lit," the man lying down commented unexpectedly.

That had been the harsh pattern of their life together when they were a single unity, like a rustic plank-bed on which spells from the past had succeeded in revealing some sort of meaningful order. Luigi Ippolito Chironi, descended from Chironi ancestors who, it seemed, had bred horses that carried the blessed backsides of two Popes and the much less blessed backside of a Viceroy . . .

A blazing light suffused the room because a black stain had now opened in the centre of the solar orb. The One and the Other looked at each other. The One, stretched out, reverted to being absent, but continued to watch the Other from between almost closed eyelids. The Other, with his wrinkled brow, presented a tenacious wait-and-see to that absent gaze. As it always had been, and always would be.

Time to say goodbye.

Getting to his feet, Luigi Ippolito yanked open the wardrobe to study himself as he stood there in his full magnificence. He was in a position to claim everything owing to him, but realised there was no point in doing that because there was no longer anyone else left to demand from him what was his. Not Cristian; killed twice, first by Domenico and then by Maddalena. Nor Domenico; destroyed by his own mournful disquiet. Nor Maddalena; who after visiting her son in the seminary, had disappeared without trace. By now she had been gone for more than a year, vanishing utterly – as only Chironi women can.

Now Luigi Ippolito was free to give up this ecclesiastical life and return to Núoro. Or was he?

He remained silent, ignoring the constant noise of the spotlight. Suddenly there was nothing anymore, nothing to think about and nothing to remember. It had all been a dream – or perhaps it hadn't. Perhaps he had reached the exact point where any change had become impossible.

But how to convey such a narrative of silences? Everybody knows that stories are only ever told about things that have actually happened somewhere. One must just hit the right note, give one's voice internal warmth like leavening dough, superficially calm but teeming within. Enough to separate the grain from the chaff, thinking almost without thinking. Because being aware that one is thinking can reveal the mechanism, and revealing the mechanism can bring the story to life.

So he must undertake his first responsibility as a Chironi which, as someone said, consisted in remaining certain that keeping the flame alive was better than being compelled to worship ashes.

The writing desk stood by itself in the shady corner of his room. Destiny had allowed him paper and a pen. And the sky outside was white as milk. Luigi Ippolito watched himself heading for the desk with the folder, the only thing he had inherited from his mother. He opened it at the first page. The shade on the desk contrasted with the fierce whiteness of the paper. A perfect light. That was, perhaps, an invitation . . .

So he took up his pen and began to write:
First come the great-grandparents: Michele Angelo Chironi and Mercede Lai.

He glanced at this, and immediately changed it, drawing a line through the word "grandparents" and replacing it with "ancestors".

First come the ancestors: Michele Angelo Chironi and Mercede Lai. Before them . . .

. . . Nothing.

LITERARY SOURCES

Sebastiano Satta, *Canti barbaricini*, La vita letteraria 1910
Epicurus, *Letter on Happiness* (Italian edition by Angelo Pellegrini,
    Einaudi, 2014)
William Shakespeare, *Henry IV* (Italian translation by Cesare Vico
    Ludovici, in *Teatro I*, Einaudi, 1964 [used by Fois in his original
    Italian text of the novel])

MUSICAL SOURCES

Umberto Bindi, *Il nostro concerto* (by Giorgio Calabrese & Umberto
    Bindi) in *Umberto Bindi*, 1960
Renato Zero, *I migliori anni della nostra vita* (by Maurizio Fabrizio
    & Guido Morra) in *Sulle tracce dell'imperfetto*, 1995
Claudio Rocchi, *La realtà non esiste*, in *Volo magico n.1*, 1971
Franco Battiato e Alice, *I treni di Tozeur* (by Franco Battiato,
    Giusto Pio & Rosario Cosentino), in *I treni di Tozeur*, 1984
Gazebo, *I Like Chopin* (by Pierluigi Giombini & Paul Mazzolini)
    in *Gazebo*, 1983

The scene of the meeting between Luigi Ippolito and Erminia appeared in an earlier version under the title *Di quando sei tornato* (written for the Festival Gita al Faro, 2014).

The story of Gessica and Priam appeared in an earlier version under the title *Certe favole si capiscono troppo tardi* (written for the Goethe Institute, 2012).

It may well be that there are real people who have exactly the same names as people in this novel: if so, this is entirely accidental and has no relation to reality.

M.F.

MARCELLO FOIS was born in Sardinia in 1960 and is one of a gifted group of writers known as "Group 13" who explore the cultural roots of their country's regions. He writes for the theatre, television and cinema, and is the author of several novels, including *The Advocate* (2003), *Memory of the Abyss* (2012), *Bloodlines* (2014) and *The Time in Between* (2018).

SILVESTER MAZZARELLA is a translator of Swedish and Italian literature, including of stories by Tove Jansson and novels by Davide Longo and Michele Murgia.